P9-CJV-896

LORI WICK

Sabrina

Doubleday Large Print
Home Library Edition

HARVEST HOUSE PUBLISHERS

EUGENE, OREGON

This Large Print Edition, prepared especially for Doubleday Large Print Home Library, contains the complete, unabridged text of the original Publisher's Edition.

All Scripture quotations are taken from the King James Version of the Bible.

Cover by Dugan Design Group, Bloomington, Minnesota

Cover photos © Jerome Tisne / Taxi / Getty Images; iStockphoto

SABRINA

Published by Harvest House Publishers
Eugene, Oregon 97402
ISBN-13: 978-0-7394-9127-0

Printed in the United States of America

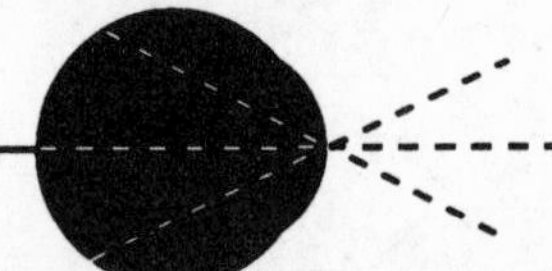

This Large Print Book carries the Seal of Approval of N.A.V.H.

For Adam Dell—
who is precious beyond words
and whose life inspires me.

Acknowledgments

- Darwin and Todd—great words this year. Thank you for your life-changing messages and the hard work you do.
- Pearly Jo—thank you for your ongoing love and support. It's lovely to have my mother be one of my closest friends. I don't know what I would do without you.
- Merry Kay—it's always a delight. You have traveled paths that have hurt, but you've helped me with what you've learned. Thank you for each word and hug.
- Carmen—your sweet spirit and good thoughts have blessed me so many times.

Thank you for your friendship and for being you.

- PubCo—you guys are amazing. Thank you for the lovely times together, for laughing in all the right places, and for hearts that believe so strongly in my books. My summer would not be complete without you. You're the best.
- Bob—did you ever picture gray hair and grown children? I'm not sure I did, but here we are. You're still the one I want to grow old with, but mostly just grow with. I hope we will have another 40 years together, but no matter how long or short the time, I want to spend it with you.

1

Denver, Colorado
1880

THE SUN WAS SETTING fast as a crowd gathered around the dead body that lay in the street. Morbid curiosity drove most of them as it was too cold to be out. And considering the neighborhood, whispers and speculations abounded.

It was easy to assume that the man had recently frequented one of the many bordellos that lined the street. Some of the crowd worked in the seamy establishments, and some had run from other streets, having heard shots, shouting, and general mayhem.

Coming into the midst of the scene was

Officer Danny Barshaw. He was a big man, with great patience for those in need of help and little for those who did not share his uncompromising respect for the law.

"Step aside, folks," he said, clearing a path with his voice and presence. People stepped out of the way, but kept close.

"Who is this man?" This would be just the first of Danny's many questions.

Folks had much to share, and for nearly 30 minutes he checked the body and gathered information from the spectators and the scene. He was writing out details and facts on a small scrap of paper when he spotted a face in the crowd marked by youth and too much makeup. The prostitute's eyes and mouth were sad as she looked down at the dead man. Danny was running out of light, and some other officers had just come with a wagon to take the body away. Weighing his options, Danny took the woman by the arm.

"Do you know anything about this?" he asked, his voice and face stern.

"No," she answered, looking afraid. "Nothing."

"Did you see anything?"

"No." The fear was still there. "I just got here."

The eyes got to him. They were too young and clear for the woman to have been in this line of work for long. He finished playing with the idea and made his decision.

"What's your name?"

"Raven."

"Your *real* name."

The woman hesitated before saying, "Bri." When she saw the officer's brows rise, she elaborated. "Sabrina."

"Sabrina what?"

"Matthews."

"Come with me," Danny ordered, not giving her time to say no.

"Where? Where are you taking me?" the woman asked, but Danny was done talking.

Now under almost complete cover of darkness, the big police officer nearly dragged the young woman away from the scene. She continued to ask where they were headed and tell him she'd done nothing wrong but learned it did no good. Sabrina eventually grew quiet and started to plan. He'd not let go of her forearm, but the moment he did, she would run. She was fast and would be gone before he could grab her again.

Amid these plans Sabrina suddenly realized she did not know where they were. He had walked them into a nice neighborhood, one not familiar to her.

Still gripping her arm, Danny arrived at a charming, small house, went up the walk, up the steps, and straight in the front door.

"Danny?" a voice called from the back. They went that way.

"Yes, and I have a guest."

Sabrina had no idea what to think when the officer walked to the rear of the home and into a kitchen, where he began to talk to a woman.

"Who's this?" the woman asked. Sabrina noticed she was attractive and smiling.

Before Danny answered he turned back to Sabrina. "Which do you prefer to be called, Bri or Sabrina?"

"Either is fine," the young woman answered honestly, although she still felt completely mystified.

"This is Bri Matthews," Danny said. "Bri, meet my wife, Callie. I'm Danny, by the way."

"Hello, Bri," Callie said, smiling at her.

Before Sabrina could respond, Danny had turned her to face him, gripping her by both upper arms.

"Now listen to me, Bri. I can give you a chance at a new life. It's up to you."

Sabrina thought he must be out of his mind, but she didn't mention this. She stared up at the intensity of the police officer's face, hoping she was dreaming.

"Callie is going to show you where you can clean up and change your clothes. Go with her now. No one will harm you."

Sabrina found herself at a doorway right off the kitchen. She was given no chance to escape but was ushered inside. The door was shut behind Callie and her.

"You can take a bath and wash your hair in here," Callie was saying, placing the kettle she grabbed from the stove onto the washboard. "Put this dress on when you're done. It won't be long enough," Callie added, having to look up to Sabrina, "but come back out when you're ready, and I'll have some supper for you."

Callie, still smiling kindly, reached out and gently touched Sabrina's arm.

"I hope Danny didn't hurt you at all. That would be the last thing he would wish to do. I also hope you'll come out and listen to what he has to say."

Sabrina had not spoken a word. She stood stock-still until the door shut, her mind unable to take in what had just happened to her.

There was no window in the room, only a single lantern that burned brightly, but she knew it was dark out. She was usually working by now.

Looking around the room, trying to figure out what she should do, Sabrina spotted the dress that had been left on a small table for her, a hairbrush beside it. She lifted it, and to her amazement, found undergarments with it, clean and neatly folded.

As she continued to touch the gingham fabric, all thoughts of escape deserted the young prostitute. The kind way Callie had touched her arm would not leave her mind. She couldn't remember the last time a woman had touched her in kindness.

Sabrina stared at the door back to the kitchen and then at the tub. Thinking she might have taken leave of her senses, she began to slip out of her dark red dress. Figuring she had little to lose, she was going to bathe, dress in the things she'd been given, go back out that door, and find out who these people were.

* * *

"Do you think she'll do it?" Danny asked Callie. Both sat at the kitchen table, not ten feet outside the room Sabrina was in, drinking coffee.

"I don't know. She's certainly young," Callie said, thinking of the large blue eyes that had stared at her, framed by an abundance of wavy black hair.

"I'm guessing she's 18 or so."

Callie had to smile. "She was certainly quiet. She looked at you as though you were mad."

Danny smiled back. "Well, we both know how true that is."

Callie smiled with very real love for her husband, never sorry a day that she'd married him, but also never knowing what life with him would bring. They both heard water in the other room and exchanged another look. They had no idea if Sabrina Matthews would listen to a word they had to say, but that didn't change what they'd started. At the very least, they had one more person they could pray for, and they knew that God could work in ways they never saw or understood.

* * *

"Do you want more?" Callie offered when Sabrina had finished one plate of chicken and dumplings.

"No," Sabrina said. Callie had not skimped on the portion, and Sabrina thought she was going to burst.

"How about some pie?" Danny offered.

Sabrina looked at him. "How about telling me why I'm here."

"I can do that," Danny said with complete ease, reaching for the pie Callie had put on the table and cutting himself a slice. "It's like this, Bri," Danny began, taking his time and talking in plain terms.

"I don't know why you're a prostitute—that's not the most important issue here—but I do know it's not a life that will be satisfying to you. No matter what the reason you got involved, it's wrong to sell your body. God has better for you."

Sabrina's heart began to pound at the mention of God. Part of her wanted to run for her life, and part of her couldn't move.

"I don't know what you know about God," Danny continued quietly, "but I can tell you that the Bible calls what you're doing sin. The Bible also says that Christ died for that sin, and if you'll trust in Him to save you, He will."

"Why are you telling me this?" Sabrina whispered. It was all she could manage.

"I looked across the crowd and saw your

face. It hurt my heart to see how young you were, but even if you were older, I would say the same thing. Was I high-handed to grab you that way? I was. Do you have the option of leaving here and forgetting this ever happened? Of course you do. But I took a chance that you might want to hear what I have to say."

Sabrina licked her lips. She did want to hear what he had to say, but a part of her felt he didn't understand. She had to say as much.

"I'm sure you've seen a lot in your line of work, but I don't know if you understand how many men there have been."

"It doesn't matter if I do or not," Danny said, seeing she was listening to every word. "God understands how many, and He's the One offering forgiveness."

"I don't think He would if He truly knew."

"Look right here," Danny said, reaching for the Bible that sat on the table. "In Psalm 31:7 it says, 'I will be glad and rejoice in thy mercy: for thou hast considered my trouble; thou hast known my soul in adversities.' And then in Psalm 69:19: 'Thou hast known my reproach, and my shame, and my dishonor: mine adversaries are all before thee.'

"Both of these verses were written by a man named David, who had done some terrible things. David was a king, and he used his power as king to have a man killed so he could have that man's wife. The sins David committed against God were serious, but he knew that God knew all about those sins.

"But there's more. David also speaks in Psalm 51 when he's broken and wanting God's forgiveness: 'Behold, thou desirest truth in the inward parts, and in the hidden part thou shalt make me to know wisdom. Purge me with hyssop, and I shall be clean; wash me, and I shall be whiter than snow. Make me to hear joy and gladness, that the bones which thou hast broken may rejoice. Hide thy face from my sins, and blot out all mine iniquities. Create in me a clean heart, O God, and renew a right spirit within me.'"

Danny stopped reading and looked at Sabrina. She looked pale and sober. He watched as she reached and shut the book, studying the words *Holy Bible* on the front and then opening it again to Psalms. She licked her lips but didn't speak.

Danny's eyes flicked to his wife, who had not joined them at the table. Tears had filled Callie's eyes as she watched Sabrina, and the slight movement of her lips told Danny she was praying.

"Are you all right?" Danny asked Sabrina after a few moments.

"I don't know. I never considered," she said, but then stopped.

"What? That God would know all the details and still be forgiving?"

Sabrina nodded and said, "I didn't think God could look on sin."

"God the Father sees everything, as does His Son, who died for our sins."

Danny and Callie watched her shiver. The room was warm, but Callie wasted no time in fetching a blanket from the living room and placing it around their guest.

"Thanks," Sabrina said absently, her eyes on Danny.

"Here is what you need to understand, Bri," Danny continued quietly. "You don't have to make a decision right now, but neither do you have to return to your old life. You can stay here with us for a while and think about this."

Sabrina blinked with her surprise. This was the last thing she expected.

"You may not have had choices," Callie said as she joined them at the table, "or felt you had choices about the life you've been living. But you do now. You can walk away from prostitution at this very moment."

"Just like that?" Sabrina voiced her skepticism. "Move in and live here free of charge?"

"Well," Danny said practically, "Cal can always use help around the house, extra hands for cooking and laundry. And when we go to church or the women come here to study with Callie, we hope you'll join in. We're not afraid you're going to eat us out of house and home or take advantage of us."

"But I might," Sabrina argued, a bit defiantly. "You don't even know me."

"That's true," Danny agreed. "You might choose to take advantage, but we're still not worried about it. We hope you'll accept this chance to change your life. We also hope you'll want the life we have in Jesus Christ."

Sabrina shivered again. Her heart yearned to reach for what he was offering, but the fear that they did not know enough about her life still loomed large in her mind.

"Why don't we do this," Danny suggested. "Why don't you spend the weekend with us? Give us a try. If you want to leave, I'll walk you back on Monday."

"Or at anytime you feel it's not what you want," Callie added.

Sabrina would wonder for hours what came over her, but she heard herself agreeing.

* * *

"You can sleep in here," Callie said later, taking Sabrina to a bedroom at the end of the upstairs hallway and lighting a lantern for her. Sabrina saw that it was neat and small with two narrow beds.

"But before you settle in," Callie continued, "I want to show you something."

Sabrina followed the other woman back down the hall to another bedroom.

"This is Danny's and my bedroom." Callie lit a lantern in here as well. "Danny will be back after he checks in at the sheriff's office, and he'll come here to this room. He won't try to get into your room. You might hear him in the hall, but he won't bother you."

"Has he ever cheated on you?" Sabrina asked quietly, taking in the neat room with one wide bed.

"No, never."

"How can you be certain?"

"In order to cheat on your mate, you have to be a liar. Danny can't even lie if he's teasing me about something. It's not who he is."

Her words gave Sabrina pause. She stared at Callie, who looked right back.

"It is just who some men are," Sabrina finally concluded.

"You make it sound as if they have no choice."

"I don't know if they do."

"All men who cheat have choices," Callie said firmly but without force. "Never forget that. And I didn't mean to make it sound as if Danny doesn't have temptations and never has to work on those. But he chooses to come home to me."

"You're a lucky woman," Sabrina said, and was surprised when Callie laughed.

"At the risk of making you think I'm going to disagree with everything you say, luck has nothing to do with it."

It struck Sabrina suddenly that this woman was remarkably comfortable with her, even knowing what she was. She was not used to that. Prostitutes were comfortable with other prostitutes, but this—Callie Barshaw, a police officer's wife—was not what she was accustomed to.

"You look tired, Bri," Callie said next, not sure if she was seeing strain or fatigue in

Sabrina's young eyes. "Feel free to turn in anytime. I'm going to."

Sabrina nodded and turned to head down the hall. Callie didn't watch her, not feeling it was her job to see that she stayed. If she was there in the morning, so be it.

* * *

"How did you sleep?" Danny asked when Sabrina entered the kitchen on Saturday morning. He and Callie had eaten two hours earlier, but he didn't mention this.

"Fine," Sabrina said, still surprised to be there.

"Did it take a while to get to sleep?" Callie asked as she put a cup of coffee in front of the other woman.

"Yes. How did you know that?"

"Your hours are different than ours," Callie said, her voice matter of fact. Sabrina stared at her.

"What's the matter?" Danny asked, although he thought he knew.

"Where did you people come from?" Sabrina asked, her mouth hanging open a bit.

Both Danny and Callie laughed, but then Danny surprised Sabrina and turned to his wife. "Do you want to tell her?"

"Or you can," she said, and Danny knew she wanted him to do the honors this time.

"What am I missing?" Sabrina asked.

"We're just deciding who's going to tell you our story."

Sabrina didn't realize it, but she leaned a little closer to Danny. Seeing it, he began.

"My father was a police officer, and I grew up with strangers in the kitchen. Some were men in hard times and drinking too much. Some were prostitutes. At other times entire families would come and live with us until they got on their feet.

"One day my father brought home a young prostitute, only 16 years old. She was both frightened and defiant, but the one thing about her that stuck out was her fascination with what my parents told her about Jesus Christ. She hadn't heard any of what they were saying before, and in time all defiance melted away and she turned her life over to God.

"She was a different person after that. She lived with us for a while but eventually found work in a mill and lived with friends of ours." Danny couldn't stop the smile that stretched his mouth before adding, "When she turned 18, I married her."

Sabrina's eyes swung to Callie, who smiled gently at her. The younger woman could only stare. Nothing about Callie Barshaw spoke of her former life. To Sabrina's eyes, she didn't look capable of such sins, but there was no reason for Danny to lie about this.

"Why were you?" Sabrina eventually found her voice and asked.

"I was born in a brothel. I'd never known any other life. My own mother died when I was only 10, but by then I had about 15 mothers. When my figure developed, I joined that life. I had been at it for more than two years when Danny's father found me."

"I tried to stop for a while," Sabrina admitted after a few moments of silence, wanting to talk about it with this woman. "I got work at a hotel in the kitchen and serving tables. But the owner kept at me. I told him no, but he wouldn't leave me alone. He touched me or backed me into a corner every day we worked together, and when his wife found out, she fired me. I gave up then and went back. I just assumed it was my destiny."

"That's not true. You have a choice, Bri. We're giving you a choice."

This had come from Danny, and Sabrina

now stared at him. For some reason, his marrying a former prostitute gave her more hope than she had ever dreamed of. Not that she was looking to marry, but what she was seeing in Danny and Callie had never occurred to her. Before today she would not have believed that a woman could walk so completely away from prostitution that a stranger meeting her would never know.

"You don't have to decide right now," Callie said, thinking she was about to get up and leave, but Callie had read Sabrina's look wrong. The younger woman's look was not a stubborn one but one of concentration. She didn't love her life, but it did make her independent, something she enjoyed.

"What happens now?" Sabrina asked, realizing she had no idea.

"If you want to continue to discuss Scripture, we can," Callie informed her. "If not, Danny has to work for a little while this morning, and I have baking to do."

Sabrina blinked. Once again, this couple had managed to surprise her. Prior to meeting them she would have said she was past surprising, but it just continued to happen.

"Do you have more questions?" Danny asked with no sign of impatience.

It was on the tip of Sabrina's tongue to ask if these people really believed God cared about what she did, but instead she asked Callie, "What will you be baking today?"

"I'll probably start with bread and then move on from there," Callie answered, as though they'd known each other for years. "Do you want to help?"

Sabrina managed a nod. Danny pushed to his feet, told them to enjoy themselves, kissed Callie goodbye, and went on his way. Sabrina wasn't given time to comment or ask questions about what would happen next. Callie asked her to start working on a muffin recipe, and because it had been years since she'd made muffins, she kept her mouth shut and forced herself to concentrate.

* * *

Sabrina was strongly tempted to pinch herself. She had no idea where Saturday had gone. The hours had flown by. Baking, seeing visitors, washing dishes, and preparing meals had left little time for talking about God. And now it was Sunday morning and Sabrina found herself in a church, a man speaking up front, Callie to her right, and Danny on Callie's other side.

Sabrina tried to listen to what the man was saying, but it wasn't working. Her eyes kept sweeping the room, afraid she would see someone who recognized her. A word floated to her here and there, but she wasn't even watching the man up front. Things all over the room distracted her, and when she wasn't watching the other people in the room, she kept glancing down at Callie's open Bible.

She was a little slow to stand up when it was time to sing a closing hymn, but this time she heard some of the words that spoke of God's holiness and gracious love. Sabrina didn't try to sing but noticed that Callie's voice was not perfect. It dipped in places and wobbled a bit, but no one seemed to mind.

Not until she was back at the Barshaws' buggy did she realize the mistake she'd made. By not listening to the sermon, she didn't even have questions to ask Danny and Callie. Not that her hosts seemed to notice. They talked about general topics on the way home and never once asked her what she thought of the sermon.

* * *

"I have to head home," Sabrina said on Sunday afternoon. Dinner was over, and she stood in the living room to tell her host and hostess.

"Will you be returning?" Danny wanted to know.

"Do you want me to?"

"Yes, we do," Danny answered.

"Why do you want to go back?" Callie asked.

"I need some things from my place."

"Why don't we take you?" the older woman suggested. "We can help you carry whatever you need."

Sabrina hesitated but managed to ask, "Have you forgotten where I live?"

"Not at all," Callie said. "We're not worried about it, so you shouldn't be either."

"And if you get there and decide you don't wish to return with us," Danny put in, "no one will force you."

Sabrina agreed, although if pressed she could not have said why. The three left a short time later.

2

"Moving out, Raven?" a woman asked when she found Sabrina's door open and that young woman packing a bag.

Sabrina looked up to find her landlady, a woman she knew only as Lil. She was not a madam, but neither was she above directing men to the women who lived in the building. She expected the rather high rent payment on time, but if a woman wanted to move, Sabrina had never seen Lil interfere.

"For a few days," Sabrina answered.

Lil's brows rose with admiration. "Good for you. I hope it pays well."

Sabrina said nothing—unsure how to

answer—and was glad when Lil walked away. She hoped what she was doing would pay well too but knew her hopes had nothing to do with money.

"Hello." Callie's voice could be heard in the hallway, passing the woman who owned the building.

"I might have a room opening," Lil began, but stopped. Sabrina was staring at the door when Callie entered.

"I thought you might want help," Callie offered.

"Did she say something to you?"

"She started to, but I didn't encourage it."

Sabrina never thought about Callie being able to hold her own in such a place, but she looked calm and confident.

"Let me tell you something," Callie began, keeping her voice low for privacy. "I was going to wait in the buggy with Danny, and then I realized there's something you don't know. You can pack it all today, Bri. You can make a complete move right now."

Sabrina shook her head ever so slightly, and Callie stopped.

"Okay," Callie agreed. "What can I help you carry?"

"Just that bag," Sabrina said as she

pointed, realizing how little of her clothing would fit into the Barshaws' world.

"All set?" Callie asked, and Sabrina nodded. The two made their way quietly to the buggy. The ride back was quiet as well. However, it didn't last. Sabrina waited only until they were back at the house to open her mouth.

* * *

"What if you're wrong?" the young prostitute asked. "What if God doesn't want me? You can't really speak for Him. No one can."

"We aren't speaking for Him," Danny explained. "He speaks for Himself in His Word, and that's why we believe He wants you."

"Where does it say in your Bible that God wants Sabrina Matthews?"

Danny went to the kitchen and brought the Bible out. He sat down and turned to the New Testament and began to read. "This is what Romans 5:8 says: 'But God commendeth his love toward us, in that, while we were yet sinners, Christ died for us.'" Danny stopped and looked at her. "Did you hear yourself in there?"

Sabrina stared at him, not wanting to answer.

"Us, we, and us," Danny answered for her. "God's love toward *us,* while *we* were sinners, Christ died for *us.* I can take you to other verses that talk about the fact that He died for all of us in the world. That's why I know that you and I both fit into the *we* and *us.*"

"You saw where I live," Sabrina said quietly. "I know you mean well, but I don't know how it can be for everyone."

Danny didn't speak again until he'd turned to the book of John. He had these verses memorized but still read them for her. "Listen to John 3:16 and 17: 'For God so loved the world, that he gave his only begotten Son, that whosoever believeth in him should not perish, but have everlasting life. For God sent not his Son into the world to condemn the world; but that the world through him might be saved.' The *world,* Bri," Danny emphasized quietly. "The forgiveness, salvation, and eternal life that God offers is not just for some but for all who believe."

Sabrina said nothing, and Danny knew he could not press her. He did, however, hand his Bible to her and a small scrap of paper. Sabrina took it without thinking, but she looked surprised.

"Sometime today I want you to read two different chapters in there. I've written them down for you. I think you need to see the way Jesus deals with women who sin. He never tells them it's all right, but He does offer kindness and forgiveness. Will you read them?"

"I don't know how to find anything in the Bible," she argued, not sure she could even open the cover and not have God strike her down for such insolence.

"There is a list of the books at the front," Danny said, fighting a smile. "Find the book and then the chapter. You'll figure it out."

Danny didn't wait to see what she did. They had been talking in the front parlor, Callie standing at the edge of the room. When Danny turned to leave, his wife went with him.

Sabrina stared down at the book, her heart pounding. Did this man really know what he was doing? What if he was condemning her to death?

Well, it will be on his head, Sabrina thought to herself, her eyes glaring at the door where Danny exited. *Let him explain to his neighbors and the people at church why there's a dead prostitute in his living room!*

But all this bravado died in a hurry. In

truth, Sabrina wanted to read the Bible. She'd seen it in Callie's lap during the church service and been fascinated. She sat down on the sofa but only stared at the book on her knees. With heart pounding and hands shaking, she eventually opened it. The list of books was at the front, just as Danny had said. Consulting the small paper, she found John 4 and began to read.

All time and space fell away as she read the story of a woman. She was a Samaritan woman who was a little way outside the city drawing water from a well. The story said that Jesus, who was resting by the well, spoke to her and asked for a drink. The woman didn't know it was Jesus, but as they talked He began to tell her things about her life, immoral things that Sabrina figured she probably wanted to keep hidden. That He'd even spoken to her, a Samaritan, was a surprise, but she didn't run away, not even when she realized He knew everything.

Sabrina had to stop and think. The woman was talking to Jesus and didn't even know it. She was standing with Jesus and He knew all about her. He knew she was living with a man and had been married several times.

A shudder ran over Sabrina. Having God know about the life she was living bothered her no small amount. The woman at the well had spoken freely to Jesus, never imagining that He knew every detail of her life.

How do I talk to You? Sabrina asked God, fear filling her that she even dared. *I'm not like this woman. I know that You know.*

Making herself not think about it, Sabrina turned to the next chapter assignment. This time she read in John 8 about a woman who had been caught in the act of adultery. Sabrina could never remember a woman coming to the brothel and catching her husband with another woman. She wondered for a moment how this woman had been caught before reading on.

Jesus did not react the way the Pharisees did. He was calm, almost disinterested, but before it was over He told her not to sin anymore, so He knew what she'd done was wrong. Sabrina knew the life she lived was wrong, but she didn't feel she had a choice. Maybe she had at one time, but not now.

Sabrina was headed back to the chapter when Callie came to mind. The way she'd handled herself at the brothel today jumped back into Sabrina's mind. She realized she had a question for Callie, one that needed an answer before she kept reading. She found her in the kitchen, sitting alone at the table.

"I need to ask you something."

"Sit down," Callie invited, and even moved a chair so Sabrina would sit close.

"How did you silence Lil today? What happened in the hall?"

Callie smiled. "At one time I would have been complimented by her offer, but now I'm insulted. My look turned cold, Bri. I stopped long enough to look Lil in the eyes, and she knew she'd stepped out of line to even suggest such a thing to me."

Sabrina thought she would give anything to be in such a position, but again told herself that it was too late.

"Are you all right?" Callie asked.

"I read those chapters. I didn't know there were immoral women in the Bible."

"All through the Bible," Callie told her, smiling a little. "Don't forget, sin is nothing new, and sexual sin is a powerful temptation that started in the book of Genesis."

"What's the book of Genesis?"

"The first book in the Bible," Callie answered, and then asked, "Did your family ever go to church? Did anyone ever tell you about the Bible?"

"No, my mother didn't like it, and my father didn't seem to care." Sabrina shrugged. "I can't remember knowing anyone who went to church. Sunday was our only day off and we stayed home."

Callie nodded and thought about this, realizing Sabrina had probably just described the way thousands of folks in Denver lived. Many worked hard all week with little time or thought for God.

The silence at the table lengthened but was not uncomfortable. Eventually Sabrina had another question.

"All those years ago, what did Danny's father say to you that helped you?"

"Let me think." Callie took a moment. No one had ever asked her that, and it had been a long time past. "I think I was most helped when he said I had choices. I didn't think I did. He said I had a choice about what I do for a living and what I believe. He turned out to be right. I eventually did believe in Christ to save me, and once I did that, I realized I did have a choice about everything."

Sabrina might have had another question, but someone knocked on the front door. Callie excused herself, and Sabrina went back to John 4. She read in verse 39 that many people in the city believed on Jesus because of the things the woman from the well had shared. At the end of verse 42, Sabrina read, "Know that this is indeed the Christ, the Savior of the world."

Savior of the world. The words reverberated in Sabrina's head, and for the first time a glimmer of hope began to shine in the corner of her mind.

* * *

"Come into the kitchen," Callie's voice sounded before she arrived. "Come and meet Bri."

Sabrina looked up in time to see Callie enter the room, a baby in her arms.

"This is my granddaughter, Delta," Callie said, laughing when Sabrina's mouth opened.

"You can't be a grandmother," Sabrina argued even as she looked at the baby, who smiled up at Callie.

"This isn't even my first," Callie explained. And without warning, the kitchen filled with people who were introduced to Sabrina. The man was Scott Barshaw, a large man like his father, along with his wife, Lisa, and their older child, Josh. Danny came from upstairs in the midst of it, and Josh ran for his grandfather.

"How's my big boy?" Danny asked Josh, who began to chatter happily into his grandfather's face. Sabrina could not have been less comfortable with all of this, but no one seemed to notice.

"We have cake," Callie was saying. "Bri helped me with the baking yesterday, and we have more than we can possibly eat."

"Why don't you give me Delta, Mother," Scott was saying, and Sabrina saw her chance. The Bible still in her hands, she slipped out of the kitchen, back to the living room, and then onto the front porch. It was cold, a little too cold to be outside, but she had to read more about Jesus and at the moment the temperature didn't matter.

* * *

"I can't find her," Callie said quietly to Danny some time later, having just come from upstairs. Her face was sad, sure she had left them, but Danny took over. He didn't know why it was obvious to him that Sabrina was outside except that he'd seen the look on her face when the family arrived. Slipping into a coat and grabbing one of Callie's, he went out the front door and found her on the first step.

"How are you doing?" he asked as he placed the coat around her shoulders and took a seat.

"It says here that Jesus turned water into wine. How did He do that?"

"He's God, and He can perform miracles."

"And then this child," Sabrina went on. "He healed a man's son without even being there."

"Jesus' miracles are recorded all through the New Testament."

"I thought I was reading the Bible."

"The Bible is divided into the Old and New Testaments."

Sabrina looked back down at the book and then out at the street. A man walked by, and it brought her back to earth.

"I can't keep staying here. I'm not making any money, and you can't live without that."

"Is that really what you want to do—go back to the night district and make money?"

"Sometimes we don't have choices."

"That's true, but not in this instance."

Sabrina didn't argue. She knew he was

right. They had told her she could stay, and she knew they meant it.

"I do have some money put away. I can pay for my keep."

"I don't expect that. I won't take money from you."

"Because of the way I earned it?"

"No. You'll need your money for new clothes."

Sabrina frowned at him in confusion.

"All of Callie's dresses are going to come up above your ankles, and your dresses don't cover you on top."

Sabrina gawked at him. She'd never met such a plain-talking man. He didn't blush or beat about the bush, and Sabrina wondered if this was the type of man it took to marry a woman in her occupation. She didn't say this, however, but changed the subject.

"Callie told me I could move out completely today. Did you know that?"

"She told me. Why didn't you?"

"I wanted to, but I was afraid of not having any money, living on the streets, and having to start all over."

"How about you look for work around here?" Danny suggested.

"Doing what?"

"I don't know. We'll ask around and see what comes of it."

"Will I have to say where I've been?"

"I don't know why you would," Danny said, not telling her that some folks, who knew the way Danny and Callie operated, would have already guessed. They would also never say anything to her. It wasn't important.

Sabrina looked back out to the street. It was such a nice neighborhood, a little like the one she'd grown up in. Such memories hadn't come to mind in a long time, and for a moment Sabrina felt sick with longing.

"Are you all right?" Danny asked, but Sabrina didn't answer. She looked back at the Bible and started again with her questions about Jesus.

* * *

A month later, Sabrina came home from work at the laundry to find the house quiet. She went to the kitchen and found a note from Callie.

I'm sorry about giving you such short notice, Bri, but Danny is taking me out to dinner. There are plenty of

ingredients for a meal, and even some leftovers. We'll see you when we get home.

Callie

Sabrina sat at the kitchen table, weary but not discontent. The familiar and comforting sounds of the house creaked around her as she sat alone for the first time in a month. She had stayed with the Barshaws only a week before realizing she wanted to make the move final. Once again the three of them had gone to Market Street, and this time she had packed for good. Lil had seen her and said she'd be welcome when she ran out of money, but Sabrina had not replied. She was afraid of that very thing but unwilling to admit that to Lil.

But money had not been an issue. The very next day Danny found her work at the laundry, only four blocks from their house, and so far she had been treated well. One man had recognized her, but he had no authority over her and looked as uncomfortable as she did about the encounter. She never saw him after the first day, and that had been the end of it.

Twice on the walk home she'd been stopped by men, one who said he knew her. But no one had touched her or tried to detain her. The hours at the laundry were long, and the work was hard, but she was still glad she'd made the trade.

Each week she attended church with the Barshaws and listened. Questions filled her Sunday afternoons, and Sabrina was learning more every week. Gone was the fear of God's anger if she read the Word. She read it every day and always hungered for more.

In fact, she reached for the Bible now. She was working her way through the Christmas story because that holiday was just weeks away. Before she could get to Luke, however, some verses in Matthew 7 caught her attention.

She read, *"Not every one that saith unto me, Lord, Lord, shall enter into the kingdom of heaven, but he that doeth the will of my Father which is in heaven. Many will say to me in that day, Lord, Lord, have we not prophesied in thy name? and in thy name have cast out devils? and in thy name done many wonderful works? And then will I profess unto them, I never knew you: depart from me, ye that work iniquity. Therefore whosoever heareth these sayings of mine, and doeth them, I will liken him unto a wise man, which built his house upon a rock. And the rain descended, and the floods came, and the winds blew, and beat upon that house, and it fell not, for it was founded upon a rock. And every one that heareth these sayings of mine, and doeth them not, shall be likened unto a foolish man, which built his house upon the sand. And the rain descended, and the floods came, and the winds blew, and beat upon that house, and it fell, and great was the fall of it."*

"This is me," she whispered to the Lord. "I've heard what I'm supposed to do, but I haven't done it. I live here in comfort and safety, but I know I'm not ready to face You. You would say You've never known me."

For a moment, Sabrina's breathing came hard. Fear crowded in, but then she remembered that she knew what to do. She did know the will of God in heaven. It was to believe on His Son, Jesus Christ. Danny had told her; Callie had said the words; and even Pastor Lederman had gone over them on Sunday.

"You died for me. You died to take my sins. I believe this, Lord. I can't save myself. I can't forgive myself, but You offer forgiveness, and I want that, Lord. I don't want You to send me away. Please save me, God in heaven. Please save me for all time."

Sabrina had no idea how long she sat there and prayed, but it must have been some time because Danny and Callie came home before she could even fix herself something to eat. She met them at the door, her face alight with peace as she told them the most wonderful thing that had ever happened to her.

* * *

"She handled it well," Callie told Danny as they readied for bed, "but all the color drained from her face, and she was so quiet the rest of the evening."

Danny looked as pained as he felt.

"It just keeps happening, Danny. We're not that far from the night district, but our neighborhood is like another world. Why are men suddenly finding her?"

"I don't know, but she has to stop answering the door. You or I will go to the door, and make it clear to whoever is standing there that *Raven* is not available for such activities. Tell them there is no Raven."

"What about work?"

Danny's head fell back. He could not protect Sabrina everywhere, but it didn't change the need he felt. He looked over at his wife, who had tears in her eyes. Danny put an arm around her and pulled her close. He didn't want to suggest what he was thinking, but at some point it was going to have to come up. Sabrina had come to them in November and believed before Christmas. It was now May. It seemed to the Barshaws that memories would fade. Sabrina had started a new life and left the old one behind, but somehow the old life was finding her, which probably meant one thing: It was time for Sabrina Matthews to leave Denver.

"I don't have to work until noon tomorrow. We'll talk about this in the morning."

"You're going to send her away, aren't you?" Callie guessed.

"If I do, Cal, it's because I love her too much to do anything else."

Callie's tears would not be stopped. Mindful that Sabrina was just down the hall, she used her husband's chest to muffle the sobs, completely unaware that Sabrina still heard them, her heart sinking with dread over what they might mean.

* * *

"Montana?" Sabrina asked quietly, her eyes having grown to the size of moons.

"Yes," Danny answered. "Montana Territory."

"Do you really think I need to go that far to escape being recognized?"

"No, you don't, but I know of a fine church family. You would fit right in."

Sabrina's look was almost comical. Callie had told herself to be strong, but she was already feeling teary. Sabrina could not help but notice.

"Is this what you were crying about last night?" the younger woman asked.

"You heard that?" Callie asked, looking crestfallen.

"I was still thinking about that man at the door. I couldn't fall asleep."

"Tell me something," Danny cut in. "Do you know these men who are approaching you?"

"Most of them, yes."

"And do they take no for an answer, or are some returning?"

"Some return," Sabrina said with a small shrug. "I don't understand why."

At a time when thoughts and hearts had been rather sober, both Danny and Callie found themselves smiling. Sabrina Matthews did not spend time thinking about the way she looked, but she was beautiful. Her skin was creamy, a bit dark in tone, but her cheeks still managed a lovely rose color. Her hair was thick with a bit of wave, very black, and her black-lashed eyes were like blue crystals. It was a surprising but lovely combination.

It took a moment for Sabrina to see her friends' smiles, and when she did, she was completely confused.

"What?"

"You're just funny," Callie said.

Sabrina frowned, trying to remember what she'd said, but she was completely at sea. Danny took pity on her and cleared it up with one name.

"Nelson Taylor."

"Oh," Sabrina said, full understanding hitting her. Nelson Taylor was a man at church who was interested in her. She had told him that she had no desire to marry and that she was the wrong woman for him, but he had said that he would never want anyone else. Each week he spoke to her, his heart in his eyes, and Sabrina knew nothing could dissuade him.

"So what do you think?" Danny forced

himself to bring them all back to the painful topic at hand. “Do you want to try Montana Territory?”

“What will I do if it doesn’t work out?”

“Come back.”

“Yes, Bri,” Callie put in, “we’ll make sure you have return fare. Short of starvation, you keep that money tucked away and come back to us if you’re unhappy at all.”

Sabrina looked into their faces, wondering how she could be away from them for one day and still be happy.

“God is in Montana Territory too,” Danny said quietly, more for himself than for Sabrina.

Sabrina looked into his eyes, knowing she quite literally owed him her life, and cried for the first time in years.

3

Token Creek, Montana Territory

"MY HEART GRIEVES FOR my friend, Abi Pfister." Pastor Rylan Jarvik spoke to the group gathered at the cemetery. Next to him lay a plain wooden box ready for interment. "I will miss Abi's lively mind and her tender heart. She hadn't always had a tender heart, as most of you know, but just last week she told me she prayed for all of you. She believed that God had great plans for the townsfolk of Token Creek and our small church family."

Rylan looked out over the faces before him. Most were from his church, but not all. He'd already said what he wanted to say concerning Abi's beliefs, but he thought a last reminder might be a good idea.

"Please don't forget that Abi is not in this box. Just last year she made Christ her Savior and God, and all that's in this box is her frame."

Rylan closed in prayer, and then folks stood and visited for a while. All enjoyed knowing Abi at the end of her life, and to a person they had a fun story to share since she joined the church family. The last one to leave the graveside was Jeanette Fulbright, who had been meeting with Abi for months. The two women had become close and grown in their knowledge of God as they studied in the book of James. Jeanette stared into the grave knowing she was going to miss her rather unpredictable friend in a very real way.

One of Jeanette's nephews came to see her back to the wagons, but before she turned away, Jeanette determined in her heart to pray as Abi had, believing that Christ had died for the folks in town and that God had something special in mind for Token Creek.

* * *

The June sun was warm on the streets of Token Creek on Wednesday morning as

Jeanette opened the door of her shop, Token Creek Apparel. She left the door standing open, enjoying the breeze as she slipped into the back to remove her hat and go to work.

Business had been a little quiet, but that suited Jeanette. When she had taken on the shop full-time, she had not counted on how much work it would be for one person. Her nephew's wife, Cassidy Holden, was always ready to give her a hand, but Cassidy was a new bride, and she and Trace lived a ways out of town where they ranched with Trace's brother, Brad, and his wife, Meg. Jeanette had no new orders this week, so that would allow her to catch up on the week before.

Jeanette started when she came from the back and realized she wasn't alone. A tall young woman had come in very quietly, standing just inside the door and looking hesitant.

"Hello," Jeanette said kindly.

"Hello," the woman greeted her. "I'm here about the sign in the window about a job."

"Please come in," Jeanette invited as she indicated a chair. No one had asked about the "Seamstress Needed" sign in the window, and Jeanette tried to tamp down her excitement. She spoke when the younger woman was seated. "I'm Jeanette Fulbright."

"I'm Bri," she began but stopped. "I mean, Sabrina Matthews."

"Do you like Bri or Sabrina?"

"I usually go by Bri."

"In that case it's nice to meet you, Bri. Tell me about your sewing experience."

"I've never used a sewing machine," Sabrina said, her gaze flickering over to the one against the wall, "but I'm handy with a needle."

"Who taught you?"

"My mother."

"Do you mind showing me some of your work?"

"Yes, ma'am—I mean, no ma'am." Sabrina stopped, took a breath, and tried to calm her racing heart. "I don't mind."

Jeanette smiled with compassion into her young eyes, knowing how nervous she must be. Jeanette wanted to hire her—she wanted it in the worst way—but even though she was drawn to her sweet vulnerability, she had her business to consider.

"How about a hem? Can you hem a pant leg for me?"

Sabrina nodded, and took the things

Jeanette handed to her—a needle, thread, and the men's dress slacks, which had already been pinned.

"Let me know when you're done," Jeanette said, moving to the sewing machine and hiding her smile when she heard Sabrina sigh.

Sabrina wasted no time. She was good with hems, and it helped to be left alone to work. Her hands shook a little while threading the needle, but as soon as she'd accomplished that, she made short work of the hem. She checked it over carefully and knew she'd done her best.

"Miss Fulbright?"

"It's Mrs.," Jeanette told her, "but please call me Jeanette. How did you do?"

By way of an answer, Sabrina handed her the pants. Jeanette studied the job and was pleased. Her style was different than Jeanette's but just as neat and strong.

"Very nice," Jeanette said honestly, but still made herself go slowly. "Tell me something, Bri. What brings you to Token Creek?"

"I'm originally from Denver," Sabrina answered. She'd had miles and hours to think of a way to answer this question. "That city holds some bad memories for me, and when I wanted to try someplace different, friends of mine from my church family suggested Montana Territory."

"Well, I think you and I would do well together," Jeanette said, having liked her answer and sensing her honesty. "But how about we give it a month's trial? If after four weeks either one of us wants things to change, we need only say."

"All right," Sabrina said, having to work not to sound as breathless as she felt. "When do you want me?"

"How about in the morning?"

Sabrina nodded, and Jeanette went on to explain when she opened and that she would need Sabrina from Wednesday through Saturday. Sabrina had a few more questions about what she should wear and how she would be paid, but Jeanette wasn't done with her own questions.

"When did you get into town?" the older woman asked.

"Late yesterday afternoon."

"Do you have a place to live?"

"Not yet."

"Why don't you plan to stay at my house? You might not find a place today, and you'll be working for the rest of the week, so staying with me will give you a chance to look around town."

Jeanette could see she'd confounded her. Sabrina looked into the older woman's eyes, inches below her own, and felt as helpless as a child. Even after life with the Barshaws and the Denver church family, such kindness from a stranger was more than Sabrina expected.

"Thank you," Sabrina managed. "I can work for you at your house if you need me to."

"As a matter of fact, I have a very fine staff that sees to everything, so you need not worry on that account. Just take your time finding a safe place to live and getting settled in."

Sabrina was given instructions on how to find the house before she thanked Jeanette again and went on her way. Barely able to breathe, she went back to the train station and stood hesitantly in the empty building. Somehow she thought it was never a place to be empty. She was on the verge of leaving when the stationmaster appeared.

"Back for your bag, Miss?" Kaleb Heydorn asked kindly.

"Yes, thank you."

Kaleb smiled at the tall woman in his midst before slipping behind the counter to fetch her heavy satchel. He wanted to ask questions but stopped himself. He was not curious by nature, but this passenger fascinated him. He knew where she'd spent the night but would never have let her know.

"Here you go," Kaleb said as he handed her the bag.

"What do I owe you?" she asked, reaching for the reticule that hung from her wrist.

"This one's on the house," he said.

"Thank you."

Kaleb nodded and watched her slip out the back door. He didn't follow but was fairly certain where she was headed.

* * *

Sabrina stepped out of the back of the train station, and walked across the gravel to a small copse of trees. She headed to the partially grassy area where she'd slept the night before and sank onto her knees.

I have a job, she prayed, her entire frame awash with relief. *Thank You. You provided. You went before me, and Jeanette Fulbright hired me.* For long moments Sabrina could not form words—her thanks to God simply filled her heart.

She had left Denver, declining a letter of introduction from the Barshaws. They had wanted to write a letter to the church family, one that she could deliver herself, but Sabrina had decided to do this on her own. Landing a job on her first day had simply not occurred to her. And she would sleep in a house tonight, not on the ground or in a train. Sabrina began to dig in her satchel for paper and a pencil. It was time to write a letter home.

* * *

"What are you doing?" Jessie Wheeler asked of Hannah, her older daughter, when she found her digging behind one of the counters of Wheeler's Mercantile.

"Looking for a rag."

"Why do you need it?"

"I'm going to dust that shelf over there."

Jessie, who owned and operated the mercantile, looked over at the shelf her daughter pointed to. It did need dusting, but the bottom ones always did. She had two customers in the store but ignored them in order to bend down on her daughter's level.

"I think you should go and play," Jessie said gently to the child, who tended to take life very seriously. "You just finished with school. Don't you want to enjoy your summer a little?"

"But who will dust the shelf?"

"I don't know right now, but I do know this: The dust will wait for us."

Hannah smiled a little. It was her mother's standard answer, and even though she had heard it many times before, it usually did the trick.

"All right," Hannah agreed, albeit reluctantly. Jessie watched her leave and then noticed Sabrina at the counter.

"May I help you?" Jessie offered.

"I need to mail this letter," Sabrina said. "Can I do that here?"

"You certainly can." Jessie took the letter and glanced at it. "The post to Denver won't go out until tomorrow."

Sabrina nodded, knowing that Danny and Callie would never expect to hear this fast. She almost smiled when she thought about their faces.

Jessie took care of the letter, including payment, and then asked Sabrina if she was new in town. It was obvious that she was, but Jessie still thought it the best start to a conversation.

"Yes, I am—just yesterday. Do you by any

chance need someone to work for you?" Sabrina mustered up the courage to ask.

"Not full-time. I'm sorry."

"Actually, Jeanette Fulbright just hired me, so I'm free only on Mondays and Tuesdays."

Jessie looked at her, not having expected this.

"I think I should tell you," Sabrina said before Jessie could speak, "I don't have any experience working in a store, but I'm not usually clumsy and I catch on pretty fast."

Jessie couldn't stop her smile. The other woman's voice was soft and at times sounded uncertain, but she stood and moved with the air of a confident person.

"I might not need you every week," Jessie began, "but if you want to come by on Monday morning, I can tell you that day."

Sabrina smiled and sighed.

"I'm Jessie, by the way," that woman said.

"I'm Bri Matthews."

"Well, Bri Matthews, I'll see you on Monday," Jessie said, and smiled again when Sabrina, looking utterly delighted, went on her way.

* * *

Sabrina stood outside the large home at the far end of town, wondering if this could possibly be the place. Jeanette had told her where the house was and that it was large, but Sabrina had not expected this.

She started up the walk, not in a hurry, and was surprised when a woman came out the front door. She was partway down the walk before she noticed Sabrina.

"Hello," the woman greeted and kept moving.

"Hello," Sabrina said in return, stepping aside so the woman could pass. Sabrina watched her walk away. Clearly she thought nothing of Sabrina's presence. This gave the newest resident of Token Creek courage to go up and knock on the front door.

* * *

"Did a young woman come—tall, with black hair?" Jeanette asked of Heather the moment she arrived home from the shop.

Heather, who had worked for Jeanette for many years, smiled before saying, "Bri is in the kitchen helping Becky."

"Oh," Jeanette said quietly, not having expected this. "How did that come about?"

"She heard Becky say she was going to make bread pudding and went in to learn how."

Jeanette had to smile. She had been quite

sure she'd done the right thing in hiring Sabrina Matthews, and for some reason this only confirmed that fact. She went to the kitchen herself and found Sabrina rapt.

"How long does it take to bake?" Sabrina asked.

"It takes 45 minutes to an hour," Becky told the new houseguest. "On a warm day like this, probably closer to 45."

Both Becky and Sabrina saw Jeanette just then. Both women smiled at her, but they were different types of smiles. Becky's said she was amused but pleased. Sabrina's was excited and a bit uncertain of being found disturbing Becky.

"Did you learn how?" Jeanette asked, defusing the situation for Sabrina.

"Yes. My mother used to make bread pudding, but I didn't remember the recipe."

"It's one of my favorites," Jeanette said. "Are you ready for supper, Bri?"

Sabrina nodded. She'd not eaten much that day and was very hungry. It was a relief when Jeanette wasted no time and immediately led the way to the dining room where they were served.

"After supper," Jeanette began once they had plates full of pork, sweet potatoes, and applesauce, "I'll take you to the porch to meet my sister. She is not capable of taking care of herself. She won't respond to you, but you may speak normally to her."

"Has she lived with you long?"

"Ten years," Jeanette said. "Her sons, along with their wives, run Holden Ranch outside of town. You'll probably meet them on Sunday," Jeanette finished, taking for granted that Sabrina would attend the church service with her.

"Does your sister respond to her sons or to you?"

Jeanette thought it an astute question but had to shake her head no.

"Her injury was quite severe. We didn't think she would live. She's not been herself since."

"I'm sorry," Sabrina said, thinking that it must be sad. It was like having someone die but still living with you. Sabrina wondered how Jeanette coped with such a situation.

"Did you get settled in your room?" Jeanette asked next.

"Yes, thank you. It's very pretty," Sabrina said, thinking of the rust and dark green decor and the light oak furniture.

"I'm glad you like it, and I meant it when I said to take your time finding a place to live."

"I asked Jessie at the mercantile if she could use me a few days a week, and she said to check with her on Monday. I may have to wait until Tuesday to look for an apartment."

"That's fine. Jessie is also a good one to ask. The mercantile is sometimes a hive of information. She might be able to tell you about apartments available in town."

The women went back to their meals, and Jeanette was given time to think a little more about who this young woman was. She was surprised that she'd looked for work on the days the dress shop was closed but still impressed. That, along with her questions about bread pudding, made Jeanette think she might have a lively one on her hands.

Sabrina would have laughed if she could have heard Jeanette's thoughts because they were all too true. Her mind was running with a thousand questions, but she didn't want to seem nosy or impertinent. Heather and Becky were easy to talk with, but Jeanette was a bit intimidating. She was obviously a woman of wealth, and Sabrina didn't think for one moment that she acquired this house, with its staff, by making and selling clothing a few days a week.

"All set?" Jeanette asked.

"Yes, ma'am," Sabrina answered, unaware her hostess had been studying her.

"My sister's name is Theta," Jeanette explained as they walked. "Heather sees to her every need. We'll just head right out here on the porch."

The large sunporch, technically a small conservatory, was warm and comfortable. Plants sat here and there, but the room was not overrun with them. In the midst of comfortable furniture in various shades of green sat a woman in a chair with high arms. Jeanette immediately began to speak to her.

"Theta, I want you to meet our houseguest. This is Bri Matthews. I just hired her to help me at the shop. Bri, this is my sister, Theta." Jeanette put a brief hand on her sister's shoulder, and Sabrina quietly greeted the silent, staring woman.

"It's nice to meet you," Sabrina said, and then glanced around. "This is such a pretty spot to sit and enjoy."

"Isn't it?" Jeanette agreed, taking a seat and inviting Sabrina to do the same. "I love this room. In mid-July or if we have Indian summer it gets a bit warm, but it still might be my favorite room in the house."

"Have you lived in Token Creek all your life?" Sabrina asked, feeling a bit more relaxed with Jeanette's easy manner.

"I came here after I was married. Theta and her family moved to the area a few years later."

"How nice to have your family near."

"Do you have family?"

"Just a sister, and we've lost all contact."

"Well," Jeanette had to say, sensing just a moment of pain in her new employee, "I hope you find family here."

Sabrina thanked her, her heart hoping for the very same thing.

* * *

"How are you?" Trace asked Cassidy, who, in her second month of pregnancy, did not like the smell of the toast Trace had accidently burned.

"I think all right," she said, not wanting to lose the breakfast she'd just eaten and having gone to sit on the front porch for some air.

Trace smiled. "You moved pretty fast there, Cass," he said, sitting down beside her. "I didn't know you could manage that."

Cassidy chuckled before saying, "I think desperation helps."

Trace put an arm around her. She was a bit thinner than when they'd married, and he wondered if she would put it all back as his sister-in-law, Meg, had done with her pregnancy. Meg had become delightfully round by the time Savanna had been born, and Trace had to admit that he wouldn't mind that for Cassidy at all.

"What are you thinking about?" Cassidy asked, and Trace realized she'd been watching him.

He smiled, knowing he was on thin ice but admitting, "I was wondering how fat you're going to get."

Cassidy's mouth opened and Trace laughed.

"I knew the truth would get me in trouble."

"That's what I get for asking what you're thinking," Cassidy said, turning a cold shoulder to him.

Trace moved her hair and kissed her neck.

"Ask me what I'm thinking now," he invited.

Cassidy turned and looked into his warm, brown eyes and found she didn't have to ask at all.

* * *

"Okay, Bri," Jeanette said the moment they were ready to work on Thursday morning, "I want you to finish the pants you started yesterday and then press them."

"Is it going to trouble you to check the hem before I press it? I want to make sure."

"That's fine, Bri, but I'm not worried about your work."

Sabrina nodded and started in. Jeanette watched the look of concentration on her face, her mind on an event that had happened earlier that morning. Theta had experienced a little trouble with the stairs, and Sabrina had stepped in, taking one side with Heather on the other. Jeanette had not been present, but Heather had told her all about it.

"Do you ever think about the person who owns the legs that might wear these pants?" Sabrina asked.

"I'm not sure I do," Jeanette admitted.

"Oh, okay."

"What were you thinking?" Jeanette was too curious to let that pass.

"Well, just that they might be the legs of a father or a grandfather, and there might be children who sit on the man's lap. Or they might be a pastor's legs, and he might hold his Bible on his knees. Or I suppose he could be a bank teller with no time to sit down at all."

Jeanette had to laugh, not bothering to mention that she knew exactly who ordered the pants, and he was none of those things.

"What did I say?" Sabrina asked.

"I'm just laughing at your possibilities. I must admit that my mind never went that far."

"Clothing could probably tell interesting stories."

"I'm sure you're right," Jeanette had to agree. "I've always thought that of the walls of a home or bank but never of clothing."

"Shoes too," Sabrina said thoughtfully. "All the places they go." Sabrina kept working steadily on the hem but added, "Of course, there is an awful lot of talking in this world as it is. I'm not sure we need to add shoes and clothing to it."

Jeanette had to laugh again.

"Am I talking too much?" Sabrina asked, suddenly looking very young.

"Not at all," Jeanette answered honestly, still chuckling a little. "I've been working alone for several months, and I just realized how much I've missed the company."

"Well, do tell me if I need to hush," Sabrina added.

"I don't think that will be a problem."

As it was there wasn't time to find out. Not five minutes passed before Brad and Trace Holden came in the door. It was time for Sabrina to meet Jeanette's nephews.

4

JEANETTE WASTED NO TIME. Just as soon as she'd hugged the men, she did the honors. "Bri, please meet my nephews, Brad and Trace Holden."

The men had both removed their hats, and Sabrina stood to meet them.

"Are you twins?" Sabrina asked when the introductions were complete.

"No." Trace took this one. "He's *much* older."

Sabrina smiled, catching the teasing glint in his eyes and the way both Brad and Jeanette smiled.

"You found yourself a tall one," Brad said

to Jeanette, but his smile was for Sabrina. "Makes you look shorter than ever."

A laugh escaped Jeanette before she could catch it, and then she tried to look outraged. It didn't help to look over at Sabrina, who had bit her lip to keep from laughing.

"I need Cassidy and Meg here," Jeanette said. "They're at my level."

"Cassidy is my wife," Trace offered, no small amount of pleasure in his voice. He had seen Sabrina looking confused. "And Meg is stuck with Brad."

"Stuck or not," Jeanette added, "they have the most adorable baby in the territory."

"A boy or a girl?" Sabrina asked of Brad.

"A girl—Savanna."

"That's a pretty name. How old is she?"

"Her first birthday is next month."

"Any steps yet?" Jeanette asked.

"No, but she's crawling everywhere."

The four talked for a few minutes more, and then the men said they had errands to run. Jeanette went back to her sewing machine, but for a few moments Sabrina sat still with her thoughts.

I didn't expect this, she said to the Lord again. She'd repeated this in her mind many times in the last 24 hours. *They're so kind and welcoming. I miss Callie and Danny, but I don't feel alone.*

It flashed through Sabrina's mind that they might want nothing to do with her if they knew of her recent past, but she pushed such thoughts aside. It did no good to think about it, and because she didn't know how these folks would respond if they knew, it was also an insult.

"How is that hem coming?" Jeanette asked.

"Almost done."

"What did you think of my boys?"

"I like them," Sabrina said, and then added quietly. "It makes me sad for your sister."

"It is sad," Jeanette agreed. "I think I'm glad that she doesn't seem to know what she's missing."

"And she's a grandmother," Sabrina realized.

"That was hard at first. Savanna was born, and all I could do was cry for Theta's loss. Now Meg just learned she's expecting again, and Trace and Cassidy's first is due early next year."

Sabrina would have asked if Jeanette thought that was going to be as hard for her, but a woman came in looking for some thread. From there, Sabrina did not know where the day went.

* * *

"Okay, Jessie," Jeb Dorn called when he came from the mercantile storeroom, "I think I've got things patched."

"I hate mice," Jessie said, frowning to make her point.

Jeb, who was Jessie's older cousin, smiled. Jessie had felt that way for as long as he could remember.

"I think what you saw is old. You know they don't come indoors in weather this warm."

"I can't think how I missed the signs this past winter."

"It helps to have things off the floor. You've done a good job with the shelves in there."

"Thanks, Jeb."

"Do you want me next week?" Jeb asked. He made furniture for a living but also helped Jessie when there was a need.

"I think I'm all right," Jessie answered. "I might have hired someone."

"*Might* have hired someone? How does that work?"

Jessie told Jeb about the young woman who had stopped in, and how Jeanette had just hired her. Jeb took the information in stride. Outside of mice, there was nothing Jessie Wheeler feared or couldn't turn her hand to. If she'd hired someone to help, it was in the best interest of her business. Jeb reminded her that he could help if this woman didn't work out, wished her a good afternoon, and went on his way.

* * *

"Savanna." Brad's stern voice halted the baby's movements. She stopped and looked over her shoulder at him. "I don't want you in the kitchen. Mama's not out there. Stay in here to play."

Expecting to be obeyed, Brad sat on the sofa next to Meg. He was not surprised to hear his daughter crawling toward the sofa before she pulled herself up and worked her way around to his legs.

"How's my girl?" Brad asked as he scooped her into his arms and kissed her neck. His answer was a round of giggles. Supper was over, and Meg admitted to being weary. She didn't say much while Brad and Savanna played and was near to falling asleep when the kitchen door opened.

"Are you up for some company?" Trace called in.

"Sure," Brad shouted back. "Come on in."

Meg sat up a little, and Brad realized what he'd done.

"Are you going to be all right?"

"I think so," she said and then smiled. "And my falling asleep in front of Trace and Cass would be nothing new."

Brad's smile was compassionate. He was done in as well but always welcomed the company.

"How are you?" Cassidy asked after she'd settled in the living room and had a chance to look at her sister-in-law's weary face.

"Just a little tired. How about you?"

"I took a nap today, so I'm not doing too badly."

In the time it took to say this, Savanna had made it to her Uncle Trace's legs, first crawling and then pulling herself up by using his pant leg. Trace was one of Savanna's favorite people—looking and sounding so much like her father—and clearly the feelings were shared. Trace took the little girl onto his lap and smiled into her face.

"How's my Savanna?" Trace asked.

The little girl could not sit still. She climbed Trace's chest until she could be close to his face, her little arms going around his neck. Trace hugged her close, the three other adults watching until the conversation went to the men's Bible study.

Chas Vick, one of the church elders, had started studying with the single men in the church family, ages 16 and up, and Rylan was working with the married men. Brad had expressed an interest in the qualifications for elder, and all the men were studying those passages.

Brad and Trace took some time talking about the last verse they had studied, and some minutes passed before they realized they were losing their wives. Meg's eyes were already closed, and even Cassidy was drooping.

"I'll talk to you tomorrow," Brad said, remembering they also had a baby to put to bed.

"Will do," Trace said, handing Savanna over and pulling Cassidy to her feet. Brad didn't try to rouse Meg. He put Savanna to bed and then came back for his expectant wife. By the time his own head hit the pillow, he was more than ready to sleep hard all night.

* * *

"How did Bri do today?" Heather asked Jeanette that night. They had just seen Theta into bed.

"Very well. She works fast and is easy to have around. She doesn't talk nonstop, but I can tell she's thinking."

"Do you think she's passing through, or will she stick around?"

"I assumed she was staying. Why do you ask?"

Heather looked thoughtful before saying, "She's the kind of person we could all lose our hearts to, and it would be hard to have her leave."

"Even if she does," Jeanette said reasonably, "we would still lose our hearts. We always do."

Heather had no choice but to agree, each woman heading to find her rest.

* * *

Sabrina blew out the lantern in her room, but sleep was far away. Without warning she was back working in Denver, her mind on the way it had been. For long minutes she tried to dispel the images, but they would not go away. Conversation and actions she never wanted to remember floated through her mind.

Feeling almost desperate, Sabrina began to mentally sing. She recalled one of the hymns she'd heard in Denver and began to sing the few words she could remember. Another song came to mind, one she knew better. She even hummed a little, staying very quiet but needing to hear the music.

Thank You for saving me from that life. Please save me from the memories. Please help me to concentrate on You and what I have now and not on who I was then.

Sabrina could think of no other thing to ask. Aching to put the thoughts away from her, she sang and prayed the same words over and over again until she dropped off to sleep.

* * *

Jeanette had told Sabrina she could take 45 minutes for dinner on Friday. Work had gone smoothly all morning, and they had accomplished quite a bit. Sabrina swiftly ate the meal Becky had sent with her and headed to Jessie's store with a question.

"How are things going at Jeanette's?" Jessie asked.

"I think fine. We accomplished a lot this morning, and she gave me extra time for dinner."

"Did you need to shop?" Jessie asked.

"Actually, Jeanette mentioned that you

might have heard of apartments to rent, and I wanted to ask you about that."

"Well, I know there was one open at Hulett's," Jessie said, looking thoughtful, "but his usually go pretty fast. And Sandgren usually has one, but that's on Willow Street, three blocks off Main Street, and not the best building in town."

"Exactly where are those buildings?"

Jessie gave directions, and Sabrina wasted no time. She thanked Jessie and started out, soon learning that the mercantile proprietress had been correct—the apartment owned by Mr. Hulett was already spoken for. Sabrina was not put off. Even though she had to head down an alley, she still wanted to speak with Mr. Sandgren before she had to be back at work. However, it didn't prove that simple. She got into the alley Jessie described, but wasn't sure she was in the right place. A man suddenly came from the building in front of her, and Sabrina spoke to him.

"Excuse me," Sabrina began. "Do you know if there are apartments for rent upstairs?"

"They're all full," the man said, his eyes lighting with interest as he stared at the tall, black-haired woman. "But I live upstairs," he added with a smile, "and I wouldn't mind a roommate if she looked like you."

Sabrina saw her mistake too late. Her look became frosty as she thanked him and turned away.

"You don't have to rush off," the man was swift to say as he started to follow her. "Come inside out of the heat. I own this place, and I'd be happy to give you a drink."

"Is this the saloon?" Sabrina turned back long enough to ask.

"Yes, ma'am. What did you think?"

"Clearly I didn't," Sabrina answered with a certain level of chagrin, starting down the alley again.

"You could tell me your name," the man said, falling into step beside her.

"Yes, but I won't."

"You could tell me where you live."

"True, but not likely."

"Where are you headed?"

"Please don't follow me," Sabrina tried one last time, but the man didn't listen.

* * *

Rylan heard the woman's voice and the words and wasted no time getting to the alley that ran along the back of the livery. He looked out to see Bret Toben from the saloon. He was speaking to a woman with black hair, or rather the woman was speaking to him.

"What country are you from?" the woman asked Bret.

"What country?" Bret looked as confused as he felt. "I was born right here in Montana Territory."

"Since you seem to be having a hard time understanding English, I made a simple assumption."

Rylan watched Bret throw back his head and laugh. The lady turned with a roll of her eyes and started off again, but Bret persisted.

Sabrina was done. She had told him in every way possible that she did not want to know him, and still he followed her and tried to find out who she was. This time she not only rounded on the man but stepped toward him. He was so surprised by this move, coming from a woman who looked him right in the eye, that he had no choice but to back up.

"Thank you for the information you gave me," she said now, all kind tones gone. "But I'm leaving the alley now, and you *will not* follow me."

Bret eyed her. There was no mistaking her meaning. Her eyes were dead serious. Bret, well built, good looking, and successful, had never in the past been forced to push his attentions on a woman and realized he wasn't going to start now. With a slight bob of his head, not showing his regret that she was going to get away, he turned back to his saloon.

Sabrina had started off again, her head down with thought, when she spotted a pair of large boots. She drew up in surprise and jumped a little as she came to an awkward halt.

"I'm sorry I didn't see you," Sabrina spoke, having to tip her head back to see the man's face.

"I didn't mean to startle you," Rylan said. "Are you all right?"

"Do you have the time?" Sabrina asked, having already forgotten that asking questions of strangers could get her into trouble.

"Let me see," Rylan said, reaching for his pocket watch. "I've got ten minutes after one."

"Am I more than five minutes from the dress shop?" Sabrina asked.

"Jeanette's? No. In fact if you come

through the livery here, you'll have two minutes to spare."

"Am I just half a block off Main Street?" Sabrina asked, her heart sinking even before he answered.

"Yes."

"Oh, thank you," Sabrina said, thinking she was going to have to get her head on straight. She was so intent on finding an apartment that she hadn't noticed where she was, or the saloon, or that she was talking to a livery worker. His leather apron and huge size should have given him away, but Sabrina had been single-minded in purpose.

"Tell Jeanette that Rylan said hello," Rylan said when Sabrina came out on the street side of the building.

"Oh!" Sabrina said, surprised again and then shaking her head a little as she realized this should be no surprise. Jeanette would certainly know everyone in town.

"I will tell her, and thank you for the time."

Rylan smiled at her rather dazed expression, wondering absently which woman was the real one. The one who stood up to the saloon owner in the alley or the one who looked disoriented by his mere mention of

Jeanette Fulbright. Rylan went back to work, realizing he would probably never know.

* * *

"We close at one o'clock?" Sabrina clarified.

"On Saturdays, yes," Jeanette answered. "I know I could be busy all day, but I was waking up very tired on Sundays, and I don't want that. If the folks of Token Creek have a sewing need, they'll simply have to get here before one."

Sabrina nodded her acceptance, but she was busy doing rapid sums in her head. If Jessie didn't need her on Monday and Tuesdays, her finances were going to get interesting. At the same time, maybe Jessie would need her more on Saturday afternoons. Sabrina went back to cutting the gingham for a child's skirt, reminding herself that she was off that very afternoon and could gain an answer to at least one question.

* * *

"There's a new woman in town," Jeb Dorn told his wife, Patience.

"Tell me about her," Patience requested, as interested as Jeb knew she would be.

"She's working for Jeanette, and when Jeanette's shop is closed, she'll be at Jessie's."

"How did this come about?"

"A woman came to town this week and applied to Jeanette for the help she's had posted in her window."

"And Jeanette hired her, just like that?"

"Evidently, but because Jeanette isn't open all week, the woman also asked Jessie if she could use her."

"Did you meet her?"

"No. I know her name is Bri, and I was there when she came to see Jessie this afternoon. Jess was up to her ears in customers and hired her on the spot."

"Where is she living?"

"I didn't get that far."

Patience thought about this for a moment. Both Jessie and Jeanette hired this woman. That in and of itself spoke volumes. Patience could hardly wait to meet her.

* * *

"I need an ax," the man said, and Sabrina came up from the floor where she had been kneeling, her mind scrambling.

"I believe they're over here," she said, hoping she was remembering right. She led the way, her mind intent on her task, but the man had not followed. He was distracted by something he'd spotted on a shelf. Sabrina took that time to locate the axes, grabbing two different types and taking them back to the aisle with the dry goods and clothing.

"How are these?" Sabrina asked.

The man turned as though just seeing her but was immediately taken with the axes.

"We have the heads and handles separately too," Sabrina said, having noticed this on the shelf.

"Where are they?" the man asked as if she was hiding something from him.

"This way," Sabrina said, stepping back this time and waiting for him to lead the way.

* * *

"Oh, no," Hannah said to her mother at the counter.

"What's the matter?"

"Bri got Macky."

"Oh, no," Jessie echoed. "What does he need?"

Hannah smiled before saying, "Everything in the store."

Jessie tried to look stern, but in truth that was the type of customer he was. He always paid in cash and never quibbled about the price, but he always came in looking for one thing and left with everything but that item. And always on their busiest day, taking everyone's time and energy.

"I'll go," Hannah said, but Jessie stopped her.

"I think Bri will be all right, but let me know if you see something."

"Mama." Clancy was suddenly at her side. She was Jessie's younger. "I need this."

Jessie looked down at the small hair comb and worked not to smile. Clancy had very fine, flyaway hair.

"Why do you need it?" Jessie asked.

"For my hair."

"I know it goes in your hair, but—" Jessie started and stopped. This was a new phase for her daughter. She was suddenly aware of things in the store and was sure she "needed" them.

"I'll tell you what," Jessie went for the compromise. "Put it right here in the basket under the counter, and when the store closes, we'll talk about it."

"You won't sell it?"

"I won't sell it."

"It's time to go," Hannah said to her mother and sister.

"All right. Have fun with Patience, and stay right together all the way there and back."

"Jeb always walks us home," Hannah assured her, and Jessie bent to kiss both girls goodbye.

She was glad they were going to spend the afternoon with Patience. Most days she would miss them around the store, but this was Saturday, and there was no time for missing anyone.

* * *

Sabrina walked back to Jeanette's that evening with coins in her pocket. This was Jessie's routine, to settle up with her employees on Saturday when the store closed. She even went so far as to tell Sabrina she could plan on Saturdays each week and any Mondays and Tuesdays that were busy enough. Sabrina was well pleased with this plan and knew that for the moment she would have enough to live on.

"Well, Bri!" Heather said when the younger woman came in the front door. "What did you do with yourself this afternoon?"

"I worked for Jessie at the mercantile."

Heather's mouth opened. It was the last thing she expected.

"Did Jeanette know about that?"

"I don't think I mentioned it. It wasn't a certainty until today."

"Are you tired?"

"A little."

"Well," Heather said, trying to recover—this woman was more independent than she expected—"Becky almost has supper on. You can rest your feet and tell us about working at the store."

Sabrina thanked Theta's faithful companion, suddenly missing Callie and the way she had taken care of her. She went to wash for the meal, thinking she must be more weary than she realized as she was strongly tempted to cry.

* * *

Sunday morning did not go well. Theta had a rough go of things, and Heather didn't even attempt to join Jeanette and Sabrina when they left for church. As it was, the two women were late. They slipped into the rear of the sanctuary, glad there was an open spot near the back, and sat down just as a song ended.

Sabrina was taking in the room, the neat pews and tall windows, when Rylan stepped into the pulpit. Sabrina stared at him, just keeping her mouth closed. After a moment, even though Rylan was speaking, she leaned toward Jeanette.

"Is that the pastor?"

"Yes. Rylan Jarvik."

"Does he have a brother who works at the livery?"

"No, it's the same man."

Sabrina had to think about this. She didn't know why she was put off by this, but she was. It was simply so different from Denver. Why did this man have to work at the livery? She didn't know pastors ever did that. Sabrina sat thinking about this for a long time. And in that time, she missed most of the sermon.

5

"BRI, THIS IS CASSIDY. She's married to Trace."

"It's nice to meet you," Sabrina said, still not sure what she thought of all of this. Danny had said there was a fine church family, and Sabrina had liked everyone she'd met, but she hadn't planned on the pastor being a livery worker. And huge into the bargain. He didn't look like a pastor at all.

"Are you enjoying Token Creek?" Cassidy asked, and Sabrina forced her mind back.

"I am, yes. I find that I like small towns," Sabrina said, realizing how true it was. It was fun to have a few dozen streets and know that soon nearly every face would be familiar.

"And this is Jeb and Patience Dorn," Jeanette said next, turning to the couple that had come up. "This is Sabrina Matthews. She goes by Bri."

"It's nice to meet you, Bri." Jeb put his hand out. "I'm Jessie Wheeler's cousin. I saw you at the store."

"I remember," Sabrina said, liking him very much.

"And how did you like the store?" Patience asked.

Sabrina smiled. "It was interesting. And busy!"

"Always on Saturday," Patience agreed. "Sometimes Jeb helps out as well."

The five of them talked for a while before Trace came looking for Cassidy. Jeanette invited them for dinner, but they had plans. The two women ended up walking home together, and for some reason, Jeanette could not bring herself to ask what Sabrina thought of the morning. There was a note of disquiet about her that Jeanette could not decipher. Sabrina had not shared her story with Jeanette, but she sensed that the younger woman shared her faith in Christ.

She knew better than to make assumptions, but there was something humble and open about Sabrina that caused Jeanette to think she believed.

However, she had not seemed to enjoy the sermon. She'd been very still, opening her Bible only at the end, and hadn't even tried to sing the closing song. She seemed to like the people she met, but Jeanette could tell there was something serious on her mind.

"Are you all right?" the older woman finally asked. They were on Jeanette's front walk and Sabrina had come to a stop.

"I think so. I suddenly miss my church in Denver."

"Anything in particular?"

Sabrina looked at her, wondering how honest she could be.

"I guess I'm just a little confused. Why does your pastor work at the livery?"

"Because we're a small flock, and even though the families give generously, they don't have a lot of excess. Rylan has never wanted us to be taxed with giving for his salary."

"So he wouldn't have enough to live on if he didn't do that?"

"That's right."

Sabrina's heart twisted with compassion. She still didn't know if she was comfortable with this new pastor, but she certainly understood not having enough money.

"Does it bother you that he works at the livery?"

Sabrina bit her lip and admitted, "He doesn't seem like a pastor to me."

Jeanette had to smile even as she asked herself if this younger woman had heard a word of the sermon. Rylan had preached from the book of Colossians, and there was no mistaking the amount of time he must have studied.

"He does look more like a livery worker than a pastor," Jeanette admitted, finally moving to the front door, "but I hope you won't judge him on his looks. I hope you'll give him a chance."

It was just what Sabrina needed to hear. She had realized that she'd been judging him by his appearance and knew there was no excuse for that.

"I will certainly give him a chance," she said with quiet conviction. "And thank you for explaining."

Jeanette didn't comment, but she did look into Sabrina's face before she opened the door and felt sure once again that this young woman was special.

* * *

"Which place?" Rylan asked of sheriff Nate Kaderly when that man came for him on Sunday evening. The two men had gone to an apartment building on Willow Street because a man was dying. The sheriff had been called on an unrelated matter when someone else mentioned the man's plight. As was the sheriff's habit, he went for Rylan.

"Back here." Nate led the way. The apartment was at the rear, up a set of outside stairs that had seen better days. Nate did not knock but opened the door slowly and led the way inside. He had not dallied, but they were too late. The man was gone, his body already going cold.

"Who was he?" Rylan asked.

"Someone called him Ivan, but I didn't know him. Do you want to be alone—I mean, to pray for him?"

"I'll tell you something, Nate," Rylan said kindly. "I try to pattern my life from the Bible, and there is nothing in God's Word about praying for the dead. By the time a person leaves this earth, he's made his choices."

Token Creek's sheriff looked interested, but he didn't ask questions or comment. He mentioned going for Abe Wyner, the town's undertaker, but that was the end of it. Rylan did not linger in the man's small apartment, but he did pray. Not for the dead man—he'd meant what he'd said—but for Nate Kaderly, who, as caring as he was of others, never saw his own need.

* * *

"Hannah," Sabrina asked the little girl on Monday morning, "where do I put these pants? The shelf is getting full."

"Oh, there's a place in the storeroom for those. I'll show you."

Sabrina followed Jessie's daughter and when she got to the shelf in the back took some time to arrange things neatly. This was the way Jessie found her.

"You're as good as Jeb. He likes things neat."

"Don't you?" Sabrina asked.

"I love things neat, but when the store is busy, I don't feel I have time." Jessie's hand came up. "And so the storeroom looks like this."

"It's not so bad," Sabrina said, and she was right. Thirty minutes of work would put it to rights.

"Mama." Clancy was suddenly there, a hatbox in her hand.

"Yes, Clancy."

"I need this."

"A hatbox? You don't have a hat."

"But I will when my head is biggest."

Sabrina's hand came to her mouth. Jessie did not look at her, but Sabrina could see that she was fighting laughter as well.

"Why does Clancy have a hatbox?" Hannah arrived and wished to know.

"Clancy," Jessie addressed her youngest daughter, ignoring Hannah for the moment. "You may have that, but nothing else."

"What if I need something?" the child argued.

"I don't want to hear about it—not for a week."

Clancy looked stubborn but turned to Hannah.

"How many is that?"

"How many days?" Hannah clarified.

The women left Hannah counting on one hand and Clancy still frowning. If they stayed, they were both going to laugh.

* * *

"So this is where you work."

Sabrina heard the male voice behind her and turned to find the man from the alley.

"Can I help you?" Sabrina asked.

"I hope so. I'm Bret Toben, by the way."

"Sabrina Matthews," she told him, her voice not overly friendly. "What can I get you?"

Several replies sprang to Bret's lips, but he squelched them all.

"Tobacco, please."

Sabrina had not done this herself and started to go to find Jessie, but Bret's voice stopped her.

"She keeps it right here."

"I know where it is," Sabrina explained, "but I don't know how to cut it."

"I buy the whole twist," Bret said, lifting one down from the rack. "And Jessie charges me a nickle."

Bret held the coin out to Sabrina, and she took it. She ignored the fact that he let his fingers linger as long as he dared and went behind the counter to the cash register.

"Hello, Bret," Jessie said suddenly. "Is Bri taking care of you?"

"Bri?" Bret said, looking at that lady. "You didn't tell me about your nickname."

"I don't think we're going to have that many conversations," Sabrina said, not unkindly.

"Is it me or the fact that I own a saloon?"

"Does it matter?" Sabrina asked.

"It might," Bret hedged, even as he knew she was right.

Jessie smiled at Bret, who was much too used to attention from women. He caught the smile and gave one in return. He would have enjoyed the challenge of getting a few more words from Sabrina but decided to head on his way. Tipping his hat in a way he knew was charming, he bid the ladies goodbye.

"So tell me," Jessie asked as soon as he was gone, "is it him or the saloon?"

"Both, I suppose. I can tell he's not my type."

"I wonder who is your type," Jessie said, voicing her thoughts aloud.

Sabrina could have told her that was the last thing she wondered about, but she had no time. Clancy showed up, clearly put out, having been told by her sister that she couldn't need anything for seven days!

* * *

Old Ivan Lamour died.

The words, coming near the end of the

workday, were not easy to hear, but they meant that an apartment had opened up in town. Sabrina did not want to cause anyone at Jeanette's to worry, but this was something she had to check on. Jessie had warned her that the location on Willow Street was not the best, but Sabrina said she still wanted to look. And this time she found the building without incident. She knocked on two doors before someone answered, and that woman directed her to yet one more door.

"Do you have an empty apartment for rent?" Sabrina wasted no time asking the man who opened the last door.

Pale, watery eyes looked her up and down, clearly surprised, but Butch Sandgren was not about to pass up a paying customer. And she was young and pretty.

"This way," Butch said after a moment, and led the way around the back. He had done nothing with the place since the body had been taken away. His plans did not include much, so he had no issues with showing it as it was.

Sabrina had seen worse certainly, but not by much. Her own place in the bordello had been better.

"How much?" she asked, thinking it needed far more than cleaning.

Butch named a price that sent Sabrina to the door.

"Thank you for showing me the apartment," she said, but Butch's voice stopped her.

"I could lower it some."

"How much?" Sabrina asked, also planning to ask about paint and the stairs outside.

The two dickered for several minutes, Sabrina having to give in some, but Butch certain he was giving in more.

"I would like to move in right away," Sabrina said, "but I also want the repairs started right away."

"How am I supposed to paint if you're in here?" Butch asked.

"I'll do the painting myself if you buy the paint. But the stairs have to be started right away. And this lock—" Sabrina went to the door. "I want that fixed no later than tomorrow evening."

Butch could not believe he was agreeing to all of this, but she kept looking at him expectantly, and her voice was very nice.

"All right," Butch said. "But I want my rent today."

"I was thinking I would pay the first month as soon as the stairs were fixed."

This plan did not sit well with the landlord, and more dickering ensued. Nevertheless Sabrina left well pleased, hurrying back across town to Jeanette's to tell that household her good news.

* * *

"But Bri," Jeanette said when she found her voice. "We're in no hurry to have you move out. Why don't you take a little more time finding a place?"

"Thank you, Jeanette, but I think it will suit me very well, and the price is good."

"Bri," Heather had to speak up as well. "That section of town can be very rough, especially after dark."

"I'll be careful," Sabrina assured her, smiling at her caring.

The women were not done. They tried through supper to talk Sabrina out of the move, but she had made up her mind. And that was not the end of it. In the morning at the store, Sabrina mentioned to Jessie that she had taken Ivan Lamour's apartment, and her reaction was the same.

"You rented it?" Jessie asked in surprise. "It's not in the best part of town."

"But it's affordable, and I'll be careful," she repeated herself, confident that she could do it.

Jessie was on the verge of telling her who some of her neighbors would be, prostitutes and the like, but a customer needed her. She forgot about it until things were so slow that Sabrina was asking if she could leave early, having already picked out and paid for the paint she was going to use. Jessie stood at the door of the mercantile store, broom in hand, wondering if she should have said more.

* * *

"Becky!" Sabrina said, coming around the corner of the building and finding her sitting on the bottom step.

"Is this the place?" the cook demanded.

"It is. Come up and see it."

"Bri." Becky stopped her with a hand to her shoulder, her voice soft and serious. "I'm here for one reason, maybe two."

"All right."

"I'm here to talk you out of this, and if that doesn't work, I'm here to clean."

Sabrina had to smile.

"It does need work, Becky," Sabrina explained gently, "but I'm pleased to have found it, and I want to be able to take care of myself, which means finding a cheap place."

Becky nodded, seeing that she was not going to change her mind. Becky had known that she wouldn't but was glad she'd tried. Following Sabrina up the stairs, she resigned herself to whatever came next.

* * *

"Hello, Rylan," Jeanette said when that man ended up at her door that evening. "Come in."

"Is this a bad time?" Rylan asked, having planned to just check on Theta, but Jeanette looked slightly distracted.

"As a matter of fact, your timing is perfect. Can you help Timothy lift a bed into the wagon?"

"Certainly. In the back?"

Before Rylan knew it, he was on the heavy end of a bedframe, lifting without a problem, and hoping Timothy was not taking too much on himself. Timothy assured him that he could take it from there, but the mute appeal in Jeanette's eyes was impossible for Rylan to ignore.

"Why don't I go along and help you on the other end, Timothy?"

"Oh, you don't have to do that, Pastor."

"My evening is suddenly free," Rylan said, climbing aboard with a swift change of plans.

Timothy didn't argue but put the team into motion and headed toward Sabrina's new apartment on Willow Street.

* * *

"How does this look?" Sabrina asked, having painted one wall on the living room end of the apartment. The bedroom was separate, but the rest of the apartment, living room, kitchen, and dining area, was one square room.

"It looks good," Becky complimented, "but I don't know how you're going to stand to sleep in here with that smell. You'd better come back to Jeanette's tonight."

Sabrina laughed at Becky's thinly veiled attempt to get her away from the apartment. The two had cleaned for hours before Becky had gone back to Jeanette's for a few hours to work on supper, muttering all the time about Sabrina not having enough furniture or even a decent bed to sleep on. The one that had been left was not something Sabrina was willing to lie on, and the women had dismantled it, carted it out, and thrown it away.

"I think I hear the wagon," Becky suddenly said.

"What wagon?"

"Timothy is bringing a few things," Becky said before disappearing out the door and calling down to Timothy to be careful of the stairs.

Sabrina was in the midst of cleaning up her paint supplies when she realized someone had come in. She turned to find Rylan Jarvik filling the doorway.

"I don't think we've officially met," that man said, his voice deep. He came toward Sabrina, his hand out. "I'm Rylan."

"It's nice to meet you," Sabrina said automatically, realizing he was even larger than she first realized and the hand that took hers was gigantic.

"I didn't get your name," Rylan began, but Becky was suddenly there.

"Now, Bri, where do you want this little chest?"

"What is this for?" Sabrina asked.

"Watch that wall, Timothy," Becky said, taking charge. "She just painted."

For some reason, Sabrina was embarrassed. There was something about Rylan Jarvik that flustered her. Maybe it was the way she'd first seen him at the livery, or the way she hadn't heard a word of his sermon, but whatever the cause, it made her want to duck away the moment she saw him.

"I'm going to help Timothy with the bed," Rylan was saying. "What wall do you want it on?"

Sabrina had no idea. She hadn't thought that far and now stared at him without saying anything. Rylan didn't know what was hard about the question, but when she didn't answer, he simply went back down the stairs to help the other man.

"What's the matter?" Becky asked.

"I think I'm just surprised," Sabrina answered when she found her voice.

"Watch that step, Timothy," Sabrina heard Rylan say from outside. She turned to Becky.

"I have to run down to see the landlord. Just put things where they make sense to you."

"All right. I'll take care of it."

Sabrina waited only until the men were out of the way before escaping. It was true that she did need to ask Mr. Sandgren about the repairs on the stairway, but she also hoped Rylan Jarvik would be gone when she returned.

* * *

"Do you call her Sabrina or Bri?" Rylan asked Jeanette a few hours later.

"Bri."

"And she was living here until today?"

"Yes. She took us by surprise," Jeanette admitted, a frown on her face. She was working to accept Sabrina's move, but it was proving difficult. "I told her she could take her time and look for a place, but then she rented from Sandgren."

"And you wanted her where?"

"Ideally, above my shop, but I've got that rented. At the very least I hoped she would get into one of the places Hulett has."

Rylan nodded. He understood, even if he didn't completely agree with Jeanette. Parts of town were not as safe, and he realized how that might bother her. Clearly Sabrina didn't share Jeanette's feelings either.

"Bri came with you on Sunday, I noticed," Rylan said next.

"Yes. It was hard for her. She said she missed her church family in Denver."

"She's a long way from home."

"She is," Jeanette agreed. "I guess Denver holds some hard memories for her, and a friend suggested she try Token Creek."

It was a long way to come in Rylan's mind, but he didn't comment on that. He also wondered who might have suggested Token Creek. He had lots of family and friends in Denver and would not have been overly surprised to learn that he knew the very person.

"More pie?" Jeanette offered.

Rylan, who had forgotten to eat supper, accepted. Heather, who had just taken Theta to bed, joined them. The three of them talked until well after dark.

* * *

"How was your first night?" Jeanette asked when Sabrina got to work on Wednesday, not able to resist giving her a hug.

"It was great. Thank you for the bed and other pieces. You're too generous, Jeanette," Sabrina added, only to have that lady laugh.

"Now you're going to make this harder."

"What's that?"

"I've got something else for you," Jeanette said, going in the back and returning in a moment. "This was never picked up, and I think it might be long enough for you."

Jeanette held out a navy skirt, with a wide waistband that looked to be just Sabrina's size.

"I can't just take this from you, Jeanette."

"Sure you can. I want you to have it."

Sabrina held it up to the front of herself. It looked an exact fit.

"I have a white blouse that would be perfect with this," the younger woman said quietly. "Thank you, Jeanette."

"You're welcome. You'll have to wear it tomorrow so I can see it."

"I'll do that."

Jeanette peppered Sabrina with questions about her new place and neighbors she had not met. As the two started on the day's work, they continued to talk, but Jeanette kept quiet about her true feelings, still doing mental battle over Sabrina's independence.

* * *

"The lock on my door still isn't fixed," Sabrina said to Butch Sandgren that evening, thinking at this rate she would never have to pay her full rent.

"The piece has to go to the livery, and I haven't got time," he said. "Take it yourself and let me know what it costs!"

No words could have been more depressing to Sabrina. The last thing she wanted to do was run into Rylan. Nevertheless she made herself take the piece to work with her the next day. Maybe Jeanette would say she was headed that way, and she could ask her to drop it off.

6

SABRINA SAW NO HELP for it. Jeanette had not said a thing about going to the livery, and if she didn't go there during her dinner break, there would be even more days with a door lock that didn't really work.

Dreading it with every step, Sabrina went that direction, not bothering to eat the food Becky had sent with Jeanette for her. She stepped inside, unsure where to find someone, and then realized Rylan might not be working today. Feeling a bit bolder, she went in the direction of a wide doorway that sat past the stalls, thinking she'd heard noise and someone might be in the forge. Rylan chose that moment to come from that fiery room.

"Excuse me," he said, pulling up short when he would have walked right past and using his sleeve to wipe the sweat from his brow. "I didn't see you, Sabrina."

"No, it's my fault," Sabrina said. She had turned as they spoke until she was partway into the room, backing away from Rylan with sudden nerves. "I'm having a problem with my lock. Mr. Sandgren said to bring it here."

Rylan took the piece she held out and inspected it.

"Is this from the door into your apartment?" he asked quietly.

Sabrina nodded, meeting the eyes she had to look up to see.

"You don't have a lock on your door?"

"Not at the moment."

For several seconds Rylan knew what Jeanette had felt—fear for this woman's safety. He studied the lock again, seeing how easy it would be to fix, and then looked back at Sabrina.

Without warning Rylan stepped forward, took Sabrina by the shoulders and propelled her into the water trough that sat some four feet to the left. Sabrina gasped as water came to her waist, sloshing nearly to her shoulders. She looked up at the man bending over her and got angry.

"Rylan Jarvik!" Sabrina spat. "What in the world? This is a brand new skirt!"

"You were on fire," he said, but Sabrina didn't hear him.

"Jeanette gave it to me yesterday!"

"Here, let me help you."

Sabrina glared at him but allowed him to help her from the trough. Rylan lifted her easily and set her beside the water trough this time. Soggy as she was, she came fully upright, ready to tell him again how she felt until he bent a little and repeated himself.

"You were on fire. Your skirt was on fire."

Sabrina looked as surprised as she felt, and tried to turn to see the back of her skirt. That was when Rylan spotted the front of her. The white blouse had become transparent with the water.

"Let me get my jacket," Rylan began, but Sabrina didn't understand.

"It's not that cold. I'll just head home and change."

"Wait," Rylan said, but Sabrina was already headed for the alley. Rylan caught her at the door and put the jacket around her. Sabrina turned back, no longer angry but more confused than ever.

"This was my fault," Rylan began before Sabrina could speak. "I had no business letting you near the forge. I'm sorry."

Sabrina would have been made of stone not to respond to the regret she read in Rylan's eyes.

"Thank you for putting it out," Sabrina said, relaxing a little for the first time. "I wasn't burned." This said, she began to remove the jacket to hand to him, but Rylan's hands came to her shoulders.

"Your blouse . . ." he began.

"Did it get burned?" Sabrina asked, trying to see again.

". . . is wet," Rylan finished.

Sabrina finally heard the words and froze, but only for a moment. Moving swiftly, she pulled the jacket around her and found herself fully enveloped. Not until she was covered did she look back into Rylan's eyes.

"I'll just run home and change."

"No hurry about the coat. And again, I'm very sorry."

Sabrina thanked him again and went on her way. She cut down the alley and across side streets to gain her front door as fast as she could. Jeanette would be wondering what happened to her, and this was not the way she wanted to be seen.

* * *

Pete Stillwell, owner of the livery, timed his visit perfectly. He came in to check on something in the livery office, which freed Rylan to go to see Jeanette. Rylan was sweaty and in work clothes but knew this was warranted. And thankfully Jeanette was alone. Rylan swiftly explained the incident to the dress shop owner, and even though she didn't want to, she took the money Rylan gave her.

"Please replace the skirt. It's all my fault, and I want to take care of it."

"I will, Rylan, but I'm fairly certain Bri will understand."

"She's a stranger here, Jeanette. I hate the thought of anything happening that would make her regret her move or feel uncomfortable with me or any of us."

Rylan did not stay much longer. Jeanette thanked him for his understanding and then prayed for Sabrina. She would not have thought about Sabrina's reaction in those terms and realized that Rylan might be right. Jeanette kept working but with an eye to the window, anticipating Sabrina's return any minute.

* * *

Sabrina picked up Rylan's jacket, set it back down, and then picked it up again. Before it was over, she ended up leaving it, wanting to get back to Jeanette's as fast as she could. She took the same shortcut but didn't go back through the livery, hurrying back as fast as her long legs would carry her. She nearly burst through the door, an explanation on her lips, but Jeanette stopped her with three words.

"Rylan was here."

"He explained?"

"Yes. Are you sure you're not burned?"

"I'm fine, but I don't know if the skirt can be fixed."

"He left money to replace it."

"He didn't have to do that."

"He wanted to," Jeanette said, not adding that Rylan was more concerned about Sabrina's reaction to what happened than the skirt. Jeanette knew that sharing this was not a good idea, but she hoped that Sabrina would share on her own.

"Did he tell you my blouse got wet?" Sabrina asked.

"He said you took his jacket, so I made an assumption."

Sabrina suddenly sat down. This was not the way she had envisioned things. She had never planned to bare her body for a man again, and now the pastor of her church had seen her in a wet, white blouse. She had been wearing a shift, but that hadn't been a great deal of help.

"Are you going to be able to forget about this?" Jeanette asked, wondering what the look on Sabrina's face meant.

"I think so. It might be embarrassing to see Pastor Jarvik."

"He's a gentleman to the soul of his being. He would never deliberately do anything to embarrass you."

"Will he be embarrassed when he sees me again?"

"I don't think so. I think he'll be as kind and caring as he always is."

The kind of man who comes here and pays to replace my skirt. Sabrina didn't say this aloud but nodded and picked up the man's shirt she was working on. Jeanette didn't press her any further, assuming if she wanted to talk some more she would.

* * *

It had taken a little doing. Sabrina had not cooked for more than a week, and the stove was new to her, but eventually she put some supper on the table. It was nothing like Becky could produce, but the bean stew was edible, and so was the flat bread that went with it. She had only one pot and a few dishes, but in time she knew she would build on that.

"Cleanup is easy," she said to herself as she began to boil water for the handful of items that needed washing and then laughed at her own joke. A moment later, someone knocked at the door. Sabrina found Rylan on the landing.

"Hello," she said quietly.

Rylan held up the lock she'd left at the livery. "I thought I'd stop by and fix this for you."

"I forgot all about it," Sabrina admitted. "Thank you."

"You're welcome," Rylan said, going to work on the door while standing just inside. Sabrina watched him for a moment, not sure what she should do.

"Something smells good," Rylan finally commented.

"Oh, it's just a stew I made. Would you like some?"

"I've eaten, but thank you."

"It was my first time," Sabrina said, not sure why she added that.

"To cook here or anywhere?"

"Here."

"How did it go?"

"I think all right. Becky cleaned the stove the other day, so it doesn't even smoke."

"That Becky is a wonder. Have you had her biscuits?"

"No, I don't believe so."

"When I'm desperate, I make broad hints, and she takes pity on me."

Sabrina laughed. It was such a funny comment coming from this confident, seemingly self-sufficient man.

"You can laugh," Rylan said, still working on the door, "but after you've had them you'll find yourself desperate enough to beg like the rest of us."

Sabrina had to smile, even though he wasn't looking up to see it.

"I like her bread pudding," Sabrina said. "She even taught me how to make it."

"I haven't had that," Rylan said. "I'll have to drop a few hints for that one too."

Again Sabrina wanted to laugh. He was so honest about wanting to eat Becky's cooking, without a bit of shame for what he called begging.

"Well, now," Rylan said, and Sabrina looked up to see him watching her. "You do know how to smile."

"Do I not smile very much?" Sabrina asked, feeling uncertain.

"Now that I think about it, a certain blacksmith tried to burn you to death today, so it's no surprise that you didn't smile at him."

"It was just a mistake," Sabrina said.

"That's true, but if I can be honest with you, I've never let anyone get near the forge, and for the very reason you discovered today. I don't know how I let my guard down."

"I didn't realize I was so close."

"I think a cinder must have been on the floor. I assume the bottom of your skirt was burned?"

"The hem, yes."

Rylan nodded and then said, "All done. It should work now."

"Oh, that was fast."

"Have a good evening, Sabrina," Rylan said, finding "Bri" a little too familiar.

"Thank you. Oh, just a moment." Sabrina remembered the jacket and went to get it from the corner of the living room. She handed it to Rylan, who looked at her directly.

"Thank you. I'd forgotten all about it."

Sabrina nodded and thanked him again. She closed the door and locked it, thinking Jeanette had been right. He had done nothing to embarrass her.

* * *

"What is this?" Butch Sandgren asked, when Sabrina gave him only a portion of the rent money on Friday after work.

"That's half the rent, minus the money it took me to buy the paint and have my lock fixed."

The anger in the man's face was unmistakable when he said, "I can have you kicked out."

"By whom?"

"The sheriff."

"Before or after you explain to him about our agreement?" Sabrina asked, feeling a bit shaken by his anger.

"What agreement?"

"You haven't fixed my stairs, and I've been living here for ten days. If they break, I can't even get to my apartment. Not to mention I could be hurt."

Butch calmed down. He did mean to fix the stairs and had genuinely forgotten.

"All right. I'll get to it next week."

"Thank you," Sabrina said, and turned to go on her way. She was about to round the corner, back to her stairs, when a voice spoke to her.

"More folks should stand up to him. If they did, he'd fix this dump."

Sabrina looked around, but all she saw was a window.

"Who said that?" she asked the window, and waited for a woman's face to appear, a cigarette hanging from her mouth. She was not very old, maybe in her mid-twenties, but her eyes were hard.

"I said it. Are you the new woman upstairs?"

"Yes. Bri Matthews."

"I'm Crystal."

"Hello, Crystal."

Crystal shook her head in self-derision before saying, "Butch went on and on about how pretty you are."

Sabrina didn't try to comment on that.

"And then I still let him visit me."

"Maybe you shouldn't," Sabrina said with

enough confidence that Crystal stared at her.

"I think someone's at my door," Crystal suddenly said. Sabrina could see the front door—no one was there—and saw it for the excuse it was. Still she took the hint.

"I'll say goodnight then."

"He was right," Crystal said before Sabrina could move away.

Sabrina looked at her and waited.

"You are pretty."

That said, the face disappeared back inside, and Sabrina slowly climbed the stairs to her room.

* * *

"Can Bri stay for supper?" Hannah asked her mother on Saturday afternoon.

"As long as she likes venison stew," Jessie agreed.

"I'll ask her," Hannah volunteered. Sabrina said that she did but still checked with Jessie in the next hour.

"Are you sure you have enough?"

"Plenty, but I think I'd better warn you that this is our night to walk by the creek."

"What does that mean?"

"Oh, that we'll all get at least a little wet."

"I think I can live with that," Sabrina said with a smile, thinking about her recent bath in the livery and thankful she wasn't wearing a white blouse.

Sabrina would have asked Jessie a little more about it, but Patience Dorn was coming her way with a young woman who was holding a baby.

"Hello, Bri," Patience greeted. "I don't think you met my niece on Sunday. This is Meg. She's married to Brad. And this is their daughter, Savanna."

"I've heard about you," Sabrina said, smiling at the adorable baby in Meg's arms.

"How do you like working for Jeanette?" Meg asked.

"I like it very much. Saturdays are my favorite because the contrast of being there in the morning and here in the afternoon is so interesting."

"She means tiring," Jessie teased, and the women went to work on Meg's list. Patience took Savanna into the rear of the store with Hannah and Clancy, and Sabrina was given a chance to get to know Meg.

"How was Theta this morning?" Meg asked.

"Actually, I found an apartment," Sabrina told her. "I'm not at Jeanette's now."

"Oh, I'll bet they miss you. Becky loves to have someone to take care of."

"Well, she sends enough food my way that in some ways she still is."

"That's Becky all right. Oh, are these on sale?" Meg asked, having spotted canned plums and apricots.

"They are on sale, yes."

"Brad loves these," Meg said. "And I don't find them that often."

"I don't think I've ever tried any."

"They're not bad. Sometimes the syrup is a little sweet, but it's a treat when I run low on our own canned goods."

Savanna was heard giggling just then, and Sabrina was going to ask about life with a baby in the house, but someone came in the door. Sabrina couldn't see Jessie, so she went to see if she could be of any service.

* * *

"We throw rocks," Clancy told Sabrina on their walk to the creek.

"Into the water?"

"Hard," Clancy clarified, and Sabrina had all she could do not to laugh. Both girls were delightful, but Clancy had such a funny way of expressing herself. Clancy took life very seriously at times, and the little girl's sincerity was very fun to watch.

"You can get wet," Hannah filled in now, "but just a little."

"I'll try to remember that," Sabrina said before turning to Jessie. "How long have you been doing this?"

"A long time. After being in the store all week, I just need to get out on Saturday evening."

"What do you do in the winter?"

"We come until it's too cold. We usually make it into November but never into December."

"Do you get much snow?"

"We get enough, but the cold is the hardest part. It's unforgiving."

Sabrina got cold easily and did not look forward to that time. It was hard to imagine it getting cold on a warm day like today, but it had been the same in Denver—hot enough to boil you in summer and anything but come winter.

Before she knew it, they were at the creek. It had been closer than she realized, and as she listened to the water ripple over stones, making white waves in some spots, she wondered that she hadn't come here before. The scene caused her to remember all the things Danny had taught her about God the Creator, and that made her prayerful. It also made her wonder what Jessie believed.

"Over here, Bri," Hannah invited, and Sabrina joined that little girl at the water's edge. From there the time flew, everyone getting a little wet, until Jessie urged Sabrina on her way, making sure she started home long before dark.

When the girls had been out of earshot, though, Jessie had been plainspoken about Token Creek on Saturday nights and Sabrina's neighborhood getting more than its share of action when folks started drinking. Sabrina, snug at home, didn't think much of it until the sun set and it got noisy. She fell asleep just fine, but even as she prayed for Jessie and the girls, it occurred to her that Jessie had been right and that going out on Saturday nights was probably not the best of ideas.

* * *

"What's up?" Trace found Cassidy in the living room, the lantern turned high and a letter in her hand.

"Jessie had a letter from my mother. Meg brought it back."

Trace sat close to his wife. "How is she?"

"Her back has been hurting again, but other than that, all seems well."

"Can she visit when the baby comes?"

Cassidy smiled before reading, " 'You had to ask. Just try to keep me away.' "

"I wondered if she might not feel that way."

"Once she gets here, I won't want her to leave."

"Maybe she'll feel the same way."

"And you would really be all right with that?"

"Well, it would take some getting used to, but I think we would be fine."

Cassidy smiled at him, thinking he was wonderful, before she finished the letter and snuggled close to Trace's side. She had sudden visions of her mother moving to Token Creek and being strong enough to help Jeanette with the shop and maybe even live in the apartment above. Cassidy knew it was just a dream, but part of her wondered if someday it might come true.

* * *

"Sit by me," Jeanette invited when Sabrina came into the church building on Sunday morning. Sabrina was happy to have Jeanette's company, and between her and Heather, they caught Sabrina up on all news concerning Becky, Timothy, and Theta before they wanted to know how Sabrina was doing in her apartment and was she safe enough?

The women were still visiting when Rylan stepped into the pulpit, but for a moment, Sabrina sat in quiet wonder and prayed. They welcomed her like an old friend, treating her with such love.

Had Sabrina but known it, Jeanette and Heather were so thankful to see her they could have wept. They had not asked her what she believed, but Jeanette had simply taken her along to church on that first Sunday. And now here, living on her own, she had still joined them for the service for the last two weeks.

Rylan had started his sermon, but all the women took time to pray and praise God for providing in such an amazing way.

* * *

Sabrina sat after the sermon ended, reading over Colossians 1:17 and trying to understand what Rylan had meant when he mentioned creation. She was still working on it when Chas Vick came up to speak with Jeanette. Their conversation did not need much time, and as soon as they were done, Jeanette introduced him to Sabrina.

"It's good to meet you," Chas said. "Are you visiting, or have you moved to Token Creek?"

"I moved here a few weeks ago," Sabrina said, liking him and feeling free to share. "I work part-time for Jeanette and part-time for Jessie at the mercantile."

"Well, you're a busy lady. Between those two stops, you must see everyone in town."

"Especially at the mercantile," Jeanette added.

"It is busy," Sabrina agreed.

"Where are you living?"

"I'm in one of the apartments on Willow Street."

"One of Butch Sandgren's?"

"Yes."

"He's a character, isn't he?"

"That's one way to put it," Sabrina said dryly, thinking there was another side to Mr. Sandgren that was not so charming.

"Listen," Chas suddenly said. "If you're free for lunch and can stand four kids, we'd love to have you."

"Oh, thank you," Sabrina answered, not having expected this.

"Let me find my wife," Chas said, and left before Sabrina could say another word.

Sabrina looked at Jeanette, who smiled at her.

"You'll like the Vicks. Miranda is wonderful, and you'll fall in love with all four children."

Sabrina could only nod, still trying to take it all in. Miranda Vick came over, and Sabrina left with them a short time later. Not for many hours did she remember she had a question about that one verse.

7

"When you continue to study these qualifications," Rylan said to the men on Monday night as they met in his living room, "don't lose sight of the cross. When you see 'hospitable' in the verse, see the cross. When you read that we need to be sober and vigilant, again, remember the cross.

"It's easy to see this list as a group of things to master and check off. If we forget that the main goal is living a godly, holy life before God, then Christ's amazing work on the cross will diminish. Working at these things with the cross in mind empowers us to a greater purpose: to lead our families and the church of God to greater holiness."

Brad had a question for Rylan just then, and so did Daryl Rathman concerning why it was important for elders not to be new in the faith. They ended in prayer as they always did, and because it was early still, the conversation turned to some physical matters.

"How are you doing financially, Ry?" Trace asked. "Are you planning to stay at the livery?"

"I am, Trace, but not because I'm strapped. I still like the fact that it eases the burden for our church family, but it also gives me great opportunities in the community. Pete depends on me a little too much at times, but I think it's worth it."

"How is the paint fund coming?" Daryl asked.

"I think we're almost there," Rylan said. "You'd have to check with Chas to get an exact figure."

The men talked about a number of things in the next 30 minutes before going on their way. Rylan saw them off from his porch, always so thankful for the time they had, before going back to his living room, quiet and empty now, and praying until bedtime for each and every man.

* * *

Dear Bri, Callie's letter began. Sabrina was reading from a rocking chair in front of the mercantile.

> **I can't tell you what it did to my heart to hear from you. I have cried and prayed for days, and to know that you have been taken in by a woman there in Token Creek made me cry and pray all the more. I know there must be much more news, so please write again. Everyone here misses you, but Danny and I do most of all.**
>
> **Tell us all about the church family and friends that you're making. As you can imagine, we are anxious to hear all. Lisa is expecting again, so that's our big news. She feels well but is weary with Josh and Delta to care for.**

Sabrina read quickly until she got to the last paragraph, the one where Callie told her what God had been teaching her.

Lately I've been looking at Genesis and marveling at God as Creator. This is not a new topic for me, but my thoughts have been new. When I am tempted to hide from God because of my sin or some flaw, I have to remember that He knows all. He's the Creator. I don't know why it's taken me this long to see it in that light. I can read that He created everything, but I forget how personal that is. He created Callie Barshaw and knows every part of her frame. He made her compassionate and sensitive, and He also knows she wants to have her own way. He sees what's good about her and can stay and what has to be trained out.

The peace I feel about this new realization has freed me to go to God in a new way. I have long prayed in repentance, but this is new. Now I'm praying with such respect for who God is but with none of the fear of being "found out." I praise Him for continuing to train me because I need it so much.

Callie closed the letter soon after this, urging Sabrina to write again. Sabrina folded the letter and put it in the pocket of her apron, but for a moment that was all the more she was capable of. She was in the same boat as Callie, seeing God as Creator but not in a personal light. It was going to take some thought. There were still parts of her heart that she thought were secret. In her mind she knew that God knew all, but her heart was not fully convinced.

Jessie had not needed her this Tuesday as things at the mercantile had been very slow, but she'd still gone and checked for mail and then sat in the rocking chair on the wide boardwalk out front to read the letter. This was where Hannah found her.

"Hi, Bri."

"Hello, Hannah," Sabrina greeted quietly, still thinking about Callie's words and how personal they were to everyone. God was the Creator of each of them.

"What are you doing?"

"I just read a letter from a friend. What are you doing today?"

"I might get to play with Heidi."

"Heidi Vick?"

"Do you know Heidi?"

"Yes. I had dinner at Heidi's house on Sunday."

"They have a baby," Hannah told Sabrina, though she already knew, "and a dog."

"Isn't that fun?"

"Clancy used to be a baby, but not anymore."

"You're both big girls these days," Sabrina said, and without warning a memory of her sister came flooding back. They had been about the same distance apart in age, and Sabrina would have been the Clancy of the two.

"Are you sad?" Hannah asked suddenly, and Sabrina thought she was much too aware for her age.

Before Sabrina could answer, Rylan had come up the step and joined them. Neither female watched him approach, but Sabrina saw in a moment that he and Hannah were old friends.

"Pastor Rylan," Hannah said, running to take his hand, "I might get to play with Heidi today!"

"That sounds fun. Do I get to come?"

"No," Hannah answered, looking truly regretful about this. "You're too big."

"I could get on my knees," Rylan suggested, his eyes exaggerated.

"No," Hannah said, but she was laughing. "We play dolls. Boys don't like dolls. Franklin never does," Hannah added, referring to the oldest of the Vick children.

Rylan's free hand came out and he gently cupped her cheek before turning to Sabrina.

"How is that lock working?"

"Very well, thank you."

"Good."

"Do you need to shop?" Hannah snagged Rylan's attention again.

"I just need a few things," Rylan answered, but then turned right back to Sabrina.

"Not working today?"

"It's slow, so Jessie gave me the day off. Oh, and thank you for the skirt money. Jeanette is making me a new one this week."

"I'm glad," Rylan said, but then a teasing light entered his eyes. "Does she have enough fabric?"

Sabrina laughed but didn't answer, and Hannah took Rylan by the hand again and led him inside. Sabrina had not forgotten about the verse this time but wasn't sure if she should ask him or not. She wrestled with the idea as she walked back to her apartment but never did come up with an answer.

* * *

"We can fish," Clancy told Sabrina later that day.

Hannah had gone to the Vicks. Sabrina had written back to Callie, and after doing some laundry that she hung around her apartment, had taken pity on Jessie and invited Clancy to spend the afternoon with her. They had seen Sabrina's apartment, walked to Jeanette's, and were now strolling along the creek.

"I don't know how to fish."

"You don't?"

"No, I'm sorry."

"Mama knows how to fish, but she has to work the store."

Sabrina thought it would be nice if she could take Jessie's place, but there was still enough she didn't know about the mercantile to make that impossible.

"Oh, look," Clancy said. "It's Mr. Vick and Pastor Rylan."

"Wait, Clancy," Sabrina called to her, but the child had darted ahead. Sabrina picked up the pace, sure they were interrupting and feeling especially so when both men came to their feet. They both had their Bibles on the grass, and Sabrina felt more than a little awkward.

"And Hannah got to play with Heidi at her house, but I couldn't go," Clancy was saying when Sabrina came up. "Bri can't fish, but we still looked at the water."

"I'm sorry we disturbed you," Sabrina began, but the men were having none of it.

"You can't fish?" Chas said, sounding sad. "I didn't know that when I invited you to dinner. This changes everything."

"Not to mention Sunday morning," Rylan added. "Everyone will have to be told."

Sabrina began to laugh, but Clancy was not catching the sarcasm.

"Mama could teach you," the little girl offered, and the adults sobered.

"That would be very fun," Sabrina said to her, "but you need to understand that Pastor Rylan and Mr. Vick were only teasing me."

Sabrina took the moment to glance at Rylan, and because Clancy wasn't looking at him, he was still tragically shaking his head. Sabrina put a hand to her mouth, but a small laugh still escaped.

"I think we'll keep walking," Sabrina suggested, reaching for the little girl's hand. "Goodbye," she said, not wasting any time.

"You're taller than Mr. Vick," Clancy stated once the men had said goodbye.

"Do you think so?"

"But not taller than Pastor Rylan. No one is taller than Pastor Rylan."

The men watched them move on their way for just a few minutes, the words floating back to them. They sat down again on the grassy area where they met during the summer.

"How did dinner go on Sunday?" Rylan asked the other elder.

"It went well. Miranda asked her about her church family in Denver, and it sounds like her faith is real. New, but real."

"Did she say why she left Denver?"

"Yes, she said that city is full of hard memories for her, and one of her friends suggested the church family here."

Once again Rylan thought about what a long way it was to move and then wondered what type of life someone as young as Sabrina would wish to leave. Thoughts of someone mistreating her, possibly a family member, came to mind. It bothered him no small amount, and he had to remind himself that he knew none of the facts.

"She's certainly hardworking," Chas said next. "And pretty."

Rylan laughed. "You're impossible, do you know that?"

"Well, you let Cassidy get away, and you're not getting any younger."

"I wasn't the least bit in love with Cassidy, and you know it."

Chas let it go, but Rylan knew it would come up again. This was Chas, and lately that man had decided that Rylan needed a wife.

* * *

"You must be working at the dress shop today," Crystal said on Wednesday morning.

"Is that you, Crystal?" Sabrina spoke to the empty window until the woman's face appeared.

"Yeah."

"What did you say?"

"You must be working at the dress shop today."

"Why is that?"

"You never wear white to work at the mercantile."

"How do you know where I work?"

"I know lots of things."

Do you know God's Son died for you? was the first thing that came to Sabrina's mind, but she didn't know if she could say that. She pictured Crystal retreating back inside and never speaking to her again.

As it was, Sabrina wasn't given time. Two men came around the corner, boards and tools in their hands.

"Right here," the one said, and Sabrina could see that they were headed for her stairs. "Come on."

"I'll be right there," the other man said, taking his time moving past the women as he checked them over. He finally stopped and spoke.

"Where are you going to be in a few hours?"

"Why?" Sabrina asked, her voice cold.

"We'll be getting paid for this job and the four of us can—"

"How dare you!" Sabrina spat at him before he could finish. "Move along."

He was none too happy about the way she sent him off, and the words that came from his mouth brought Sabrina's chin up. He saw the anger in her eyes, however, and moved on his way.

"You shouldn't have done that," Crystal said in a voice that lacked conviction.

"What exactly?"

"Spoken for me."

Sabrina leveled her with her eyes and said, "You need to want better for yourself."

Crystal didn't reply, and Sabrina was too upset to say more. She told the other woman she had to get to work and went on her way.

* * *

What was I thinking? Sabrina railed at herself and God all the way to Jeanette's. *I take this apartment because it's cheap, and now my neighbor is a prostitute. She looks just like we all did, desperate and hungry. I can't handle this, Lord. I didn't even think ahead. I just heard the price of the rent and took it.*

And she didn't want to hear what I had to say! She's probably trapped with nowhere to turn. I don't have the money to help her, and I certainly can't promise her that she can find other work! Token Creek is so much smaller than Denver. She might never escape that life in this little town.

By the time Sabrina reached Jeanette's shop, her color was high. At any other time, Jeanette would have noticed immediately, but the sewing machine was giving Jeanette trouble, and she had an errand for Sabrina.

"Please find Rylan. He should be at the livery today. Ask him to come when he can and check this for me. If you should happen to see Cassidy, Brad, or Trace, they also know what to do. I doubt if any of them are in town, but you never know."

Sabrina went back out the door, telling herself she had to put Crystal and the conversation with that man behind her. She had a job and a specific task to do at the moment. Not even remembering to pray for Crystal, she simply tried to put the whole morning out of her mind.

* * *

"I think that will do it," Rylan spoke to Mr. Falcone from the bank. He had brought his horse in to be shod, and Rylan had just finished the job.

"Thank you, Rylan. I paid a pretty penny for this girl, and I don't want her going lame."

"Well, she's certainly beautiful," Rylan said, stroking the mare's shoulder. He looked up in time to see Sabrina slip inside the wide doorway and stand out of the way. He would have headed that way, but Mr. Falcone was not done.

"Her left front fetlock seems a bit swollen to me. Did you notice anything?"

"I didn't. Is she favoring that leg?"

"I don't think so, but if you could check it."

Rylan easily lifted the hoof in his hands,

and checked the area, but he found no swelling.

"I'm not seeing it, Mr. Falcone, but the Marling brothers would be the folks to ask. They're the experts in town when it comes to horses."

"Yes, I'll do that. Thank you, Rylan."

Rylan moved toward Sabrina as soon as Mr. Falcone left, but that woman had her back to him. She seemed to be studying something on the wall, and Rylan ended up standing with her, watching a spider at work.

Sabrina still hadn't realized that Mr. Falcone had left when she spotted iron hooks on the wall below the spider's web. Some were larger than others, and Sabrina took a small one from the nail it was hanging on and turned to find Rylan a few feet behind her.

"Do you sell these?"

"Yes. The large ones are six cents, and the one in your hand is three."

"How do you hang them?"

Rylan took it from her hand and showed her the top.

"You can loop this over a nail, or put the nail in first and then drive it in tight."

"Do you sell nails?"

"Well, I think if you buy a hook and need the nail, we just give you that."

Sabrina nodded thoughtfully, thinking about the spot in her kitchen where she could hang her pot. She had no place for it but the stove.

"Is that why you came in?" Rylan asked, fairly certain of the answer.

"Oh! No, it's not." Sabrina looked as surprised as she felt. "Jeanette's sewing machine isn't working, and she asked me to tell you."

Rylan nodded. "Tell Jeanette that Pete probably won't be in before dinnertime, but as soon as he arrives, I'll head that way."

"Thank you," Sabrina said. She started toward the door.

"Did you want the hook?" Rylan asked, something in him wanting to talk to her a little more.

"Not this week," Sabrina said. "Maybe next."

"What happens next week?" Rylan was too curious not to ask.

"I'll have a little more money and maybe a hammer."

"You can always borrow a hammer from me," Rylan said, wondering why the first thing he wanted to say was that he would put the hook up for her.

"Oh, thank you. I'll remember that."

"I'll see you later," Rylan said, making himself turn away. The temptation to keep talking to Sabrina Matthews was arrestingly strong.

* * *

This one goes to Mrs. Potts. She's on Bond Street in the blue house. And this one goes to Mrs. Gornik, two doors down.

Because the machine was broken, Jeanette was doing handwork and Sabrina was making deliveries. This was not normal for Jeanette's shop—or so she told Sabrina—but she thought it might be best until the machine was working again.

And the day was nice—not a cloud in the sky and warm. Sabrina loved the feel of it on her face and the way it seemed to soak into her black hair. She was enjoying the sensation so much she suddenly realized she was lost. She thought she had found the right street, but there was no blue house. She looked across the way, spotted Patience Dorn pegging out laundry in her backyard, and went that way.

"Good morning," Sabrina greeted.

"Well, Bri, how nice to see you."

"Do you know where Mrs. Potts lives? I'm to make a delivery."

"Go two streets over, and you'll find her in the blue house."

"Thank you."

"Before you go, Bri, are you free for supper tonight?"

"I am, thank you. What time?"

"Just come after work. We eat about five-thirty, or whenever Jeb gets in the door."

"I'll plan on it."

"We'll see you this evening."

Sabrina made the deliveries without mishap and was almost back to the shop when she spotted Bret Toben. He tipped his hat to her but kept moving. Sabrina was nothing but relieved. Bret would have been disappointed to learn that his act of indifference hadn't worked at all.

* * *

"Here you go, Rylan." Miranda Vick passed him the potatoes as soon as she'd served Heidi, and her older brother, Franklin. Parker, younger than Heidi by almost two years, already had his food, and the baby, Nellie, would eat from Miranda's plate.

"Thank you, Miranda. I've been looking forward to this all day."

"As have we. Parker has something to tell you."

Rylan looked at the little boy sitting next to his father, and smiled in anticipation.

"I know Jesus," Parker said, the smile in his eyes matching the one on his mouth.

"Well, Parker," Rylan said, not mentioning that Chas had told him all about this the day before. "That is very fine news. Can you tell me about it?"

"Mama talked to me, and I believe Jesus died for my sins."

Rylan had to clear his throat. This family was very special to him, and this news was very near and dear to his heart. It didn't help that Miranda had tears in her eyes, and if the clearing of Chas' throat was any indication, it also seemed to be suddenly full.

"We have a great, saving God, Parker, who loves you very much," Rylan said with quiet conviction. "I know your parents are going to teach you all about Him. Are you excited to learn?"

The little boy nodded, and everyone turned to their food. The emotions were still there, but for the moment it was best to ignore them. Rather than having Parker see him cry, Rylan was glad to have Miranda's delicious meal to turn to. It was yet another thing that God provided and a reason to give Him thanks.

* * *

"So Meg spent her summer here, and that's how she and Brad fell in love?" Sabrina clarified, having enjoyed the story Patience shared.

"That's right. She'd been coming to spend her summers with us for years, but Brad never noticed her before the summer of '77."

"And they were married that fall," Jeb added.

"And now they have a baby," Sabrina put in.

"Isn't she adorable?" Patience asked, not afraid of anyone disagreeing.

"Yes, she is. I noticed that she smiles all the time."

"Have you seen her with Brad or Trace?" Jeb asked. "She adores her father and uncle."

The whole evening went this way. Jeb and Patience shared their lives with Sabrina and put in gently asked questions of their own. Sabrina was as open with them as she had been with everyone else, but for some reason, talking about Denver this night made her ache. She missed Danny and Callie and wondered for the first time in a long while what might have happened to her sister.

For this reason, she walked back to her apartment very slowly. There was plenty of light in the sky when she left the Dorns, and she assured Jeb she would be fine, but she dawdled and before she knew it, the air was cooling and the sky was growing dim. She was on Willow Street, her building just ahead, when she heard a commotion, a man yelling, a woman crying, and the pathetic, tinny cry of an infant.

8

SABRINA DIDN'T THINK, AND she didn't hesitate but went to the door of the house in front of her and opened it. A man was standing over a woman, his arm raised to strike her, and strike her he did.

"Stop that!" Sabrina ordered and started toward him, but the man only reached back long enough to slap her away.

Sabrina was thrown back, her face hurting, but she was made of sterner stuff. As soon as she scrambled to her feet, she attacked the man from the back, raking his face with her nails. He turned from hitting the woman and bellowed, throwing Sabrina off in the process before running for the door.

Sabrina went to the woman, who had fallen into one corner. She was unconscious, her face a mass of bruises. She heard noise behind her and turned for another attack, but it was a woman.

"What happened?"

The light was too dim, but Sabrina knew that voice.

"Crystal, is that you?"

"Yeah."

"Go for the doctor and the sheriff. Hurry!"

It was no small task, but Sabrina lifted the small woman and took her to the bedroom. She laid her across the rumple of bedclothes and covered her as best she could. Not until all this was done did she go back to the living room and pick up the tiny creature in the basket. Her heart caught in her throat when she realized how small it was.

Oh, God, please, Sabrina's heart prayed. *It's so tiny. Please God—please help it.*

Sabrina suddenly felt the warmth and the wet all at the same time. The baby's skin was very warm, but the thin blanket was soaked through. The lantern was dim, but she rummaged near the basket and found a dry cloth. Stripping off everything, the baby in a crying frenzy, Sabrina rewrapped the infant and snuggled her close. A girl, a small baby girl, so new her umbilical cord was still long.

She had only just quieted her when a man came in the door. He identified himself as Sheriff Kaderly and asked what had happened.

"A woman's been beaten. I put her on the bed."

Nate said nothing else but went toward the bedroom. Sabrina sat in the room's only available chair, held the baby close, and begged God for some kind of miracle.

* * *

Rylan had not been home ten minutes when one of Nate's deputies, Lewis Varner, came for him. Not for a shooting this time but for a woman who'd been beaten. There was a newborn in the house, and the woman was in a bad way.

Rylan came into the small home, little more than one room and a bedroom, and found Sabrina sitting in one corner, the baby in her arms. The emotions that rushed through him at that point were a surprise, but he didn't take time to question her. Nate had come to the bedroom door, expecting him, and Rylan went that way.

Doctor Ertz was present, and the woman was talking a little. Rylan came in and waited while the doctor saw to her needs. He then pulled a chair close the bed.

"I'm Pastor Rylan Jarvik. Can you tell me your name?"

"Eliza," the woman whispered. "My baby . . ."

"Your baby is in the other room. A friend of mine, a woman, is holding her. Would you like to see her?"

Rylan saw the sheriff leave to get Sabrina. Rylan kept his eyes on Eliza and saw the relief when she spotted her infant, now quiet in Sabrina's arms.

"How old is the baby?" Rylan asked.

"Two days."

"What's the baby's name?" Rylan asked next.

"Mirabel."

"You need to feed her," the doctor ordered, having checked the baby before Sabrina went in. "She needs milk."

"I'll help her," Sabrina said, and waited only for the men to clear out. It took a little doing—she learned this was Eliza's first baby—but eventually the baby was settled at her breast.

"You're the new one," Eliza said when the baby had latched on. She looked up at Sabrina through swollen eyes.

"The new what?"

"The pretty one who's in the wrong neighborhood."

"Don't believe everything you hear," Sabrina said, watching the baby eat.

Eliza gave a small sigh and closed her eyes. Sabrina stayed for just a moment more and then slipped from the room.

Not until she came from the bedroom did the men see the marks on her face. Nate, who had been joined by another deputy, Thom Koeller, wasted no time asking Sabrina what had happened.

"I can't remember all of it. He was hitting her, and I grabbed him."

"And he hit you," the sheriff supplied.

"I fell back, so he must have. I scratched his face. I remember that."

Rylan watched her intently during all of this, thinking he didn't know another woman in town who would be as calm as she was in the midst of this situation. The sheriff was starting to say something more, but Sabrina quickly excused herself. Nate did nothing to stop her, but Rylan followed her outside.

"Crystal," Sabrina called to the woman who had walked past. She came back. Very little light spilled out of the house, but it was enough to show Rylan the type of dress the other woman was wearing.

"Who was that man?" Sabrina asked.

"He takes care of Eliza sometimes," she said, not willing to give his name. "I don't think he knew about the baby."

"Will he be back?"

"Sure." Her voice was matter-of-fact. "He lives there when he's in town."

"She needs someone to sit with her."

"I'm working."

"Take the night off," Sabrina ordered, her tone flat.

"I'll go in," Crystal said after a long-suffering sigh, "but not with the sheriff there."

"I don't think he'll be much longer. Stay close."

"Yes, Mother," Crystal said in angry sarcasm, but Sabrina ignored it.

"I'll check on her tomorrow."

"Why?"

"Haven't you heard?" Sabrina's own sarcasm came to the fore. "I'm the pretty one who's in the wrong neighborhood."

Crystal couldn't help herself. She laughed.

"Who's that?" she asked when she had her breath, and Sabrina turned to find a huge shape behind her.

"Hello," Rylan said calmly. "I'm Rylan Jarvik, Sabrina's pastor."

"I've heard of you," Crystal said. "You helped Maggie last year."

"How is she?"

"I think better."

"Tell her I said hello," Rylan said and then spoke to Sabrina. "I'm going to go back in to see if Eliza wants me to pray with her. Then I'll walk you home."

"It's not that far," Sabrina began, but Rylan took her hand and led her back inside. He didn't relinquish that hand until he was back in the bedroom. The chair was still close to the bed but vacant, and Rylan sat back down.

"Your baby seems happy to be back with you," Rylan said, his voice kind as he gazed down at the sleeping infant.

"She's a good baby."

Rylan nodded. "Sheriff Kaderly sends for

me when someone's been hurt or grieving, but I don't have to stay. I can pray for you if you like, but it's your choice."

"I haven't talked to God in a long time. I never make it to church."

"Since God is everywhere, we don't have to be in a church building to pray. We can call out to Him wherever we are."

"I don't want God here," Eliza said. "It's not a nice place."

"He's here, Eliza, all the time, but I won't force you to talk about it."

Eliza's head shifted uncomfortably on the pillow, and Rylan rose.

"Hey, Pretty," Eliza said, but Sabrina didn't turn.

"Sabrina." Rylan had caught it and called her name. "Eliza wants to speak with you."

Sabrina turned to the woman in the bed and went a little closer.

"Thanks for taking care of my baby."

"You're welcome. Crystal's going to come tonight. I'll check on you tomorrow."

Eliza stared at her but didn't comment. Sabrina didn't either. She turned and walked from the room and found Rylan waiting for her. Without a word, he led the way outside, clearly planning to walk her the short distance home as he'd said.

* * *

"How did you come to be in that house?" Rylan asked when they both stood at the bottom of Sabrina's stairs. There was a bit of a moon, but they were basically talking in the dark.

"I heard a woman cry out and went in."

"From your apartment?"

"No, I was walking by."

More retorts than Rylan could keep track of sprang to his lips, but he didn't utter any of them.

"Does Sheriff Kaderly always send for you?" Sabrina asked, finding this rather interesting.

"Yes. He has for so many years that it seems normal to me."

"And what do you do?"

"Just what I did tonight. I come and I pray with folks if they want it."

"Do they ever?"

"Some have. In fact some folks in the church family are people I met with during times like this."

Sabrina wanted to ask if any were former

prostitutes, but she kept the question to herself.

"Are you all right?" Rylan asked.

"Yes, are you?"

"I didn't get hit tonight," Rylan explained. "And unless I misunderstood what happened, you haven't even had time to put a cool cloth on your face."

"You're not like I thought," Sabrina said thoughtfully, feeling safe to admit it in the dark.

"How's that?"

"I don't know. I just didn't picture you being so kind."

"It's easy to be kind when you care about people."

"I can see that you do."

"I think I would have to say the same about you. After tonight, I don't know how I could think anything else."

"That's a good thing, isn't it?" Sabrina asked, suddenly feeling uncertain.

"I think it is," Rylan said, even as he wanted to tell her that she couldn't keep breaking up fights, that tonight she might have gotten off easy.

"Thank you for walking me home, Pastor Rylan."

"You're welcome. I hope you sleep well."

"Thank you. Goodnight."

"Goodnight, Sabrina."

Before he could move away, she told him she would see him Sunday. Rylan didn't correct her, but he planned on seeing her before then. He would be at Jeanette's tomorrow, as soon as he could manage it, to check on her face.

* * *

Rylan was at Chas' door first thing in the morning. Chas was the elder he was closest to, the one who tended to ask him the toughest questions and hold him most accountable. Rylan was feeling things about a woman he barely knew, and he needed prayer. He started by explaining his evening to Chas and then waited.

"She went in and stopped this man's attack?"

"Yes. I haven't seen her today, but he hit her and there was some bruising."

Chas stared at him, and Rylan's heart spilled over.

"There's something special about her, Chas. I've never been drawn to anyone like this."

"And your heart wants to gallop."

"It does," Rylan agreed, laughing at the very words he'd used in the pulpit many times. "I mostly stopped today to talk to you because I need your prayers. I need to think clearly and not be blinded by emotion."

"Well, you certainly have my prayers. Do we know what happened with this woman or the man?"

"No. My next stop is the sheriff's office. The woman was not open to talking about God, so I probably won't see her again. However," Rylan remembered, "Sabrina was headed back today."

"She said this?"

"Yes, and she had another woman go there last night." Rylan had to stop and shake his head. "I wish you could have seen and heard her. I've never seen the like."

Chas didn't know what to say. There was certainly a whole lot more to Sabrina Matthews than a tall woman with a pretty face, but finding out the facts and details might not be so easy.

Chas felt speculation coming over him and knew there was no point. As he'd told his friend he would do, he started to pray.

* * *

Sabrina knocked softly and carefully opened the front door of the house down the street. Not looking at all good, but on her feet, Eliza stood in the living room, the baby in her arms.

"How are you?" Sabrina asked.

"How do I look?"

"Awful." Sabrina didn't mince words. "I assume that's how you feel."

"Have you got a cigarette?" Eliza asked.

"No, sorry."

"Crystal probably does."

"Did she come last night?"

"Yeah. She left an hour ago."

"Can I get you anything? Maybe some breakfast?"

"No, but thanks."

There was a note of finality to her voice that Sabrina could not help but hear. The baby gave a little squeak of a cry then, and Sabrina, seeing no help for it, backed toward the door. She knew how resilient women in this life could be and also that she was looking at one. It wouldn't have surprised her if the man from last night was already back in the bedroom, sleeping off a rough night of beating his woman.

Seeing that there was nothing left for her to do or say, Sabrina went on her way. She had to slip back into her apartment to get her reticule and then get to Jeanette's. Eliza did not want her help, and she had a job to do. She was almost to Jeanette's before she remembered that she could pray for Eliza and the baby every time they came to mind.

* * *

"How is the machine working, Jeanette?" Rylan asked as soon as he was in the door of the shop.

"Just great, thank you," Jeanette answered with a smile.

"I'm glad to hear it. No Sabrina today?"

Jeanette's smile disappeared. "She's in the back. She insisted on working back there."

Rylan started that way, but Jeanette was not done. She called after his retreating back, "I might not be done with you, Rylan Jarvik. I might want someone else's side of the story."

Sabrina had certainly heard all of this, so she wasn't at all surprised when Rylan appeared. There was one small window at the back, and Sabrina had positioned herself under it to give her the best light to sew.

"How's the eye?" Rylan asked the moment he saw her.

"I'll live," Sabrina said lightly.

Rylan went to the window and bent in such a way that he could see her face in the full light. She had a shiner high on one cheek bone and a scratch on the same side. Sabrina watched him take in the marks and then look her in the eye.

"I don't think I want you to do that again," Rylan said slowly.

"Well, I don't plan on it," Sabrina said.

"But it might happen?" Rylan asked.

Sabrina had to smile a little at his tone, and Rylan did not press her. Instead he asked her if she'd seen Eliza and the baby.

"Yes. She was on her feet but looking as awful as she felt."

"I stopped to see Kaderly. They found a very drunk man with scratches on his face and hauled him in."

"She won't press charges," Sabrina said.

"But you could," Rylan said, having already discussed this with the sheriff.

"Not if she cares about him. As soon as he gets out, she'll welcome him back."

Rylan nodded, knowing how true it was. Sabrina thought she might try talking to her again but wasn't sure if that was a good idea.

Both were still thinking to themselves when Jeanette made an appearance.

"What am I going to do with her?" she asked Rylan. "Getting herself hurt like that! I tell you, Bri, you need to move home with me."

Sabrina smiled at her but didn't comment. Rylan had all he could do to keep his mouth closed. She was not the least bit afraid after what happened, and she lived in that neighborhood.

"Well, ladies," Rylan said, feeling a need to get out before someone asked him what he thought. Also, Jeanette's back room was not a large place. He barely fit on his own without two other people joining him. "I've got a sermon to work on. If you need me to check that machine again, Jeanette, I'll be at home."

"Thanks, Rylan," she said, still a bit put out. "I hope you preach on folks letting others take care of them."

Sabrina laughed out loud over this. Rylan would have joined her, but he caught sight of Jeanette's scowling face and decided to make his exit.

* * *

Sabrina found herself glad that folks only saw what they wanted to see. By Saturday afternoon when she was working at the mercantile the bruises had faded but the scratch was still slightly discernable. Jessie had noticed, and Sabrina had given a brief explanation, but not until late in the day did anyone else say a word. Unfortunately the person who paid the most attention was Bret Toben. He wanted more tobacco and a razor, but before Sabrina could find what he needed, he'd stepped in front of her.

"Who scratched you?" he asked quietly, all charm and teasing gone. Indeed, he looked angry or concerned; Sabrina could not tell which.

"It's a long story," Sabrina answered as she slipped around him to find the razor. But Bret wasn't done. He followed Sabrina to the back of the store.

"I think I want you to tell me about this. What time are you off?"

"It's kind of you, Mr. Toben, but I'm fine."

Her tone and expression told Bret he wasn't going to get anything out of her, but he still wasn't done. Bret got and paid for his things, but he left with a whole lot more. He didn't care how long it took, he was determined that someone was going to tell him what happened to Sabrina Matthews' cheek.

* * *

"How are you doing with your memorization?" Rylan asked at the end of his sermon, having assigned a new verse from Colossians each of the last few weeks. "Does anyone want to give chapter two, verse six a try? Okay, Franklin," Rylan said, smiling at how fast the boy's hand went up. "Let's hear it."

"Colossians 2:6," the little boy stood and started. " 'As ye have therefore received Christ Jesus the Lord, so walk ye in him.' "

"Excellent," Rylan praised. "How about chapter one, verse ten? Heather, go ahead."

" 'That ye might walk worthy of the Lord unto all pleasing, being fruitful in every good work, and increasing in the knowledge of God.' "

"Very good," Rylan praised. He called on several others to say the verses as well and then assigned a new one, Colossians 4:5, for the following week. When he was done, Chas came to the front.

"The Fourth of July is just about a week away," he announced. "Token Creek will have its annual picnic and races, and we hope everyone will be there. That, however, is not the last big event of the summer. I am pleased to tell you that we have saved enough money to paint our building."

Chas waited for all the laughter, cheers, and clapping to die down before continuing.

"We'll have certain days we set aside for painting, and if you can make it, we'll welcome you. If you have been working with your son or daughter, and he or she knows how to use a brush, that's fine. Otherwise we would like these painting sessions to be for the adults."

A few folks smiled and laughed at Chas' expressive face, but all understood.

"We'll organize the dates in the next week or so and let you know about those." This said, the congregation was dismissed. As might have been expected, nearly all talk was about the upcoming holiday and the painting parties that were sure to be just as good a time.

* * *

The next week sped by. The days were very warm now, and for some reason, the closer they got to the Fourth of July, the more raucous Token Creek became. Nate came for

Rylan twice during the week, the first time when a gun went off by accident and a child was shot and injured. The second time the sheriff came for Rylan was on Saturday night. It wasn't that late, only about ten o'clock, and the crying woman did not want him there, so Rylan was headed home in fairly short order.

His mind was busy with the activities of the streets and praying for various people he saw. Not until he cut down a side street that bordered the Lucky Nickel saloon did he hear a familiar voice. Rylan came to a dead stop and listened to Sabrina speaking.

"Do you want to come back to my place and talk, Paula?" Sabrina asked.

"Crystal said you would talk to me here."

"I will," Sabrina replied matter-of-factly, "but we're less likely to be interrupted if we're at my apartment."

"You're in Crystal's building?"

"Yes, upstairs."

"Hello," the woman said when she spotted the man coming near them. He did not look familiar, but in her line of work it was always good to be friendly.

"Do you want to talk to him?" Sabrina asked, having no idea that the man approaching was there for her.

"Sabrina," Rylan said, and she turned.

"What are you doing here?" she asked, well and truly surprised.

I could ask you the same thing, Rylan thought, but he said, "Can I see you ladies home?"

"Who is this?" Paula asked.

"A friend of mine. I think he's just concerned that I'm out here after dark."

Rylan had come up to stand beside Sabrina. Nothing would make him leave without her. He only hoped it wouldn't come to a confrontation.

"I'm Rylan," he said as he put his hand out and Paula reached automatically to shake it.

"Are you the pastor?"

"Guilty as charged," he said, trying to keep the situation light. It must have worked because Paula laughed a little.

"What would you like to do?" Sabrina decided to press her, not sure what she thought of Rylan's presence.

In truth, Paula wasn't bothered by Rylan, but neither did she want to talk tonight. She'd already had a few drinks, and her head wasn't quite clear.

"I'll come see you sometime," Paula said. "I'm sure Crystal can show me the way."

"Sure," Sabrina agreed, telling the woman she would see her around. She had already told the Lord that whatever happened tonight was in His hands and that she would not try to take things into her own.

9

SABRINA STARTED BACK DOWN the street toward home, knowing Rylan was right behind her. She wondered if now was a good time to ask questions on that one verse, and then she remembered that he might have to get up early to ready his sermon.

"I don't suppose there is any point in telling you that I can get home on my own."

"You suppose right."

Sabrina didn't hear any anger in his voice, but neither did she hear any flexibility. She kept her mouth shut and, when Rylan took the lead, walked slightly behind him.

Rylan was taking them on an indirect

route he felt was the safest. He didn't fear for himself, but should they come across a group of drunken men who wanted him to share the woman he'd "found," it could get ugly. Rylan hoped and prayed they wouldn't see anyone at all. He almost breathed a sigh of relief when Sabrina's stairs came into view.

"I'll see you tomorrow," Rylan said, standing to one side so she could take the stairs. The moon was almost full tonight, the sky clear and full of stars. He could see her quite easily and that her head turned when someone walked by. She looked much too interested, in Rylan's opinion, and he stepped a little closer so he could keep his voice low and still make himself clear.

"Whatever you're planning needs to wait. Go upstairs and lock yourself inside. I'm not asking, Sabrina Matthews. I'm telling."

Sabrina's chin came up just a bit, but she said not a word. Taking the key from her pocket, she climbed the stairs, unlocked her door, and then looked back down. Rylan was standing just were she had left him, watching her. Still not speaking even to thank him, she slipped inside and locked the door. She would fall asleep before she could figure out how she felt about Rylan Jarvik's actions tonight.

* * *

Rylan let himself into his house but got no farther than the living room. He didn't bother to light a lantern but made his way to the rocking chair, sank down, and began to pray.

I know she cares about these folks, Lord, but she has to have more care of herself. Denver is no different. It might even be worse in some areas. The contrast between how sheltered and yet how knowledgeable she is completely confuses me. I so appreciate her wanting to reach out, but if she's hurt or killed, I don't think my heart could take it.

Why do I feel responsible, Lord? She came here, and our church family has taken her in, but it's more than that. I feel I must protect her, as if I'm the only one who can.

Thoughts came to mind just then that Rylan had not been willing to entertain. For the first time he let his mind go to possibilities that he would hate to be true but would make sense.

Fatigue settled on him like a heavy garment. He knew he needed to turn in. His congregation was counting on him to bring truth and hope in the morning, and he could not let them down. Lighting the lantern now so he could ready himself for bed, Rylan turned in, asking God one more time to care for Sabrina and to keep her safe this night.

* * *

"Will we ever be on time for the service again?" Meg asked Brad when they were finally in the wagon and on the road. "I get up earlier and earlier, but something always happens."

"You can't predict when you're going to be sick, Meg. You're being too hard on yourself."

Meg didn't comment, but it certainly bothered her.

"You definitely amused a certain child," Brad said, a smile tugging at his lips.

"Why *is* that?" Meg asked, even as she shifted Savanna on her lap. "She can't stop giggling when I vomit."

"It will be a few years before she figures out that there's nothing funny about it."

"She laughed at Cass one time, but Cass didn't notice and because she was feeling so lousy that first month, I never mentioned it."

This said, Meg looked up to find Brad smiling a little.

"Do you think it's funny too?" she asked.

"Not your being sick, but the hysterical giggles from our daughter are very contagious."

Meg had no choice but to smile. Savanna's laughter was fun, and Brad was right, it would be some time before she fully understood.

* * *

"We won't try to start painting until the week after the Fourth. Plan on the twelfth and continuing on the thirteenth, but those are the only two days that week," Chas announced at the end of the service. "Rylan will usually be on hand, but if he's not around, I should be available. See me if you can bring ladders. If you can spare an hour or two to paint, you don't need to see me, just show up with your brush."

Chas thanked the congregation and dismissed them. Folks began to mill around and talk, but Sabrina had missed breakfast and didn't take long to head for the door. She wasn't even to the street when Rylan caught her.

"We need to talk," he said quietly, wasting no time with formalities. Sometime that morning he realized he had to get back to

Sabrina about the night before and saw no point in waiting.

"All right," Sabrina agreed, knowing it was about last night. She was still working out in her mind what happened and thought talking about it might be a good idea.

"Why don't I come by about four o'clock, when it's not so warm," Rylan suggested. "We can take a walk or go over and use one of Jeanette's parlors. She won't mind."

"All right," Sabrina agreed again, and Rylan wished he knew what she was thinking. Her eyes were amazing, the most crystal blue he'd ever seen and clear as a child's, but he could not always read them. To him it seemed that she could become inscrutable at will, like right now.

"I don't suppose you want to tell me what you're thinking," Rylan couldn't resist saying.

"I don't know what I'm thinking," Sabrina admitted. "I'm still trying to work out what happened."

"Since I'm in the same boat, I'm glad we're going to talk."

Sabrina nodded.

"I'll see you at four."

"I'll be ready," Sabrina said. She started

again for home but did so very slowly, her hunger now at the back of her mind.

* * *

"Did I see Rylan speaking to Bri after the service?" Cassidy asked Trace when they had a moment alone. Jeanette had invited them over for dinner but had left for a minute to check on Heather and Theta.

"I noticed that too. He seemed to follow her out of the church."

"Has he spoken to you about her?"

Trace was only able to shake his head no before Jeanette rejoined them, but that man could see in his wife's eyes that the subject was still on her mind.

* * *

Rylan was at Sabrina's door promptly at four o'clock. Without a lot of words they began to walk to the outskirts of town, catching the creek line some ways out. It was still fairly warm so when they passed under the shade of a large tree, Rylan came to a stop. He sat on the long grass, and Sabrina sank down some eight feet away.

"Can you tell me about last night?" Rylan asked.

"You mean, before you got there?"

"Yes."

"I had seen Crystal earlier in the day, and she had asked me if I'd ever met Paula. I guess Crystal told her about what happened with Eliza, and Paula said she had questions about God."

"And you felt you had to talk to her downtown on a Saturday night?"

"To tell you the truth, I forgot it was Saturday night until I was partway to there."

"How did you know where to go?"

"Crystal."

"Had you just gotten there?"

"Yes, maybe five minutes ahead of you."

Rylan opened his mouth to ask another question, but Sabrina cut back in.

"What were you doing out?"

"There was a shooting, but the woman didn't want me there."

"I heard gunfire earlier."

"And you didn't run out to see what you could do?" Rylan asked, his eyes wide to add to the sarcasm.

"It's not like that," Sabrina objected, but then stopped. She looked out over the creek, feeling foolish. Rylan read her face and wished he hadn't teased her. He was going to say as much when Sabrina spoke, not looking at him and almost in a whisper.

"They don't know about the shed blood of Christ. They don't know that He died for them and that He's waiting to take their sins away and save them for all time. Someone has to tell them."

"Sabrina," Rylan began, touched by her words. "I think what you're trying to do is amazing, but it can't be at the risk of your own safety."

"I'm not afraid," she said quietly but with utter conviction.

"I can see that, but maybe you should be."

Sabrina finally looked at him.

"Listen to me," Rylan tried again. "There must be a way to do this during the day."

"You go out after dark," Sabrina argued, and Rylan had to laugh. Sabrina turned her head again and wouldn't look at him, but she wanted to laugh too.

"Tell me you know that was a ridiculous thing to say."

"Yes, it was," Sabrina admitted, her face still in profile.

For a long moment there was quiet between them. Rylan knew what he wanted to say, but he also wanted to hear more from Sabrina if she wanted to share. When she didn't, he began.

"I want to tell you something I've had to learn about Token Creek," Rylan began, and Sabrina finally looked his way.

"Real hunger will come to the fore. I used to pursue people but no longer. They know who I am and where they can find me. They know how available I am. If someone is truly tired of his sin or stops long enough to feel the hunger inside, he'll seek out the truth. I have to keep living a holy life, but God will bring the people and give the increase. I don't have to put myself in danger to share Him."

Sabrina had to think about this. She probably had been too zealous, and Rylan was right, going out after dark if she didn't have to was risky.

"Thank you for not saying I need to move back to Jeanette's."

"On the contrary, except when you go out after dark I think you handle where you're living very well. To be honest, I've never known a woman with your guts. I just don't want you to be foolhardy."

Sabrina nodded. He had given her much

to think about, and she knew he'd said it with a concern for her safety. In truth she did need to be more responsible. If she was hurt because she had not been careful, someone would have to care for her, and that would be selfishness on her part.

"Can I ask you one more question?" Rylan said.

Sabrina nodded.

"Did you really think I would let you walk home alone last night when you suggested it?"

"Well, it was getting late, and I didn't know how early you had to be up when you preach."

This was the last thing he expected. Stubbornness maybe, or not wanting to be ordered around, but certainly not concern for his getting enough rest.

"What's the matter?" Sabrina asked, trying to read his face.

"You just surprised me."

"Oh."

They looked at each other for a moment.

"Do you get up early on Sunday mornings?" Sabrina asked.

"Yes, I do."

The black-haired woman nodded.

"Why don't we go to Jeanette's," Rylan suddenly suggested.

"Is she expecting us?"

"No, but maybe Becky made bread pudding."

Sabrina could not stop her laughter. It rang out over the creek line and made Rylan laugh in return.

"And one of these days," Rylan said when they were on their feet and headed back toward town, "maybe you'll tell me how *you* came to believe in the shed blood of Christ."

Sabrina said that she would, and that she wanted to hear Rylan's story as well. Rylan certainly agreed even as he prayed. *Please help me to hold myself in check, Lord. She's special, very special, but I can't rush this. There are too many things I don't know, and I'd rather lose a limb than hurt her.*

Sabrina, completely unaware of the pastor's thoughts, knew it was finally time to ask Rylan about some of his sermon points. Naturally he was more than happy to answer.

* * *

"Things a little quiet on the streets?" Bret asked of Crystal when he wandered over to the corner table she was sitting at on Sunday night. The Boar's Head was not overly busy, and she had a drink in front of her.

"Just resting my feet," Crystal said, thinking he was too good-looking and knew it.

"Do you see much of Bri Matthews?" Bret asked next, trying to appear nonchalant. Crystal's smile turned a little mean before she answered.

"You're out of your class there, Bret. She's a nice girl."

Bret's eyes grew cold. He did not like the word no, and he didn't like to be told he wasn't good enough. With a move he couldn't quite pull off, Bret shrugged and shifted in his chair, glancing around the room in disinterest.

"I just noticed a scratch on her face and wondered what happened."

"Oh that." Crystal took the bait and didn't even know she'd been caught. "Zeke was drunk and giving Eliza the once over. Bri came at him, and he hit her too."

The anger that flooded through Bret was a surprise to him. Women like Sabrina Matthews were not for hitting, and Bret thought men like Zeke were worthless even when they weren't drunk.

"What was Bri doing there?"

"I guess she heard the fight and went in to check."

Crystal finished her drink then and pushed to her feet. She halfway hoped that Bret would want a little more of her time, but she was suddenly weary of men talking to her about Sabrina. Without saying goodbye, Crystal went to the bar. A man had come in that she hadn't seen before. Maybe he would want to talk about her and no one else.

* * *

"Over here!" Clancy called the moment she spotted Sabrina. "Over here, Bri."

Sabrina wasted no time. She had made her bean stew again, and a loaf of bread, and arrived at the town's Fourth of July celebration hoping to sit with someone she knew. Tables were lined up along the creek, and the meal was potluck.

"How are you?" Sabrina asked when Clancy rushed to hug her legs. She bent enough to hug the little girl in return.

"Mama made cake."

"Did you help?"

"Only with licking."

Sabrina laughed as she asked, "What kind of cake?"

"Spice. It's Hannah's favorite."

"Where is Hannah?"

"She's with Heidi." A sudden frown appeared. "I don't have anyone."

"Well, that tells you where we stand, Bri," Jessie put in, more amused than offended by her daughter's words. "Here, give those to me and I'll take them to the food tables."

"What shall we do?" Sabrina asked, having handed off her dishes and taken a seat at Jessie's table. Clancy took a seat beside her, and for a moment the little girl only smiled at her.

"You look pretty," Clancy suddenly said.

"Well, thank you, Clancy. I like your dress too."

"Mama sent for it."

"That must have been fun."

"Oh, look!" Clancy jumped to her feet. "It's Mrs. Vick, with Nellie."

Sabrina saw that Miranda was headed her way. She had a picnic basket in hand and Nellie on her free arm.

"Is there room here, Bri?" she asked.

"I think so," Sabrina said, not sure who else was joining Jessie.

"We've got Rylan with us too," Miranda added, and Sabrina was surprised to feel her heart skip a beat.

"Hello, Miranda," Jessie greeted as she returned. "Going to join us?"

"If you have room."

"Certainly. Where is Rylan?"

"He and Chas are on their way."

Jessie looked at Sabrina and said, "For some reason Rylan and I always end up at the same table. It's become tradition."

Sabrina didn't have time to reply. Miranda had spread a blanket near the table and put Nellie in the middle of it. With a baby to play with, Clancy soon had plenty to do, but she also wanted Sabrina on the blanket with them. Watching both the baby and little girl play, Sabrina completely missed the slow way the men joined the group.

* * *

"She took it well," Rylan said, having told Chas all the details. "She listened to everything I had to say. She argued a little, but when that fell flat, she still stayed and listened to me."

"And you think you got through?" Chas asked. "She's going to be hurt if she keeps this up."

"I won't swear that she'll never find herself in another scrape, but I don't think she'll repeat her actions of Saturday night. And she asked me some very thoughtful questions about Colossians. I can tell she's taking a lot in."

Chas stopped. They were close to the crowds of townspeople now, and he did not want to be overheard.

"And how well are you thinking about all of this?"

"I can honestly say I don't know anyone else like her. I'm still very drawn, but I think I'm keeping my heart in check."

Chas might have had something else to say, but Mayor Lake was trying to get everyone's attention. It was time to eat.

* * *

"Aren't you going to join the lifting competition, Rylan?" Jessie asked when plates were nearly empty.

"I was thinking I would pass."

"Why is that?" Sabrina asked.

"My work at the livery puts me at an unfair advantage."

Everyone took this at face value, and the topic was dropped with Rylan, but Franklin wanted his father to compete. Chas put up with some good-hearted ribbing for the next few minutes, bringing laughter all around.

Sabrina was reaching for her glass when

Rylan leaned a little closer from the chair next to hers with a question.

"Do you know who Bret Toben is?"

"From the Boar's Head Saloon, yes."

"Do you have much contact with him?"

"A little. He was in the alley one day when I was looking for an apartment. It was that first day I saw you."

"I remember."

"Why do you ask?"

"He just keeps looking over here, and I don't think he's interested in Jessie."

Sabrina thought about this and remembered their last conversation.

"He saw the scratch on my face, and it seemed to bother him."

He's not alone, Rylan thought, but instead he asked, "Where do you see him?"

"At Jessie's, but I got the impression that he'd given up."

"On what?"

"Trying to see me."

Before Rylan could respond to this, Mayor Lake was standing on a chair and announcing that the races and competitions were about to begin.

* * *

Rylan did not get out of the lifting competition as he'd hoped, but Sabrina missed the whole thing. She told Miranda she would sit with Nellie, who had fallen asleep on the blanket. Part of her wished she hadn't volunteered, and another part of her knew it was for the best.

You can't have feelings for your pastor, Sabrina, she told herself. *You're all wrong for him. He can't have a woman with a past like yours, and he's just being kind. He cares and checks with you only because he's your pastor. It's his job.*

"Is she still out?" Jessie asked, having come back by the table to find her glass.

"Yes. I almost envy her."

"Oh, you don't want to sleep today," Jessie said. "You might miss something."

"That's true."

"You might even fall in love."

Sabrina didn't even try to keep her mouth closed. Jessie drank her water as though she'd not said a thing, but Sabrina could see the amusement in her eyes.

"What did that mean?" the younger woman demanded, only to have Nellie move around a bit. "What did that mean?"

Sabrina repeated herself, much more softly this time.

"Only that you'd have to be blind not to see what a fine man Rylan Jarvik is. Good-looking too, and taller than you. Bret Toben is also good-looking, but he doesn't go to church, and I can tell that's important to you."

"How many people know you're a match-maker?" Sabrina asked, but Jessie only laughed. Nellie moved again, and the women fell silent. Sabrina was glad for that. She had things to think about, and they had nothing to do with men. Rylan had talked about the things he was known for in Token Creek and the fact that people knew they could come to him when they were hungry enough.

Crystal had told Paula about her, and now Jessie knew that going to church was important to her. Sabrina felt hope in Rylan's words for the first time. She didn't have to go searching. She could keep studying her Bible, being part of the church family, and caring for others when she had the opportunity. Maybe someday even Jessie would come to her, when her reputation was as well known and fine as Rylan Jarvik's.

10

"WE START PAINTING THE church building a week from tomorrow," Rylan mentioned to Pete Stillwell at the end of the day. "I'd like that Wednesday off too if you can spare me."

"When am I going to persuade you that you need to buy the place, Rylan?" the older man asked, not for the first time. "I tell you it's time. I'm almost 50, my nephew isn't interested, and none of the girls want to manage it."

"It's out of my budget, Pete, and you know I don't want to smith full-time."

"You're the best employee I've ever had," Pete said, moisture coming to his eyes.

Rylan stayed quiet. Pete cried only when he'd had a little too much to drink. The Fourth of July celebration did that to many people

"Does Wednesday work?" Rylan asked again.

"Sure, sure. I'll be there."

Rylan was glad Mrs. Stillwell chose that moment to join them. Pete ended up telling his wife the days he needed to work, and Rylan did not have to worry the shop would go unmanned. If he did forget, his wife would see he got there.

By the time Rylan was ready to head home to the parsonage behind the church building, Sabrina had cleared out. He told himself that worry was not an option, but he certainly hoped she planned to head to her apartment, lock the door, and stay there.

* * *

The Tuesday that was planned for painting was busy, too busy for Jessie to give Sabrina time off, but when Jeanette remembered that Sabrina knew how to paint, she encouraged the younger woman to go home and change into work clothes so she could join the paint party on Wednesday.

Six people had made it out. Rylan was at

the front of the building with Chas, Jeb, and Patience, and for some reason, Sabrina went to the north side, ending up next to Trace Holden.

"How are you, Bri?" he asked.

"Doing well, thank you. How is Cassidy feeling?" Sabrina asked, working on the corner where Trace had directed her.

"Mornings can still be a little rough, but overall she's doing very well."

"Do you hope for a boy?"

Trace smiled. "I would have said yes before meeting Savanna, but not anymore."

"She's pretty fun," Sabrina said, thinking that she was rather partial to little girls but that it was probably because of Hannah and Clancy.

"You know," Trace said, turning to her, "it's like you've always been here."

"In Token Creek?"

"Right. We were at Jeanette's on Sunday, and she couldn't stop talking about you, even though she said you're not always careful enough and was ready to send Timothy to move you back to her house."

Sabrina had to laugh, but it was more than just amusement. There was relief there too. She did feel like she belonged, even in this short time, and she was glad to hear others felt the same way.

"I think there's a little too much fun going on over here," Rylan said, coming around the corner and looking stern. "Now, Trace, Sabrina is here to work. Stop distracting her."

"Yes, sir," Trace said, turning to wink at Sabrina.

"I didn't know you were going to be a taskmaster," Sabrina teased Rylan.

"Well, now you do, so hop to it."

Sabrina spotted a piece of wood that was hanging just far enough out of reach that she couldn't get a grip on it. Rylan noticed and came to her rescue with his brush.

"Thank you," she said.

"You're welcome. A little person like yourself can't be expected to get that high."

"No one has ever called me little."

Rylan stared down at her before saying, "I guess it's all relative."

"How tall are you?" Sabrina asked.

"Without my shoes, six foot, four inches."

"How about you, Sabrina?" This came from Trace.

"With my shoes, five foot, ten inches."

"Are your parents tall?"

"My father was. They're both dead."

"Tall siblings?"

"Just a sister, and she is taller than I am. Are you the tallest, Pastor Rylan?"

"By a good three inches. They're not sure what happened to me. The men in my family are big, but not quite this tall."

"You missed a spot," Sabrina said, and Rylan turned to her in surprise.

Trace shouted with laughter at the stunned look on his pastor's face before asking, "Now who's the taskmaster?"

"Well, you did," Sabrina said, trying not to laugh at the look Rylan was giving her. She felt free to smile when he looked painfully disgruntled and went back to painting, starting with the spot he missed.

Jeb came with the ladder a short time later, and the first thing he noticed was Sabrina's dress.

"You should have worn something old, Bri," he told her, not unkindly.

Sabrina was not able to tell him that most of her clothing was new because her old clothes had been indecent. Instead she said, "This is the dress I wear to paint in my apartment. So I thought it would do."

"Are you painting your apartment, Bri?"

Patience, who had come to their side, asked.

"Well, I started. I haven't gotten very far."

"What color?"

"Blue. It was Jessie's last gallon, and she gave me a good price." Sabrina did not add that she hadn't been entirely certain she could trust her landlord to honor his agreement to pay for the paint, and that was why she'd looked for a good deal.

The men began to work up high, and Sabrina and Patience covered the area below, chatting about this and that and working in companionable silence. Long before they were done, Sabrina's arm was screaming at her, but before anyone finished for the day, they had covered almost two sides.

* * *

"Well, now." Bret caught Sabrina when she cut down the alley on the way home. "I see Mrs. Fulbright is having you paint her shop."

"No, I was working on the church building," Sabrina answered, looking down at the paint she'd gotten on her sleeve.

"You look a little warm," Bret said, keeping his distance but not bothering to monitor his gaze. Even in a paint-stained dress, Sabrina was worth a second glance. "Why don't you come in."

Sabrina could read his thoughts as though he'd said them and decided to speak plainly.

"To what end?"

Bret did not see this coming and would have spoken plainly as well, but there was a dangerous glitter in Sabrina's eyes. Instead he opted to change the subject.

"I heard how you got your face scratched."

"Did you?" Sabrina sounded as disinterested as she was.

"You should be a little more careful."

"I'll remember that," Sabrina said, and moved on her way. Bret repeated the offer to come inside, but Sabrina didn't answer. She was too busy telling herself no matter how tired she was, she needed to stay out of that alley on her walk home.

* * *

"It might seem that we're spending too much time on this one aspect," Rylan said to the men who had gathered at his house on Thursday night, "but I want us to go back to verse eight of Titus 1. I think we moved too fast over the command for bishops—elders as we see in verse five—to be sober.

"We immediately run over this since none of us drink, but there's far more to this command. An elder is a sober-thinking man. This is a man who knows how to say no to himself. It's not just about drink, but also food and thoughts that are not in control.

"We need to take a long, hard look at our hearts when we see this word. We need to humbly ask God if we're sober men. You're all married. You can ask your wife if she believes you are sober." Rylan smiled a little. "She'll probably mention the fact that you don't drink, and that will give you an opportunity to talk about it."

The men were quiet for a moment, Rylan letting them have their thoughts. Brad was the one to speak.

"You always encourage us to ask our wives. Whom do you ask, Ry?"

"Well, I expect to hear from any and all of you if you see something amiss in my life, but I usually check with Chas. He's good about asking questions that make me think."

"When did you first realize this was not talking only about drinking?" Jeb Dorn asked.

"It's probably been a few years. I was

studying this and caught the fact that verse seven covers wine. I got to looking long and hard at these verses and the ones in First Timothy, and realized the bigger issue here.

"And if I might add, it's tougher than avoiding alcohol. It takes constant thinking, but that's what we men of Christ have to be, well-thinking men who are serious about the work on the cross and what it means in our lives and in the lives of our families."

The men talked for another 30 minutes, and because it was late, spent only a short time in prayer. Rylan, however, was at the advantage this night. He was already home and had no wife or children to see to. He took the next hour to pray for each man who studied with him, asking God to give them greater humility and a yearning for holiness. Only after he'd pled his heart did Rylan seek his bed.

* * *

Sabrina found herself alone in the dress shop on Friday morning. She had handwork to do, and at the moment, it was quiet. Heather had been ill in the night and was not able to see to Theta. Becky was there to help, but Jeanette had not wanted to leave her on her own. Sabrina didn't mind. She had talked with Crystal the night before and had a lot to think about.

"Did you talk to Paula?"

"Just for a few minutes."

"Are you going again?"

"No. If you see Paula, you can remind her where I live, but I'm not going back out after dark."

"I think Toben is interested in you."

"Is he?"

"He's rich, you know."

"He could be Midas—I'm not interested."

"You like that big guy?"

"My pastor? Of course I like him."

Crystal studied the other woman, but Sabrina didn't help her. She sometimes wondered why she bothered.

"Eliza is moving."

"Where to?"

"I don't know, but I think she's afraid Zeke will hurt the baby."

"He probably would."

"Why did you do it?"

"It's just who I am."

"You don't have a scar."

Sabrina touched her cheek. "No, it's all gone but the memories."

A moment of silence fell before Crystal said, "I gotta go."

"Crystal," Sabrina stopped her with the one word. "I pray for you."

There was a long stare and no comment. Sabrina was about to turn away when Crystal thanked her.

Thinking back on it now, Sabrina still wondered if she'd done the right thing. She knew Jeanette kept a Bible in the back, and because she was almost done with her work, she went and found it. She turned to Colossians and read from the first chapter, verse ten: "That ye might walk worthy of the Lord unto all pleasing, being fruitful in every good work, and increasing in the knowledge of God."

There's so much I don't know, Lord, please teach me. Help me to walk worthy and increase in knowledge of You.

Sabrina went back to work, but she asked God for these very things until Jeanette arrived.

* * *

Sabrina had not thought about what Rylan's reaction would be. She came to church on Sunday morning, a little earlier than usual, only to have Rylan take one look at her and pull her off to one side of the foyer area.

"What happened to your cheek, Sabrina?"

"Oh." Her hand came up to her cheekbone. She'd almost forgotten. "A box fell from a shelf in Jessie's storeroom."

Rylan looked so surprised that Sabrina smiled up at him, clearly amused.

"Was I almost in trouble?"

"Almost," Rylan had to admit, knowing it was time to face the fact that his reactions to this woman were anything but calm. He honestly thought she'd been out again, and he was ready to put her under lock and key.

"Would that have been so bad?" Sabrina pressed him.

"It all depends on the circumstances."

"So there are rules now?"

"There have always been rules. I thought we were in agreement on this."

"We are," Sabrina agreed, "but I've also been thinking about the fact that if we never go outside of our circle, when will we share Christ?"

"You're right, and it's easy to forget that.

It's also easy to forget that going outside the circle has to be done wisely."

"I'll remember. I'll just tell Jessie I need to stay out of the storeroom."

Rylan tried to look stern, but a smile peeked through. Sabrina's smile had turned a bit cheeky when she saw she'd gained the upper hand, and Rylan chuckled a little.

Trace and Cassidy, just coming in the door, noticed the smiles between the two in conference, and Cassidy did not waste a moment. She turned to her husband, her brows raised, her meaning clear. Trace knew she wanted him to question Rylan, but he wasn't ready to do that. It was too much fun watching from afar and asking God if this might be the one He had for their pastor.

* * *

"What happened to your cheek?" Jeanette asked, looking instantly upset.

"A box fell on me in Jessie's storeroom."

"Oh, you poor dear," Jeanette said, gently touching Sabrina's other cheek and telling herself to calm down.

Heather joined the women at that moment, and Sabrina had to explain again.

"Don't forget the women come to our

house tomorrow, Bri," Heather reminded her.

"I don't think I'll be there. Jessie has me organizing part of the storeroom, so even if we're slow, I'll probably be doing that."

Heather asked a few details, and the women were still discussing that when the service began. Sabrina made a mental note to visit at Jeanette's as soon as she could. There was never enough time to visit the way she liked, and not being with them made her miss Callie as well as feel very far from home.

* * *

"Where is Sabrina?" Cassidy wanted to know when she and Meg got to Jeanette's on Monday.

"Jessie needed her at the store today."

The women of the church gathered at Jeanette's house most Mondays. They prayed together and shared a time of fellowship that each woman enjoyed. The children played in the room with them or in Jeanette's other parlor. Becky did her part with treats and drinks, and Heather managed to go back and forth between both groups and still keep an eye on Theta.

"You can pray for me," Jeanette requested when the ladies had settled. "Savanna's first birthday is coming up, and not having Theta know about it is bothering me."

Both Meg and Cassidy were in the room and nodded with compassion.

"It's funny when it hits me. Most days, I go along, just thankful that she's here, but when the big events come on the calendar, I ache to have my sister back."

Miranda said she would take that request, and Patience shared about her upcoming trip to New York to see her brother- and sister-in-law, Meg's father and mother. She was excited to go back after all these years, but it was a long way to travel and she said she wasn't 19 any longer.

For some reason this got everyone to laughing. It took some moments to settle back to the requests, but before it was over, all the women had shared something they wanted special prayer for. The women each prayed, interrupted only twice by the needs of children, before they broke to have the pastry Becky had made. Not leaving for almost two hours, each one was very thankful she had come.

* * *

Sabrina had been correct. She was back in the storeroom at Jessie's, restacking shelves and hopefully making more items and shelf space available. She was working steadily along when she heard a male voice. Jeb Dorn had come to help her.

"What can I do?"

"Oh, Mr. Dorn, that's kind of you, but—" Sabrina stopped when he put his hand up.

"Patience took one look at that bruise and gave me the look. If you get hurt again, I'll be in all kinds of trouble."

Sabrina laughed, but she believed with all her heart that everyone was overreacting. A vision of her face after a violent customer got done with her one night in Denver floated through her mind. The pain of the memory was intense, and Sabrina was surprised that it took this to bring it back. It would have made more sense to recall it after the night with Eliza.

"What shall I do?" Jeb asked, and Sabrina was happy for the distraction.

The two worked along, with occasional visits from the girls, until dinnertime. Jeb couldn't stay in the afternoon, but with his help, Sabrina finished that day. She nearly fell into the door of her apartment, too tired to even eat, and thinking that she was not cut out for such work. The storeroom, coupled with a day of painting last week, was making Sabrina wonder if she shouldn't try to find work at the bank.

* * *

"I'll check with Rylan first," Trace said to Cassidy as they entered town on Sunday morning, "if you're sure you're not up to something."

"I'm sure," Cassidy said with a laugh. He'd checked with her twice already. "I don't know Bri at all, and if Ry's not comfortable with it, you know he'll be honest."

Trace knew that Cassidy would never play games with a person's heart, but she was a romantic. He had told her straight up that he was not going to speak to Rylan, but he had agreed to ask him for Sunday dinner. It wasn't until they agreed to this that Cassidy also mentioned having Sabrina.

"Can you join us for dinner today?" Trace asked Rylan as soon as he got in the building, even before the service could begin.

"I can, thank you, Trace."

"Great. Cass also wants to invite Bri, but if you'd rather we didn't do that, just say the word."

"Why would that bother me?" Rylan asked in all sincerity.

"Because it might look like we're up to something. We're just inviting the two of you."

"I don't have any objections. Have you checked with Sabrina?"

"Cass will do that if you're good with it."

"I'm fine," Rylan agreed, but a little part of his heart feared rejection. If he got to the ranch and Sabrina wasn't there, he would know where he stood.

* * *

As it was, both Rylan and Sabrina rode to the ranch with Trace and Cassidy. It meant that Trace would have to take them back to town later, but he didn't mind. Rylan could have taken something from the livery, but Trace was quick to offer.

When they arrived at the house, Sabrina enjoyed the large front porch and thought she could have sat on it all day. However, when Cassidy went to the kitchen to put dinner on, Sabrina went to lend a hand.

"Is there something I can do?"

"Sure," Cassidy agreed. "Those biscuits need to go into a bowl. You'll find one in that cupboard on the wall."

Cassidy glanced over as she worked and had to make a comment.

"You must hear this all the time, but your hair is beautiful."

"Oh, thank you," Sabrina said, not having heard that for a long while.

"It looks thick."

"It is."

"I don't know how you wear it down. I have to have mine up when it's this warm."

"I don't get hot very easily. I tend to be cold."

"What are you going to do this winter?"

Sabrina laughed before saying, "Probably freeze."

Cassidy smiled at her, but an unbidden thought came to mind: *Rylan would keep you warm this winter.* She pushed the thought away, not wanting to plot against her friend Rylan or Sabrina.

"How's it coming, Cass?" Trace appeared to check on her.

"Good. The meat is almost hot, and I just have to put these sweet potatoes in a bowl."

"Let me know when you need things carried."

"Thank you."

The gesture was so simple. Sabrina was sure this couple thought nothing of it, but for her this small act made her ache. It was the type of thing Danny would do for Callie. Sabrina had resigned herself months ago to never having this special unity with a man, and she was still resigned to that, but at the moment it hurt so much she could hardly breathe.

It was a relief to have Cassidy unaware. The food was ready faster than she thought, and before she had more time to grieve, they were sitting down to dinner.

* * *

"How did you come to Token Creek?" Cassidy asked Sabrina when they all had dessert in front of them.

"It's a long story," Sabrina said, not unwilling to share, but not wanting to monopolize the conversation.

"We have time," Trace said, already seeing that his wife was very drawn to this woman and fairly certain that Rylan was working to keep the emotions from his face.

"Well, I found myself alone. My parents had both died, and my sister and I had lost touch. In fact she had made it clear that she didn't want me in her life anymore. But then a man and his wife came along, Danny and Callie Barshaw. They took me into their home and cared for me. They found me a job at a laundry. I lived with them for more than six months, and it was during that time I believed in Christ. Their faith is genuine, and they taught me from the Bible and took me to church each week.

"But Denver still held a lot of painful memories for me. Danny suggested I try Token Creek because there's a fine church family here." She smiled before saying, "And I found out he was right."

With her comments about the church family, Trace and Cassidy naturally looked to Rylan. That man waited until Sabrina looked at him as well.

"Danny Barshaw is my father's cousin," Rylan told her quietly, his eyes seeing more than he let on.

11

SABRINA LOOKED AS SURPRISED as she felt over Rylan's announcement. She was too stunned to even speak. Had this not come up before? Did Rylan not know that she wrote to Danny and Callie regularly? And why hadn't Danny mentioned his relationship to the pastor of the Token Creek church?

"So he sent Bri because he knew about your being here?" Cassidy asked.

"He's done it a few times over the years," Rylan said by way of explanation. "Although none of the folks still live here."

"Did he contact you and tell you Bri was coming?" Trace wished to know.

"No. This is the first I've heard that Sabrina knows them. And I haven't talked to Danny in years. I visited home two years ago, but my family has a farm on the outskirts of town. Danny and Callie live right in the city."

"I had to leave my hometown a few years ago," Cassidy began to share.

Sabrina could have sighed with relief to have a change in subject. There was no point in guessing.

"My mother is still there and sometimes it's still hard to be away from her," Cassidy went on.

"You should tell her the details," Trace said, and Cassidy didn't hesitate. Sabrina listened intently, feeling like the day she learned that Callie had been a prostitute. It was too easy to believe that everyone's life was idyllic, with no past pains. Cassidy's experience with her own brother sounded as difficult as Sabrina's relationship with her sister.

Sabrina did not have a lot to say as the afternoon went on. She had much too much to think about.

* * *

"You can drop us here," Rylan said to Trace as they came into town. Sabrina wasn't paying very close attention to where they were but suddenly found herself a few blocks from the church building.

"Thanks, Trace," she said, glad for a chance to walk the rest of the way home.

"You're welcome. Don't forget what Cass said. Come back and visit us."

"I will."

"Thanks, Trace," Rylan added, shaking the rancher's hand and turning to find Sabrina ready with her goodbyes.

"I'll see you next week," she started.

"Why don't I walk you home."

"It's still light out," Sabrina pointed out.

"That's good, actually," Rylan said, taking her arm and turning her in the right direction. "I'll still be able to see your face when you tell me why it upset you that I know Danny Barshaw."

Sabrina frowned up at him, but Rylan didn't comment. They walked in silence for a time, and Rylan thought that at this rate she would be headed up her stairs and he still wouldn't know.

"I write to them every week," Sabrina suddenly said. "Did you know that?"

"No. I had heard that someone from Denver suggested you head this way, and I'll be honest and tell you I wondered. I know a lot of folks in Denver, and my family is all there, so it makes sense to me."

Again more silence.

"Why does it bother you?" Rylan asked.

Because for a long, painful minute I forgot I asked Danny and Callie to let me do this on my own, and I feared that Danny wrote and told you about me.

"I think," Sabrina ended up saying very slowly, "that I was just taken by surprise. It's not at all important. In fact it's nice to have someone know them."

Rylan was quite sure this was not the whole of it, but he was not going to ask. There was something altogether fragile about this woman. It wasn't something you saw on a first or second meeting, and it was certainly not something you would notice when she was painting the church building or sitting and sewing at Jeanette's, but it was there.

"Thank you for walking me home," Sabrina said, now standing at the bottom of her stairs.

"The next time you write to the Barshaws, please tell them I said hello."

"I will," Sabrina agreed, but then just stood

there. "They've never mentioned you. Maybe they were waiting for me to say I'd met you. Which I did in my last letter, but I haven't heard back."

"Maybe they haven't kept in touch with anyone lately and didn't want to send you to someone who was no longer here."

"Maybe."

"That makes sense. Is it still bothering you?"

Sabrina frowned again, but Rylan thought it was at herself.

"It was a silly thing to be upset about."

"I don't know about that. You're a long way from home, and they're your only link."

Sabrina looked up at him. He was so understanding at times, and for just a moment, she could see Trace and Cassidy, happy in their home. She had to work very hard to keep the yearning from her face and knew it was time to head upstairs.

"Thanks again," Sabrina said, and turned swiftly away.

Rylan knew something had happened, but he had no idea what. Once she was inside, he turned for home, realizing that until he saw her again, he wouldn't know if he was the problem or it was something within herself.

* * *

Monday night found everyone at Brad and Meg's ranch house. Trace and Cassidy were certainly there, as were Jeanette, Jeb, and Patience. They had also invited neighboring ranchers, Bart and Marty Carlisle, in order to celebrate Savanna's first birthday.

That little girl had no real idea she was the guest of honor, but that didn't stop anyone's fun. She was nearly walking on her own these days, and when she managed a few steps, she usually clapped for herself and fell down. The group naturally found this hysterical and would laugh even harder when Savanna joined in.

By the time supper was eaten, the men and women had found their own corners. The women were at the dining room table, and the men had settled into the living room, the conversation taking turns with ranching, town politics, and Jeb's latest project in his workshop.

"Marty's birthday is in August," Bart Carlisle said, lowering his voice. "I want a bookshelf for her, oak."

"What size?"

"A tall one," he said, "with a dark finish."

"I've got a tall one that doesn't have finish right now. Why don't you stop in and see it."

Bart was agreeing to this even as Marty was questioning Patience about a desk for Bart.

"Bart's birthday is in September. Is it too late for Jeb to start?"

"I don't think so. Are you coming into town this week?"

"Maybe Saturday," Marty said.

"Come by and see us," Patience invited. "We're going on a trip next week, but if you come by this week, Jeb can get measurements on what you want and start it as soon as we get back."

Without warning Brad entered the dining room. The women swiftly fell silent, not willing to mention the topic of their conversation. Without meaning to, they all managed to look guilty.

"Well, now," he said with a smile, "I almost get the impression I was being talked about."

"Not at all," his wife said in such an exaggerated way that Brad laughed.

"What are you talking about in there?" Jeanette asked.

"I'll never tell," Brad said, bringing smiles to every woman's face and laughter when he wanted to know if it was time to cut the cake.

* * *

The sky was growing very dark when Sabrina heard a knock on her door. She hoped that Bret Toben had not gotten it into his head to visit, but she still opened the door, lantern in hand.

"Eliza?" Sabrina said to the woman on her landing. "I thought you'd moved out of town."

"My baby is sick," Eliza whispered. "Do you think that Pastor would still pray?"

"Yes, he would. Do you want me to go and get him?"

"Will he come?"

"If he's home, I'm sure he will."

Eliza put a shaky hand to her mouth, tears coming to her eyes. She stumbled back down the stairs. Sabrina had to put her shoes back on but stopped only long enough to blow out her lantern before she started across town.

* * *

Rylan had his Bible open, but his eyes were across the room. He was working on memorizing all of Psalm 144, and concentration was coming hard. The words were powerful, reminding Rylan of God's will and force to do as He pleased. But the psalmist was humble, knowing that he was nothing compared to almighty God.

"'I will sing a new song unto thee, O God; upon a psaltery and an instrument of ten strings will I sing praises unto thee.'" Rylan said out loud to the room just before someone knocked on the door.

At this hour he knew it would be the sheriff, and almost smiled at the fact he'd just taken off his shoes.

"Oh, you're home!" Sabrina said with relief when the door opened, her voice breathless from running.

"Sabrina, what's the matter?"

"It's Eliza. Her baby's sick. She wants you to come and pray."

"I'll get my shoes."

"All right."

"Sabrina!" Rylan was suddenly back. "Wait here for me."

Sabrina nodded, but Rylan couldn't see it.

"Did you hear me?"

"I'll wait," she agreed, still breathing hard.

Rylan was on the porch a few minutes later, and on the walk back across town he heard Sabrina at her most talkative.

"I thought she was gone. Crystal said she'd moved on. She's afraid of Zeke, for the baby. And then she was at my door. She was crying and asking for you. I know it's dark, but she asked for you, and I couldn't ignore that. The baby's sick, and she's so little. I had to come. You understand, don't you? I had to."

"It's all right, Sabrina," Rylan said, but she was still talking.

"I don't know if I can do this. My heart breaks every time I talk to Crystal or Eliza. I thought I would be so strong, but my heart feels like lead when I see them. I don't know what God wants from me, Pastor Rylan. I just want to help, but it hurts so much."

Rylan stopped and brought Sabrina to a stop with him.

"You did the right thing in coming for me. We'll just go to Eliza's place now, and then you and I will find time to talk about it later."

"I'm sorry."

"There's nothing to be sorry about. We'll talk later."

Sabrina didn't feel any better, but she knew she had to hush. Rylan didn't need her going to pieces right now. He had a baby to pray for. Without saying another word, she turned and started toward Eliza's. She calmed down enough to remember to pray, and then for the first time was able to watch Rylan Jarvik at work.

* * *

"You're warm, aren't you, little one?" Rylan spoke to the tiny lethargic infant in his hands, his touch amazingly gentle. "I'm just going to hold you right close to me, Mirabel, and pray. You just rest while I pray for you.

"Father in heaven, thank You for this little person You created in Your image. You have a plan for her, Lord. You know how long You want her days to be on this earth. You knit her frame together, and You can see every beat of her tiny heart.

"Thank You for sending Mirabel into Eliza's life. Help Eliza to trust You, Lord, even if You don't plan to heal her daughter. Help us to be wise, Lord, and to know how to help Mirabel. Help us to trust You for the mighty God You are and to understand that Your ways are perfect. In the name of Your Son, I pray. Amen."

Rylan looked up at the women who sat side by side on the ancient davenport but kept the baby in his arms.

"I'm going to find Doctor Ertz, Eliza. Mirabel has got to be seen."

"She's so hot, and she's stopped crying."

"I'll find him," Rylan said again, his heart fairly certain this child was dying. He handed the baby back to her mother and without letting himself look at Sabrina went swiftly from the house.

"I didn't think he would come," Eliza said the moment he left.

"I knew he would. I wasn't sure he would be home, but he was."

Eliza looked at her and then down at the baby. She began to cry softly, and Sabrina had never felt so helpless in all her life.

* * *

"I'll come by the mercantile tomorrow and check on you," Rylan said after he and Sabrina had walked the short distance to her stairway. There was little moon, but the sky still managed to glow with stars. It's immense beauty, however, was lost on this couple tonight.

"You were wonderful tonight," Sabrina said, almost as if she hadn't heard him. "You knew just what to do and say."

"Thank you for coming to get me."

"I wish I could do more. I wish I knew what to do."

"I think you did very well. And Doc Ertz was optimistic. He got Mirabel to eat, and he said that will make all the difference."

"She's so little," Sabrina said next, and

Rylan heard the thickness of her voice. "I don't want her to die."

"I don't want that either."

A sob broke in Sabrina's throat—she couldn't help herself.

"Come here, Sabrina," Rylan said gently. "Let me give you a hug."

The moment Sabrina felt his arms around her she was lost. She sobbed against the front of Rylan's shirt, her heart feeling as though it would break. Rylan's hold was undemanding. He kept control, but he had to resist the urge to press a kiss to the top of her head and cuddle her close.

"This is when trust and faith are tested," Rylan said quietly, bending a little toward her ear. "The same God who saved you has a plan for this little family. We can choose to believe that and take comfort in that fact."

Rylan felt Sabrina nod against him and put his hands on her shoulders. He couldn't see her very well but still held her a little apart from him and asked if she was all right.

"I think so. Thank you again for coming."

"Try to sleep," Rylan urged, and watched her take the stairs on slow, tired feet, knowing he needed to get home and take his own advice.

* * *

Sabrina did not look her best on Tuesday. Jessie noticed her pale face and puffy eyes right away but didn't say anything for a while. The girls were at each other off and on, and not until after dinner did Jessie catch Sabrina alone.

"Are you all right?" the mother of two asked.

"I didn't sleep well. My neighbor's baby is sick, and I kept thinking about her." In truth, she had prayed most of the night away but didn't know if Jessie would understand this.

"Is the baby going to be all right?" Jessie asked.

"I don't know. I checked this morning, but they were both asleep."

Jessie wasn't sure what to say. She knew who some of Sabrina's neighbors were, and it was tempting to ask why she got involved. At the same time, her heart was touched. On days like today when all the girls did was fight, she was ready to sell them to the first available customer, but in truth she knew she would never make it if anything ever happened to one of her daughters.

"Jessie," Sabrina had been watching her, and had to ask, "where is the girls' father?"

"Gone."

"Dead?"

"No, just gone."

"Were you married?"

"We were, yes."

"How long has he been gone?"

"Since I was expecting Clancy. It was so early I didn't even realize it."

Sabrina didn't react but she wanted to. This man, whoever he was, didn't know he had a second daughter. At moments like this, she didn't think men were worth it, but then she remembered Rylan last night and the gentle things he'd said to Eliza. And the new mother seemed to listen. Just having Rylan come in her time of need had seemed to change the way she'd viewed him.

"I think that's the mail," Jessie suddenly said, looking up and seeing Kaleb Heydorn from the train station. He never dallied but dropped the mailbag on the counter and went on his way.

"Do you want me to get it?" Sabrina offered, but Jessie took it.

Sabrina kept sorting the cooking utensils and tinware that had been pawed through over the weekend until Jessie returned with a letter for her. Not even needing to ask,

Sabrina knew it was all right that she read it. Getting comfortable on the rocker out front, she opened Callie's letter.

> **We are so excited that Rylan is still there. We had heard that he'd moved on, but that a good man had taken his place. How wonderful to hear he's still there. Danny loves Rylan's father, Donald. They've always been very close and admired each other, even when they've been out of touch.**
>
> **Your apartment location sounds like a challenge. I will admit that I did not picture you living in that part of town, but I think you can do this. Your heart is tender, but you don't want that life again. You never wanted that life, so I don't fear your going back to it.**

"Well, now." Rylan was speaking before Sabrina could finish. "This looks like hard work."

Sabrina smiled as he took one of the other rocking chairs. Technically they were for sale, but Sabrina doubted that anyone would ever buy. Indeed they looked as though they'd been there for years.

"I got a letter from Callie," Sabrina said. "They had heard you'd moved on."

"I can see how that might happen. Communication is tough enough face-to-face. I can understand how facts might get crossed over that many miles."

Sabrina didn't think he had any trouble communicating but felt foolish saying so. Rylan watched her for a moment but didn't want to stare, or rather he didn't want to be caught staring, so he turned his gaze to the street. The first thing he saw was the sign for the Boar's Head.

"Have you seen much of Bret lately?"

"Not since the day I painted."

"What happened then?"

"I made the mistake of cutting through the alley."

"What did he have to say?"

"The usual, come in and sit down out of the heat or have a drink."

"How did you meet him exactly?"

"I was very new in town and went down the alley. He came out a door, and I made the mistake of asking if there were apartments for rent in the building. He's been trying to talk to me ever since."

"I thought you made your feelings pretty clear that first day. You would think he'd take the hint."

Sabrina agreed, not catching on that Rylan had witnessed some of the interaction.

"I probably should get back to work," Sabrina said. She'd had plenty of time to read the letter, and Jessie was paying her.

"Did you see Eliza this morning?"

"I stopped in, but they were both asleep. Did you go?"

"I was just there. Mirabel is pretty warm again."

Sabrina's heart sank, but she was glad she'd been warned.

"I'll see you later," Rylan said as he stood.

Sabrina thanked him for coming and slipped back inside. Just as soon as she had an excuse, she hugged Clancy, glad the little girl did not notice the stricken look in her eyes.

* * *

"I brought you some soup," Sabrina said to Eliza after work that night. The front door to the house was open, but the room was still very warm.

"I'm not hungry."

"I'll leave it here," Sabrina said, putting the bowl on the table. "How is she?"

The baby was back in the basket, looking smaller than ever. Eliza didn't answer but sat looking down at her daughter, her face drawn with fatigue.

"Where are your people, Eliza?" Sabrina asked.

"Redmond, almost to Billings."

"How long have you been gone?"

"A long time."

"Were you a working girl there?"

"No." Her voice became thoughtful as she remembered. "I followed my man. His name was Lem Hawkes. He had dreams of finding copper, lots of it."

"What happened to him?"

"He was killed at the mine, penniless, and I was a long way from home."

"Is your family still in Redmond?"

"My father is. I got a letter from him last year." Eliza looked down in the basket. "He doesn't know about Mirabel."

"When Mirabel gets back on her feet, you've got to go back. He'll be pleased to know he's a grandpa."

Eliza didn't answer. She just looked back down at the baby. Sabrina could hardly stand it. She glanced around and spotted the bowl of soup.

"Here," Sabrina said, taking the bowl, finding a spoon, and handing it to the other woman. "You won't be able to feed Mirabel if you don't eat."

The other woman took the spoon in hand. Sabrina watched her, and while Eliza ate the soup, begged God for help. Only a few minutes passed before, very quietly, she began to tell Eliza her story.

12

"THIS IS LOOKING GOOD," Chas said to Rylan when he got there on Wednesday to help with the paint. Philip Leffers was working on some trim on the far side, but for the moment, the two men were alone.

"It's coming along," Rylan agreed. "I don't know how many more days I can get from Pete, so I'm glad it's going fast. I have to work tomorrow to fill in for today."

"Is he still trying to sell the livery to you?"

"Yes, mostly when he's been drinking, but I know he's still serious."

"It's too bad you don't have a half dozen

strapping big sons to help you run the place. That would make it a light load."

"I think you forget that I'm 26. It's not possible for me to have any strapping big sons."

"Nonsense," Chas teased. "With your size, they'll be strapping big sons by the time they're five."

Rylan laughed. He was used to comments about his size, and in truth it never bothered him. But lately he wondered if a certain woman would even consider marrying a man as big as he was.

"How is it going with Bri?"

"I was just thinking about her," Rylan admitted. "How does a man find out if a woman would welcome his interest?"

"That's a good question. It's a little different for each woman. I don't want to be cryptic, but I think you'll know."

Rylan nodded, the paintbrush still moving.

"I was watching her on Sunday," Chas said. "You were talking about the miracle of the resurrection, and her eyes were filled with wonder. And then afterward, she took Nellie in her arms, and when Heidi wanted attention, she pulled her close as well. It was pretty special to see."

Rylan shook his head. "I can't even look at her when I preach. She lets her guard down completely in church, and I can read every look of wonder, hope, and conviction."

Philip joined the other men just then, so they dropped the topic, but Rylan knew that Chas would get back to him. He was that kind of friend.

* * *

"Guess what," Jeanette said when Sabrina got to work on Thursday.

"What?"

"We're all caught up, and I think you can take a day off."

"Oh," Sabrina said. "Are you sure?"

"Yes, ma'am."

"Are they painting today?" Sabrina questioned, and Jeanette was thankful she'd checked. She took in the fatigue on the younger woman's face and knew she was doing the right thing.

"No, they're not. I was thinking you might want to rent a buggy from the livery and head out to see Cassidy. She told me you had a great time last Sunday."

Sabrina stared at her. Such a thing never occurred to her, but it would be fun indeed.

"I've never done that before."

"It's not hard. Cassie used to go and visit Meg every Wednesday. Pete or Rylan will set you up with a rig, and Holden Ranch is straight out of town on the left. You can't miss it. As soon as you get going it will all be familiar."

Sabrina didn't know what to say, but then Jeanette didn't need her to comment. She saw her to the door and watched her move down the street, a satisfied smile on her face.

* * *

Rylan had not made it to the forge yet. He had cleaned a few stalls and spent time trying to calm a frightened mare who was trying to kick her way out of the box. He had to shoe her before the day was out, and he wasn't exactly thrilled with the prospect.

He wondered afterward how long she'd been standing there but didn't ask. Sabrina had come in the door, much as before, and stood over by the three- and six-cent hooks.

"Hello," Rylan said, headed that way.

"I'm here to rent a rig," Sabrina said, not quite believing it herself.

"Is that right?" Rylan said, just fighting a smile and wondering how anyone could manage to look so confident and uncertain at the same time. Not to mention beautiful. The light blue dress she was wearing was not something he'd seen before.

"I'm going to see Cassidy."

"That'll be fun. Have you driven a buggy before?"

"Not for a long time."

"I think I have just the right one."

"I don't want the horse to run away with me," Sabrina said, not willing to take for granted he would know this.

"I don't think that will happen," Rylan said, already planning to send Candy. She would be calm even if her tail were on fire.

"Jeanette said Cassidy used to do this."

"Every week."

Sabrina made herself stop talking then. She was a bit panicked about it all and wondered if she shouldn't just go and see Heather and Becky. Rylan had not actually done anything yet. It wasn't too late to change her mind.

"I'm not sure," she started, and Rylan stopped. He'd been pulling the rig out into the wide alley between the stalls but set it down and came back to her.

"About driving the rig?"

"Yes, and Cassidy is not expecting me. I don't even know if she's home."

Rylan almost said he was certain she was, but he made himself walk to the door. He looked up and down the street and smiled when he saw the wagon.

"I think you might find someone from the ranch at the mercantile. Why don't you check there, and then you can ride out with whoever is going home."

Sabrina looked down the street the way Rylan had, but she didn't see anything in particular. She already felt foolish for bothering him and didn't want to ask what he'd seen.

"Do I owe anything for your time?" she asked instead.

"Five dollars," Rylan said, his face utterly serious, and a laugh escaped Sabrina before she could stop it.

Rylan's own smile appeared before he spoke again.

"Will you do me a favor? Stop back and let me know if you need the rig."

"Certainly I will, and thank you, Pastor Rylan."

"You can do me another favor while you're at it, and just call me Rylan."

"Oh," Sabrina said. "What do I call you now?"

"Pastor Rylan."

"And you call me Sabrina, don't you?"

"Um hm."

"But everyone else calls me Bri."

"I think I've noticed that."

"Why is that?"

Rylan didn't answer. He stepped out in front of the livery and shouted, "Cassie! Hold up a minute."

Cassidy brought the wagon to a halt and waited when Rylan waved to her. The livery man went back to the lady waiting behind him.

"Are you going to tell her you want to come to the ranch, or am I?"

"No, I can ask," Sabrina said, but she didn't sound very certain. Rylan walked with her to the wagon and greeted his old friend.

"You're in town early, Cass."

"Aren't I, though," she agreed with a grin. "How are you, Bri?"

"I'm fine. Are you very busy today, Cassidy?"

"Nothing out of the ordinary," Cassidy said and then caught on. "Are you free to come out?"

"I am. I was just about to rent a rig, but I wasn't sure I could drive it."

"I used to do that every week when I visited Meg," Cassidy said, smiling at the memory.

"Oh," Sabrina had a sudden thought, "if I don't rent a rig, someone will have to bring me back to town."

"What time do you want to come back?" Rylan asked before Cassidy could volunteer.

"After supper, Ry," Cassidy put in, "and you come out and join us."

"Thank you, Cassie. I'll plan on that."

Before Sabrina knew it, she was in Cassidy's wagon and going with her to finish her errands in town. She was halfway to the ranch before she remembered that Rylan had not told her why he called her Sabrina.

* * *

I have to take a nap had been Cassidy's words after dinner. Trace had gone back out to work, and she had explained that everyone told her to baby herself on this first child. After the first one was born, you always had someone else to take care of and not always time for a nap.

Sabrina did not mind the time alone. Cassidy had already showed her the stream that ran through the property, and with a blanket in hand she was headed down there to relax and dip her feet into the water. It was wonderful to take her stockings off; the air felt good; and when she put her feet into the water, it chilled her but was worth it.

Sabrina looked around the ranch, the Bitterroot Mountains all around, and wished for her Bible. But that only lasted a few minutes. Rylan had been urging them to think on Scripture, to know it, and have it always with them in their hearts.

Sabrina thought about Exodus. She had been reading in that book for a few days and was amazed at Moses' path to God. She had never heard any of this before and was awed at the way God worked. A verse came to mind from chapter 3. Sabrina did not know it by heart, but words came back to her about God being with Moses and bringing him to serve God on a mountain.

So many years ago, so many faithful servants for years, Lord. I feel small and insignificant, but You use each one of us where You will. You have a plan for me. Pastor Rylan . . . Sabrina stopped and smiled. *Rylan keeps telling me that, and I can see it now. There is so much I don't know. Help my heart to keep learning. I grow anxious when I think that Crystal and Eliza will never accept You and believe, but I can't control the time. Only You know their paths.*

Sabrina realized she had some repenting to do. She had been anxious. She had wanted to be in control and to be the one to "save" each woman she met. It was remarkably freeing and gave her a tremendous amount of peace to give it over to God. It was even freeing for her to realize how foolish she was for thinking she could compete with God.

Sabrina was still in the midst of these thoughts when she looked up to see Cassidy coming her way.

"Couldn't you sleep?" Sabrina called to her.

Cassidy laughed. "It's been almost two hours."

Sabrina didn't know how that could be possible.

"It's like that out here," Cassidy said, joining her on the blanket. "Time ceases to exist. I love it."

"I can see why you would."

"Did you sleep?" Cassidy asked.

"I had too much on my mind."

"Something in particular?"

"One of my neighbors has a baby who's

sick. She let Pastor Rylan pray with her for the first time the other night. I'm hoping she'll want to hear more and the baby will be all right."

"What's her name? I'll pray for her too."

"The mother is Eliza and the baby is Mirabel."

"I like the baby's name."

"It's pretty, isn't it?"

"Yes. Is there a father?"

"No."

Some of Jeanette's words came back about Sabrina living in a bad part of town. Cassidy had been concerned when she heard, but now she was fascinated.

"Where is the father?"

"I don't know if she knows who the father is. She's a prostitute."

"And she's your neighbor?" Cassidy asking, hoping she had kept the surprise from her voice. She didn't know what she thought the "bad part of town" meant, but this wasn't it.

"Yes. I was looking for cheap rent, and that put me on Willow Street."

"And you're staying there?"

"I'm planning on it. I would move if something nicer opened up that I could afford, but most days I'm too busy to look. Tell me something," Sabrina said before Cassidy could form another question. "Did Jeanette tell me that you opened Token Creek Apparel?"

"Yes."

"What was that like, starting your own business? Did the bank loan you money?"

"My mother gave me the money to start, so that was a tremendous help. I knew I could sew well enough to make a living, but in truth I didn't know if Token Creek would support it. They did obviously, but it was a risk."

Sabrina nodded, looking fascinated.

"Are you interested in starting a business?"

"I don't do anything well enough to try. And I don't mind working for Jeanette and Jessie. I admire Jessie—she does an amazing job—but I would hate to have to raise my girls in a store."

"She is amazing. She told me one time that it's her dream to build a home someday, but there's never any time. The store takes it all."

"Have you ever talked about what she believes? It's never come up, and I don't want to ask her."

"Did you know that Jeb is her cousin?"

"He told me."

"He and Jessie have talked about God for years, and she has a lot of respect for Jeb and Rylan, but she doesn't think she needs church or the Bible. She thinks she's a good person on her own."

Sabrina had a new thought. There was one great advantage to knowing prostitutes. They never argued that they were fine. They might not want to hear what you have to say, but it wasn't because any of them thought they were sinless.

"Well, now," Trace said loudly enough to warn them, having caught sight of Sabrina's bare feet. "This looks fun."

By the time Trace made the blanket, Sabrina had managed to tuck her stockings away and get her feet under the hem of her skirt. Trace sank down and kissed his wife and then asked the ladies about their day.

"How late is it?" Cassidy suddenly asked.

"It's suppertime, I think. At least that's what my stomach thinks."

Cassidy pressed him and found out it wasn't that late, but she still rose and started for the house. Trace went with her, and Sabrina said she would be along shortly.

She had just gotten her stockings and shoes back into place and the blanket folded when she saw Rylan coming up in a buggy. She hadn't expected him this early but thought it was nice he could get away. It took his stepping out of the wagon and walking slowly toward her for her to realize he'd not come with good news.

* * *

Sabrina could not stop trembling. Not in her wildest dreams did she picture herself standing in the cemetery next to the tiniest casket she'd ever seen. Mirabel had died in the afternoon the day before. Crystal had come for Rylan, who had gone to Eliza and prayed with her. He had stayed as long as she wanted, Crystal hovering in the background all the while. When it seemed he should leave, he'd headed to the ranch for Sabrina.

Sabrina had not cried, and Rylan had not pressed her to talk about it on the way back to town. He'd taken her to Eliza's and watched as she'd silently gone in and sat with the stunned mother.

Now the small group of mourners stood in the cemetery at the edge of town. Rylan looked over the group. Doctor Ertz had come, and Sabrina, but outside of that, these were the outcasts of the community. Saloon owners and workers, prostitutes and some of the men who visited them, stood around the small grave. Rylan hadn't been asked to say anything, but when eyes kept turning to him, he went to Eliza and checked with her.

"Do you want me to say anything, Eliza? Maybe what we talked about yesterday?"

Eliza nodded, and Rylan stepped back a little to address the group.

"Thank you for coming. Eliza and I talked about some things yesterday, and I'd like to share those thoughts with you. I don't have my Bible with me, but I can tell you that God treasures babies like Mirabel. It says in Psalms that we are knit together in our mother's womb, and for that reason, I know God watches over infants and little ones.

"For those of us who grow old enough to know what choices are, we all have to face what we're going to do with God's Son, Jesus Christ. But for little ones like Mirabel, God understands they can't choose or reject Him. And God is a just and loving God. He would never condemn such a small life away from Him. For this reason, I believe Mirabel is with God right now. Not because of who she is, but because of who He is. I take comfort in that.

"I hope that anyone who doubts they will spend eternity with God will not wait another day to take care of that. Mirabel's time was done, and we will grieve her, but we don't have to grieve without hope." Rylan paused for just a moment before adding, "If anyone wants to know any more about the things I've said, I hope you'll come to me."

Folks started to wander off, some with a word to Eliza. Sabrina stayed at her side, not wanting to talk to anyone but not sure she should leave. She glanced up and spotted Zeke in the distance, and all thoughts about staying silent deserted her.

"Zeke is here," Sabrina said, not mincing words. "You deserve better than that, Eliza. Go home to Redmond. Go home to your father. You won't have to work like this anymore. Leave Token Creek and this life behind you. And keep searching for God," Sabrina added, her throat threatening to close. "Don't ever give up until you find Him."

Eliza finally looked at her.

"I'm so sorry she's gone," Sabrina said, unable to stop the tears that flooded her eyes. "She was so precious. Don't lose yourself too. Mirabel wouldn't want that for you."

"Is there anything I can do?" Rylan asked Eliza next. She answered him, but Sabrina couldn't hear it. A moment later, Rylan took Sabrina's arm and led her away.

"I told Eliza you would help her pack."

"Certainly. Is she doing that today?"

"No, you can check with her tomorrow."

Sabrina nodded and then realized that Rylan was definitely taking her somewhere. She saw the buggy ahead and took the hand he offered to climb on board. She didn't know when she'd been so weary. All she wanted to do was sleep. It took some minutes to see that Rylan was not taking her home.

"Where are we going?"

"To Jeanette's."

"Why?"

"Because you need someone to look after you right now."

"Don't be nice to me, Rylan Jarvik!" Sabrina commanded, desperately working not to cry. "I mean it."

Rylan didn't comment—he understood—but neither did he change his course. He was taking her to Heather and Becky. They would know what to do.

* * *

"Did you know and not say anything to me?" Heather whispered to Jeanette as soon as she got home.

"No. I never even guessed. Are you sure?"

"I tell you, I've never seen him like that. Even after she fell asleep in the chair, he sat and watched her, his heart in his eyes."

Jeanette stared at Heather. All this time she'd been watching out for Sabrina, worried about her safety and completely missing that Rylan was falling in love.

"They're perfect for each other," Jeanette said at last.

"Perfect," Heather agreed, forcing herself to keep her voice down.

"And you say she's still here?"

"In the kitchen with Becky. He made her promise to stay until he came back."

As though talking about him would conjure him up, both women heard a knock on the front door. Becky could be heard going from the kitchen, talking all the while to Sabrina.

"I tell you you might as well come, Bri. It's going to be Pastor Rylan."

"I'm coming," Sabrina said bringing up the rear, and seeing that Becky was right. Rylan was at the door, stepping in to greet them both.

"Supper is almost ready," Becky said. "I'll give a final call."

"Thank you, Becky," he said as she wandered off. He didn't waste time snagging Sabrina's attention. "How are you doing?"

"Better. It helped to sleep."

"Can I be kind to you now?" Rylan asked.

"That was a terrible thing to say to you, and you're making a joke out of it."

"You were not yourself."

"But I still owe you an apology."

"I didn't tease you so you would feel bad. I truly did understand."

Sabrina looked at him. He was kind, remarkably so, and the more she was with him, the more she liked him. She knew he would never return any strong feelings she might develop, but she was all right with that. Having his friendship was all she needed.

"You're doing it again," Rylan said, keeping his voice light.

"Doing what?"

" 'Inscrutable at will' is how I would term it."

Sabrina frowned at him in confusion.

"Your eyes," Rylan explained.

Sabrina had to think about this and then asked slowly, "So I'm working to hide my thoughts?"

"I'm not sure. Your eyes can be very expressive or give nothing away. I assume that's deliberate."

Sabrina had to think some more about this. Her gaze wandered to the floor, and she frowned in concentration. Rylan wanted to laugh. It was as if he'd disappeared.

"I don't know," Sabrina said suddenly, just as Becky called for them. "I honestly don't know."

Rylan had to laugh. Seeing it, Sabrina misunderstood, her hands coming to her waist.

"Were you teasing me again?"

"No," Rylan said, but was still laughing, and Sabrina clearly didn't believe him.

With a longsuffering shake of her head, she turned toward the dining room. She wasn't sure what she'd missed, but she knew she'd missed something.

13

"WERE THERE MANY PEOPLE at the funeral?" Jeanette asked over supper. She had not been completely aware of the afternoon's events, but Rylan had caught her up. She had been genuinely sad for the mother's loss.

"Maybe twelve people," he said, trying to recall.

"Anyone I would know?"

"Doc Ertz. I think that's it."

Jeanette turned to Sabrina. "Did you know anyone besides the doctor?"

"Several. Some are my neighbors, and one I know by accident."

"How does that work, knowing someone by accident?" Heather asked. Theta had settled down quickly, and she had been able to join them.

Sabrina had to smile. How did she explain Bret Toben to a woman like Jeanette? Yes, Heather had asked the question, but Jeanette was listening to every word. For some reason, Sabrina saw Jeanette as sheltered. She probably wasn't as sheltered as she thought, but just in case she was right, Sabrina did not want to be the one to change things for her.

"Sabrina?" Rylan said, and that lady realized she hadn't answered.

"I'm sorry, Heather. I was just thinking about how I'd met Bret."

"Bret Toben?" Jeanette asked.

"Yes, do you know him?" Sabrina asked with surprise.

"Certainly. He's done business at the bank for years. He was at the funeral?"

Sabrina nodded.

"How do you know him, Bri?" Heather was still curious.

"I met him when I was looking for an apartment, and he shops at Jessie's," Sabrina heard herself saying, realizing it was easier than she thought.

"Bret has shown interest in Sabrina," Rylan had no issue saying. "It's been a bit challenging for her."

"How do you handle it?" Jeanette asked.

Sabrina would not have chosen to share this, but Jeanette did not seem as shocked or upset as she would have imagined.

"I just keep saying no."

"No to what?" Heather asked, looking concerned.

"He usually asks me into the bar for a drink."

Jeanette opened her mouth to ask what she was doing near the Boar's Head but then shut it. Jessie's was across the street and not many doors down from that saloon. And on top of that, she knew there were things that Sabrina didn't tell her because of the way she reacted and suddenly understood why.

"I need to tell you something, Bri," Jeanette said, setting her fork down and looking serious. "I didn't want you to move to that apartment. I've hated it that you're there, but you were able to speak to this poor girl who lost her baby, and I think that's wonderful. I think *you're* wonderful."

"Thank you," Sabrina said, watching Heather nod her head in vigorous agreement. The black-haired woman looked at Rylan, working to understand where that must have come from, but he only smiled at her.

Becky came bustling in before anyone could comment further, checking bowls and offering dessert. Sabrina was never so glad to see her and have the attention shift away from herself.

* * *

It's like leaving Denver, Sabrina prayed as she dressed on Saturday morning, thankful that Jeanette had been understanding about work. *I know it's not the same, but packing for Eliza makes me feel as though I'm leaving Callie and Danny all over again. I don't want to cry. I don't want to put that burden on her, Lord. Help me to think of Eliza's needs and not my own. Help me to do just what she needs and to show my beliefs as who I am. May You use that in some way, someday, Lord. Help me to trust You for that.*

Sabrina pulled her hair back with a ribbon, knowing it would be easier to have it out of her face, and went out the door. Mirabel came to mind, but Sabrina pushed the images of her small face away. She didn't know what the day would look like, but something told her it was not going to be fun.

* * *

"Do you need to sell some things before you go?" Sabrina asked Eliza after an hour of work, making an assumption.

Rylan had offered to buy Eliza a train ticket, but she didn't know if he wanted people knowing about that. She knew the pastor had feelings for Sabrina—she'd seen it with her own eyes—but not what their relationship was.

"No," Eliza said. "I'll pack today and leave in the morning."

Sabrina was glad. She thought the longer the other woman stayed around, the more likely it was she wouldn't leave at all.

"Do you want anything from the kitchen?" Sabrina asked.

"No, take what you want and leave the rest."

Sabrina kept sorting, not really sure what

the other woman needed but wanting to help in any way she could.

"What is *she* doing here?"

Sabrina turned at the sound of the male voice and told herself to stay calm. She was tempted to go after Zeke with an iron skillet but knew that was wrong.

"Get out, Zeke," Eliza said tiredly. "I told you I'm going, and I am."

"I need to talk to you."

"No. Just leave."

Sabrina didn't want to get involved. She made herself turn her back on the arguing couple. She was using the kitchen table to fold clothing and never saw the blow coming. One minute she was standing upright and the next she was out cold.

For a full ten seconds, Eliza did not react. She stared in horror at the act of cowardice on Zeke's part and then began to scream.

"What have you done? She's my friend. She's helping me! Get your worthless hide out of my house and never come back!"

Zeke had never seen her like this. She had picked up a chair and was actually coming at him.

"Eliza, if I could just talk to you," he tried, but she was having none of it. Eliza chased him to the door and then slammed it in his wake. She dropped the chair and made a beeline for Sabrina, praying for the first time in years.

"Please God, not Pretty. Don't let her be dead. Anything but that."

* * *

Sabrina felt the wet cloth on her face and struggled to wake up. Her head pounded. She started violently, but it was Eliza holding her head and not Zeke.

"Oh, you're alive, you're alive. I thought he'd killed you."

"What happened?" Sabrina asked, reaching for the back of her head and willing it to stay on her shoulders. It felt as though she'd been drinking, but she was pretty sure she didn't do that anymore.

"Here, sit up." Eliza helped her, and Sabrina looked around the small house. She made the mistake of shaking her head and had to groan a little.

"Is he gone?" Sabrina asking, realizing what must have happened.

"Yes. I chased him off."

Sabrina came to her feet and turned to

go back to work. Eliza watched her, still trying to take in all she knew about her and what had just happened. She had been dreading leaving Token Creek, even knowing there was nothing for her here, but not now. Throwing off her grief, she began to work swiftly. She didn't want to wait until tomorrow. There was an afternoon train. If she hurried, she could get word to Rylan Jarvik, and make it.

* * *

"Clancy, be careful," Sabrina said, watching the little girl climb on a ladder in the storeroom. "Don't fall."

"I won't."

Sabrina wanted to stay and keep an eye on her, but the store was full. She found the egg basket and rolling pin she'd been looking for and went back out front to assist the woman who had asked for them. And it seemed that everyone had a special order. Jessie had been bent over the catalog all afternoon.

Two boys, chasing each other through the store, had spilled the barrel of peanuts, and Hannah had been none too happy when asked to help with the cleanup. Sabrina's head still ached, and she had to work not to look at the clock every few minutes. She couldn't remember the last time she wanted a day to end so badly.

* * *

"You're all set?" Rylan asked Eliza. They had met at the train station and taken a seat on a bench against the wall, Eliza's bags at their feet.

"All set."

"Where's Sabrina? I thought she'd be here."

"She already said goodbye. Jessie was planning on having her at the store and since we were done, she went."

For a moment they were quiet. Rylan had bought her ticket, something he had not done lightly, and he was going to make sure she boarded that train.

"Do you fear Zeke will follow you?" he asked after a moment.

"No, he never has much money. He'll be stuck here for a while, and he doesn't know where I'm from."

"Good. You'll be safe with your father."

"Watch out for Pretty," Eliza suddenly said. "Zeke might still have it out for her."

"Do you think he holds a grudge from that first day?"

"Yes, and he's a coward. He hit Pretty from the back."

Rylan stared down at her.

"Zeke hit Sabrina today?"

"Knocked her out cold. She needs to get out of that neighborhood. It's no place for a girl like her."

Rylan was delighted to see and hear the train from a distance. He had some thinking to do, and the sooner he saw Eliza on her way, the sooner he could get to it.

"Thank you for everything," Eliza said, standing from the bench they'd been sharing, the train pulling into the station. "I won't ever forget."

"I'll pray for you, Eliza."

"I'll read the Bible you gave me, Pastor."

Rylan put his hand out to shake hers. He watched while she boarded and stayed until the train pulled out and she waved from the window, her face still etched in grief but with a light of determination as well.

Rylan had plenty to do, but he sat back down on the bench for a few minutes longer, asking God to reach this woman through His Word and save her for all of eternity.

* * *

Sabrina did not even have the energy to walk home. Jessie had closed the store and said goodbye, but Sabrina had gotten no farther than the rocking chairs. It was Saturday night in Token Creek—she couldn't linger for long—but it felt so good to sit down and have nothing to do.

Her head didn't hurt anymore, but she learned in a hurry that she could not touch the lump at the back. It smarted a little too much for curious fingers.

Sabrina was wondering what Zeke had used to hit her and how she was going to brush her hair when she spotted Chas Vick coming up Main Street. She hoped he didn't need something at the mercantile. If so, he would have to wait until Monday.

"Hello," Sabrina greeted him, smiling when he sat down.

"You're just the person I'm looking for, Bri Matthews."

"Why is that?"

"I've come to ask you to supper."

"Oh, thank you," Sabrina said with pleasure but knowing she had to be honest. "I'm awful tired, Chas. I don't know if I'll be very good company."

"If you're tired, that's perfect. You won't have to fix your own supper."

Sabrina agreed. She thought it a very nice offer and told herself to move out of the chair. Even the walk down the street was an effort, but Chas talked about various things, and before she knew it, they were at the Vicks' front door. Chas held the door for her to go in, and the first person she saw was Franklin.

"Hello, Franklin," Sabrina greeted him, even as Chas invited her to have a seat and make herself at home.

"Does Miranda need help?"

"No, but she'll be out in a minute to see you."

"This is my horse," Franklin began, holding up a small wooden toy. "I call him Quincy, after Trace's horse."

"I like that name," Sabrina said, thinking this was familiar and he must have told her about his toy horse the last time she was there. Sabrina made the mistake of putting her head back against the sofa. The bump hurt, so she shifted around a bit and continued to watch Franklin with his horse. She even had a vague memory of Heidi coming in with her dog but just couldn't be sure.

* * *

Rylan watched Sabrina wake up, sorry he had not been there when she arrived. The last thing he wanted her to believe was that he'd plotted against her. Pete had agreed to get an order out that was too much for the end of the day, so Rylan had run to Chas and asked for his help, wanting him to catch Sabrina before she went back to her apartment. By the time he'd cleaned up and joined the Vicks, she was sound asleep.

"Did I fall asleep?" Sabrina suddenly asked, sitting up very straight.

"Yes."

"Oh, no. I've got to apologize to Miranda."

"You'll do no such thing," the woman said, coming into the room with a plate of food. "You told Chas you were tired. Here's your supper."

"I slept through supper?" Sabrina asked, feeling embarrassed and disoriented.

"As I said, it's not important. We are in the other room. Rylan will visit with you while you eat, and then you can join us for dessert."

Sabrina watched Miranda walk from the room and then looked down at the plate of food in her lap. It took some time for her to look over at Rylan, but when she did, she was struck by his face.

"You look a little weary," Sabrina commented, not unkindly.

"I am," Rylan agreed.

"Do you know if Eliza caught the train?"

"She did."

"I'm glad."

"How was your day?"

"Long and tiring. I'm glad it's over."

Sabrina took a bite of food. She was hungry but not quite awake.

"Did you happen to see Zeke at the train station?"

"No. He wasn't around."

"He hit me today, from the back, and I don't think he'd been drinking. I don't want him following Eliza, but I wish he would just leave town."

"Why don't you stay at Jeanette's?" Rylan asked, feeling drained and hoping she would agree.

"You'll walk me home, won't you?"

"Certainly."

"I think once I'm in my apartment, I'll be fine," Sabrina said in complete honesty. "On Monday, I'll see Sheriff Kaderly and report what he did."

"Why wait until Monday?"

"I guess I didn't assume he would be around tomorrow."

"Someone is always at the sheriff's office, and we can do that when I walk you home."

Sabrina nodded, knowing she would not have thought of this.

"Are you not hungry?"

"I'm starving, but it feels funny to eat when you're just sitting there."

Rylan stood. "Let's head to the kitchen. You can finish your supper while the rest of us have dessert."

It occurred to Sabrina to wonder who took care of Rylan Jarvik. He always seemed to be taking care of her, and she wondered who saw to his needs. *Maybe he doesn't want someone taking care of him. Some men don't.*

By then Sabrina was in the kitchen, being welcomed by the Vicks with no time for any more speculation.

* * *

"You say he hit you? With what?" Lewis Varner asked Sabrina, who noticed that he wrote nothing down.

"I didn't see it. He hit me from the back."

"How do you know it was Zeke Masters?"

"He was the only person in the room who would do that."

"Who else was there?"

"Eliza Norlin."

"The prostitute?" Lewis asked, looking as repulsed as he felt.

"Yes," Sabrina said quietly.

"Will she testify that this happened?"

"She left town today."

"Well, now, isn't that convenient."

Sabrina almost looked at Rylan. She didn't know what she'd done to gain this man's animosity, but it was nearly palpable in the room. Sabrina stood uncertainly for a moment, her old fear of police officers coming up and having to be pushed down.

"What will you do?" Sabrina finally asked.

"Do? I don't know if there is anything to *do.* I have only your word on the matter."

"Why isn't the lady's word enough?" Rylan asked with far less force than he felt.

Lewis looked up at him. He knew the sheriff thought the pastor was something special, but Lewis was not taken in.

"Listen," Lewis said, looking back to Sabrina. "I'll mention it to Sheriff Kaderly, but the fact that you didn't come in for hours, with only your word for what happened, makes it a little hard to press."

Sabrina only nodded and turned for the door, Rylan at her heels. He waited only until they were outside to speak.

"What was that about?"

"I don't know. I'm glad I had a nap or I might have overreacted."

"Have you had dealings with him before?"

"The only time I've ever seen him was that first night with Eliza and Zeke. Maybe I'm being judged by where I live."

"Speaking of which . . ." Rylan began.

"I'll look for something," Sabrina agreed. "I guess it's for the best."

"I'll keep my ears open, and Jessie hears just about everything."

Sabrina didn't mention the money. She didn't want pity, but she was still figuring out what it cost to live in this town. So far she was making it, but there were many things she would like to add to her apartment. If her rent was higher, that was going to be impossible. Eliza had given her some kitchen items, and that helped.

"Are you going up?" Rylan asked, and Sabrina realized she was standing at the bottom of her stairs.

"Yes, thanks for walking with me."

"You're welcome. I'll see you in the morning."

Sabrina climbed the stairs and knew by the top that the nap had not been enough. She would sleep hard this night.

* * *

"How are you doing with praying for Token Creek?" Rylan asked the next morning at the end of his sermon. "Are you remembering? Sometimes I don't hear from Sheriff Kaderly for weeks, but lately I've been called out to the homes of many folks. There are hurting people here, lost people who need your prayers.

"A woman named Eliza lost her baby this week. Mirabel was just a tiny scrap of a thing, not even six weeks old when she died. Eliza decided not to stay in town anymore, but I'll remember her often. She took a Bible with her and knows that I'm praying for her. I want you to pray too."

Rylan closed in prayer then, still weary from the day before but also thankful for this group of fellow believers. A few of the men, as well as Sabrina, were the only ones who saw folks from all parts of town, but he knew they prayed with him and counted those prayers as a blessing to his heart.

When he came from behind the pulpit, several folks came to him and said they would remember to pray for Eliza. Rylan believed there was not a dearer church family in all the world.

* * *

"Hug my mother," Meg told Patience, wanting to cry at the thought. "And have such a good time."

"We will, and I have all the things you wanted to send."

"Tell them that Savanna is getting so big and that she loved the hat and little vest. She wears the hat every day."

"I'll tell your parents all of it, and when we come back we'll bring all the news."

Jeb was next, hugging Meg and kissing the baby goodbye. Brad shook Jeb's hand and bent to kiss Patience's cheek. The farewells said, Brad and Meg went to their wagon, but Brad could see his wife was upset.

"Wish you were going?"

"A little," Meg said, her voice wobbling. "I don't have the energy right now, and the train ride would be so long for Savanna, but I miss my parents, Brad. I can't tell you how much."

"I'm sorry you can't go. I wish they'd made this trip before we started having children. You could have gone with them then."

"Without you?" Meg asked, looking as surprised as she felt.

"Just for a visit. I would understand."

"It's not really about me," Meg admitted. "I want them to see Savanna."

Brad nodded in complete agreement because he was in the same boat. His mother lived in town, but for all of her awareness she might as well have been across the country.

It was a quiet couple who made their way home to Holden Ranch.

* * *

"Are you busy?" Sabrina asked Becky late in the afternoon on Sunday.

"What are you doing at the kitchen door?" Becky scolded, pulling the other woman inside with a shake of her head.

"My bread pudding didn't turn out." Sabrina showed her the pan. "What did I do wrong?'

Becky looked down at the unrecognizable mass and had to cover her mouth.

"You're laughing," Sabrina said, catching the action.

"No," Becky denied, but she couldn't stop her smile.

Sabrina smiled a bit sheepishly, and then Becky began to question her.

"Was the bread fresh?"

"Yes."

"And you beat the liquid throughly?"

"Yes."

"And you poured the mixture over every bit of the top?"

"Yes.

"How many eggs did you use?"

Sabrina bit her lip. "I think I forgot the eggs."

Becky gave her usual longsuffering look and said, "What am I going to do with you?"

"I'll remember next time."

"Did you find an apartment yet?"

"How did you know about that?"

"I know a lot of things," she said, not admitting that she talked to Rylan earlier that day. "So have you?"

"Not yet. I have to talk to Jessie in the morning."

"You need to get yourself moved back here. We all want it."

Part of Sabrina wanted it too, but it wasn't that simple. She couldn't live there indefinitely, or at least that's what she told herself.

"Thanks, Becky," Sabrina said, closing the conversation and heading for the door. Becky would not let her leave empty-handed. She packed a basket with food and sent that on Sabrina's free arm.

14

RYLAN SPENT THE DAY alone. He thought about Sabrina quite a bit and wanted to see her, but he didn't give in to the idea. The Vicks had asked him to join them in the evening, but Rylan was taking all Sunday afternoon to read his Bible and pray.

It was not an unusual thing for him to do, but never had he done it with such a distraction. Sabrina was beginning to be very special to his heart, and she came to mind often. He asked the Lord not to let her get between them, and by working hard to control his thoughts, she did not dominate.

He spent a long time studying in Colossians and kept up his memorization of Psalm 144. He climbed into bed at the end of the day, thankful the sheriff had not come for him and he'd had so many hours with just the Lord. It was the refreshment he needed.

* * *

"Do you know of any other apartments in town?" Sabrina dutifully asked Jessie on Monday morning.

"Not since the last time you asked," Jessie said. "What's up?"

"I don't think I can stay where I am on Willow Street. It's gotten unsafe."

"Gotten?" Jessie asked, her brows raised.

Sabrina ignored her and asked a few customers who came in that day if they knew of a place. No one was very helpful, but she told herself to keep trying.

The day dragged a bit, her mind on the apartment as well as a letter she owed Danny and Callie. She walked home, her mind adrift, only to find Zeke sitting halfway up her stairway. Sabrina could not tell if he'd been drinking, but he was angry and wanted to know exactly where Eliza had gone.

"Get off my stairway, Zeke," Sabrina wasted no time saying.

"Answer my question."

"Eliza is gone. I'm not sure where she is right now."

"Where was she headed?"

"I won't tell you that."

Zeke came at her, and Sabrina backed away. The area was quiet right now, and Sabrina's eyes darted toward Crystal's window. That window was closed, but Sabrina still called her name. Zeke lunged for her, and Sabrina fought hard, but Eliza was not there to chase him off this time, and Zeke did not give up until Sabrina was unconscious.

* * *

Sabrina woke slowly, tasting dirt and blood in her mouth. She coughed a little, trying to find air and wondering which part of her hurt the most, her face or throat. She heard movement just then and tried to move away.

"No more, Zeke," she mumbled. "No more."

"Sabrina?"

"Who is it?"

"Crystal. What happened?"

"Please," Sabrina croaked past a raw throat. "Please find the sheriff."

Sabrina wasn't sure if she hesitated or not, but she heard her run off and worked to push herself into a sitting position, glad there was still plenty of light and she could see to navigate. Sabrina sighed when she felt the building against her back.

Okay, Lord, I'm giving up now. No matter how I feel about Jeanette's house, I'll go. If she'll have me, I'll move back.

Sabrina thought she had prayed for an hour before the sheriff came, when in reality only five minutes had passed. Sabrina looked up at that man, her eyes unconsciously pleading for help.

"Crystal is finding Doc," the sheriff said, silently horrified over what had happened to her.

Sabrina wanted to thank him but wasn't sure she could push any more words past her throat.

Again time seemed to stand still. Sabrina closed her eyes and wished she could sleep and have the pain and Zeke's image go away, but then she opened her eyes and Timothy was there with the wagon. But more than that, Rylan was jumping down from the seat and coming toward her. Sabrina didn't know when anything felt as comforting as his arms lifting her and his voice telling her it was going to be all right.

* * *

Sabrina's silence bothered Jeanette. Her neck was bruised, but it was more than that. Some of the light had gone out of her eyes. She looked weary—completely spent—but would not close her eyes to sleep.

Jeanette and Heather helped her with gentle efficiency, and when Sabrina was cleaned up and tucked under the covers, Jeanette opened the door for Rylan to enter. She took a position at the corner of the bed and listened.

"Hi," the big man said, keeping his voice low and taking the chair that had been pulled up close to the bed. "I just have one question for you: Was it Zeke?"

"Yes."

Rylan nodded and would have spoken again, but Sabrina beat him to it.

"I'm sorry," she said, having held the words inside for so long that it hurt.

"Why are you sorry?"

"It's all my fault."

"Why do you say that?"

"You all wanted me to move back here, and I wouldn't. I'm sorry."

Rylan picked up her hand. It was scratched and bruised, as was her arm, but he held it gently.

"No one thinks this is your fault, because it isn't. I don't want you to think like that anymore."

"I'm more trouble than I'm worth."

The words did funny things to Rylan's heart. He shook his head no and said, "Nothing could be further from the truth. Will you do me a favor?"

"Yes."

"Go to sleep. We'll talk more tomorrow."

"You're coming back?"

"Yes."

"Are you sure you have time?"

"I'm sure."

"Don't come if you don't."

"All right," Rylan agreed, knowing they had bridges to cross over the way she viewed herself and this incident.

"Rylan," Sabrina said with the last of her energy, her throat very sore.

"What?"

"Thank you."

For just a moment Rylan took her hand in both of his. Sabrina watched him and then closed her eyes. Rylan heard her sigh and relinquished the hand. He and Jeanette exited the bedroom together and closed the door.

Jeanette stood in the hallway, her hand to her mouth in horror over Sabrina's face.

"What was that man thinking?"

There was much Rylan could have said to that, but he said only, "I need to let Nate know that it was Zeke Masters, since he doesn't know any of the details. Why can't Doc get here tonight?"

"He's not in town. His neighbor said he'll be back tomorrow."

"I'll be by in the morning if that's all right."

"Certainly. Anytime."

Jeanette saw him to the door before going back to check on Sabrina who was very much asleep.

* * *

Sabrina woke in the night, not sure how she could hurt in so many places at one time. A low moan escaped her as she tried to shift against the pillow, and she wondered how close she'd come to dying. It wasn't the first time she'd been hit, but it was the worst.

Sabrina knew she would not get back to sleep unless she could relieve herself, but it was taking some courage to move. She had resigned herself to the pain when the light of a lantern came through the doorway.

"I thought I heard you."

It was Heather. She set her lantern on the table by the bed and looked down at Sabrina.

"Did I wake you?" Sabrina asked.

"I'm a very light sleeper, and I sleep with my door open so I can hear Theta. Do you need to get up?"

"Yes."

Sabrina stifled more than one groan climbing from the bed, even with Heather's help. It was a wearying ten minutes before she was tucked back under the covers, and as though it was not the middle of the night, Heather sat down on the side of the bed and looked at her.

"I think you were very brave tonight."

"Why do you say that?"

"Unless I miss my guess, you fought back."

"I did, but he was angry, and that gives a man strength."

"Don't go back, Bri," Heather begged. "I'm afraid for you. I'm trying to trust in God for your safety, but I don't know if my heart can take your going back there."

"I won't, Heather. I don't know where I can find a place I can afford, but I won't return."

"We'll help you," Heather said, knowing

they would do everything they could to keep her with them as long as possible. "Maybe Jessie knows something."

"I just checked with her," Sabrina said.

Heather could have cried. She was already looking for another place to live, but it hadn't been soon enough.

"Can you sleep now?" Heather asked.

"I think so. Heather?"

"Yes."

"Do you think Timothy would have time in the morning to go to the apartment and get my Bible?"

"I'm sure he will. I'll ask him."

Heather slipped out after Sabrina thanked her, planning to be up early to check on her, but when she got to Sabrina's room, it was empty.

* * *

"Lord, You have a plan for Rylan and Bri," Chas said quietly. He and Rylan were in Chas' living room, the children still asleep. "Help us to trust You for this. None of us would have chosen this road for Bri, Lord, but Your ways are perfect. Your glory is the goal, Father.

"Give Rylan wisdom to think well and trust You. He might be tempted to rush in and try to be more to Bri than she needs. Help him to remember that she needs a pastor and a friend right now more than anything else. She might not be thinking well about this attack, and Rylan can't minister as he should if he doesn't guard his heart carefully.

"Turn this to Your glory, Father. Let Bri's light for You not be dimmed in this community. Help her to trust as she should and understand how much You love Zeke and how much he needs our prayers."

When Chas was finished, Rylan began to pray. He started by thanking God for Chas and his good reminders about what was important. He finished by asking God to guard his heart for other more serious reasons. This was new territory, and in truth he did not know how Sabrina would respond. If she was angry at God over Zeke's attack, it would uncover a side of her that he'd not seen before.

Rylan did not think she would be angry, but he also could recognize wishful thinking in himself. He wanted Sabrina to be the one, and in such cases blindness could be a major temptation.

The men talked for a while after they prayed, Rylan thanking Chas for meeting with him so early and on such short notice. When they had finished, Rylan started for the door. He hadn't counted on Miranda, who expected him to stay for breakfast and was already bringing mugs of coffee to the men. He stayed, reminding himself that Sabrina was probably still asleep and would not be up to company for a few hours.

* * *

Sabrina stood by the stove in the kitchen, wrapped up in a blanket, trying to heat water for a bath. She was sore, very much so, but also desperate to gain some sense of normalcy.

"Well, now," Heather said quietly, "I didn't expect to see you up."

"I need a bath," Sabrina said. "I'm ignoring the pain to have one."

Heather began to help, going into the small room off the side of the kitchen they all used for bathing. The warm weather meant she did not need to make a fire, but she set towels out and put some cold water into the tub while the rest of the water heated.

Becky eventually arrived, and contrary to her normal response, she didn't scold but took over for Heather. In less time than Sabrina expected, she was on her way to being clean, even washing her hair. She didn't try to look in the mirror, knowing that would make her feel worse. She was certain to be even achier when she was through, but at the moment getting clean was all that mattered.

* * *

"Now, little miss," Timothy spoke from across the kitchen table, not overly mindful of the fact that Sabrina was a few inches taller than he was. "Where will I find your Bible?"

That had been an hour earlier. Becky had gone with Timothy, and they had brought back much more than Sabrina's Bible. Sabrina was now dressed and sitting under the window in the small parlor, her Bible in her lap. The house was alive around her, and from time to time someone would check on her. Sabrina had not wanted anyone to wait on her, but she'd used all her energy to dress, so Heather had to brush her hair and Becky made her breakfast.

Zeke had hit her so hard on one side of her face that a tooth was loose, but Sabrina had managed some porridge on the other side. The juice she drank was the most satisfying, and at the moment she was enjoying a cup of coffee. She was reading in the book of Joshua about Rahab when Nate came.

"I'm glad to see you up, but you look like you should be in bed," that man said, taking a seat, his face showing the concern he felt over the terrible bruising and scratches on Sabrina's face and neck.

"I must admit I have felt better, but I'm not sure lying around will help."

"Can you tell me what happened?"

Sabrina did so, not mentioning that all of this could have been avoided. She didn't know if he understood how biased his deputy was, but she wasn't going to be the one to inform him.

"Had Zeke been drinking?"

"I haven't had enough contact with him to be sure about that. I don't recall smelling any alcohol."

"We're still looking for him," the sheriff said.

"Who is 'we'?"

"My deputies and I."

Sabrina was tempted to say something then, afraid that his one deputy would not actually arrest Zeke Masters even if he had the chance, but she kept her mouth shut. The sheriff didn't stay much longer, and that was fine with Sabrina. She finally admitted to herself that she was completely spent and returned to her room to sleep.

* * *

"How did you get involved last night?" Sabrina asked Rylan when she saw him later that morning. She had slept for nearly two hours and then gone downstairs to find him there. She also learned that Jessie had visited.

"Timothy and I were moving a davenport for Mrs. Cornwall when Crystal saw us."

Sabrina nodded, but she was trying to remember how Crystal got involved. It wasn't like her to lose details, but the night before was fuzzy in places.

"How are you feeling?" Rylan asked, still surprised that she was up and dressed. It was true that she had come into the room very slowly, but he hadn't expected her to be on her feet at all.

"Not so great, but I think I came close to getting killed, so in light of that, I can't complain."

"I assume he wanted to know about Eliza?"

"Yes. I wouldn't tell him anything, so he just kept hitting me. Why does a man do that?" Sabrina suddenly added. "Why does a man feel so attached to a woman that he'll kill to find her, but he's not kind to that woman? He uses her and hits her."

"It's sad and strange, isn't it?" Rylan replied. "You would think from the way he acted that he never wanted to see her again, but if she was the one thing in his life he had control over or believed he had control over, he wouldn't want to lose that."

Sabrina nodded. He was suddenly talking her language. Having control over things or even believing she did gave her confidence and security. Danny had been working with her about giving that up, but it had been coming slowly.

"Are you angry with Zeke? Or anxious about him?" Rylan asked, reminding himself that she needed a pastor right now and a friend—nothing else.

"I don't think I'm angry. Men like Zeke are confusing to me, but the idea of his needing control makes perfect sense. I won't tell you I'm not afraid of him because I am—he was strong—but I don't feel overly anxious about it."

"Why is that?"

"Danny taught me that there's no point in

worrying about what might happen. He said I just needed to be ready to handle everything God sent into my life, and if an event arrived that I wasn't ready to handle, I would learn and know better next time."

"That was good counsel. He would be pleased to know how well you listened."

"I hope Zeke doesn't come back and find me again," Sabrina suddenly said, forcing herself not to touch her aching face. "Is it all right to hope for that?"

"Certainly. No one would wish to have this repeated. I'm hoping the law will find him and he won't be on the streets again."

"I have been anxious about that," Sabrina admitted.

"What exactly?"

"That Deputy Varner won't arrest him if he finds him, and I'll be stuck facing him again."

"Did you tell Nate about that night in his office?"

"No. I pictured him not believing me, and I was too tired to argue the point."

"So he doesn't know all of this could have been avoided?"

Sabrina shook her head no. She was going to ask Rylan if he would tell him, and Rylan was going to tell Sabrina that he would do exactly that, but Doctor Ertz had finally arrived.

* * *

"Jeanette told me you were here this morning. Who was at the store?" Sabrina asked Jessie when she came after work.

"I just didn't open on time, but after I did I couldn't get away with Jeb gone."

"It was sweet of you, but you didn't have to do that. I understand you have a store to manage."

Jessie looked at her as if she was talking nonsense, almost feeling the bruises on her friend's face herself.

"What am I going to do with you?" Jessie finally asked.

"I was going to ask what *you're* going to do with Jeb and me both gone."

"I'll manage. Just get better."

Sabrina wanted to say it looked worse than it felt, but she had finally seen herself in the mirror and realized that wasn't true. She looked and felt as if she'd been beaten. The bruises and scratches on her body were not so painful, but her face still looked as bad as it felt. If she didn't want to answer dozens of questions, she would be stuck inside for some time.

"How are the girls?"

"They miss you and ask about you."

"I miss them too."

"I said you were sick, so be prepared to fend off those types of questions."

It bothered Sabrina that Jessie would lie to the girls, but part of her understood. How did one tell a child about such an act of violence? And it wasn't as if she felt good. Sick was probably a pretty close description.

The women talked for a bit longer, and in time Sabrina sensed that Jessie was angry about the attack. She understood how easy that would be and wanted to tell Jessie that her heart was in a completely different place, but they had already talked for a while, and the girls were with a neighbor.

Sabrina saw her friend off, praying for her but knowing that any conversation about how she was dealing with Zeke would have to wait.

* * *

"When did you report this?" Nate asked Rylan, searching the paperwork on his desk.

"Last Saturday night. Deputy Varner didn't find it plausible because Sabrina didn't come directly after the attack."

"Let me get this straight," Kaderly began.

"Before Sabrina was attacked on Monday, she was knocked out by Zeke, reported it, but was not helped?"

"That about sums it up."

"Why didn't Sabrina mention it to me when I spoke with her?"

"She feared you wouldn't believe her concerning your own man. Had I realized she felt that way, I would have told her otherwise."

Nate stood, every line of his being angry. He had seen Sabrina Matthews' battered face, something that could have been avoided. They might not have found Zeke—they hadn't found him yet—but at least they would have known.

"Thank you, Rylan," Nate said, clearly done speaking about it.

Rylan turned for the door. He was not worried about the deputy hating him. He had failed to do his job and must answer for that. Rylan was only thankful that Token Creek's sheriff cared too much to let it pass.

* * *

"I could do some handwork for you, Jeanette," Sabrina said from her seat in the conservatory on Friday morning. Theta was not with them. "Bring some home with you if you want me to."

"All right," Jeanette agreed, wanting to lead Sabrina's life but knowing she couldn't. It was still taking a lot out of Jeanette not to order the younger woman back to bed.

"When my face heals I'll head out and start looking for apartments," Sabrina said next. "I think if I actually go and do the asking myself, it might be best."

"Did Jessie have no leads?" Jeanette asked, feeling her heart speed up a little. She told herself she could not be desperate to keep this girl here, but she was.

"No. I just checked with her."

"You do know we're in no hurry to have you leave?"

"That's very sweet of you, Jeanette, but I can't stay here forever. You don't let me pay rent, and you won't let me help."

Jeanette was not about to change her standard on that issue, so she tried a new tack.

"We'll just check with Rylan about what you should do," Jeanette suggested, and could see by the slight narrowing of Sabrina's eyes that this wasn't going to work.

"Is Rylan in charge of my life now? I didn't know that."

Jeanette was working hard to find something to say when Rylan walked in and rescued her.

"Well, now." Sabrina's voice was deceptively soft with anger. "I'm glad to see you. Evidently you have all the answers."

"All right," Rylan said, moving carefully and forcing himself not to look at Jeanette.

"Jeanette speaks as though you're in charge of where I live. I don't recall when that happened."

Rylan did look at Jeanette then, who gave him a condensed version of their conversation. He would have tried to explain to Sabrina what Jeanette had meant, but Sabrina wasn't done.

"What no one seems to realize is I'm not safe anywhere. Zeke wants information that you and I have. He's not going to go after you, but if he wants it badly enough, he'll find me wherever I live."

This had not occurred to Jeanette, but Rylan calmly nodded his head.

"Jeanette did not mean that I was in charge, but I did mention to her one day that there might be options we haven't thought of. No one is going to force you to take an apartment you don't want. I'm not taking over for you. You can handle this yourself.

But you can also understand that we're not anxious to see you hurt again."

Sabrina nodded, feeling foolish. She had been upset over nothing, but it hadn't felt like nothing. It felt as though Jeanette was ready to say or do anything to keep her there, and that made no sense to Sabrina. She was a busy woman with a busy life, and Sabrina didn't know why she would insist on having her there to complicate things.

"I'm going to get something to eat," Jeanette said, coming to her feet. "Is anyone else hungry?"

Both Rylan and Sabrina declined, which left them alone in the conservatory.

15

"YOU'RE ALWAYS HAVING TO rescue me," Sabrina said with quiet wonderment, Jeanette barely out of the room. "I'm always in a mess and needing to be rescued."

Rylan stared at her, but she wasn't looking at him. Her eyes were across the room. Eventually they swung to look at him, and Rylan could tell she was thinking about her time in Token Creek, going over it in her mind.

"You were there that night when Zeke hit Eliza. You walked me home," Sabrina recounted. "You found me on the street talking to Paula, and then talked to me the next day so I would be safe. You found Cassie for me so she could take me to the ranch that day so I wouldn't have to drive the buggy." Sabrina stopped, her mouth suddenly opening. "You were even there the first day with Bret Toben and let me cut through the livery to get back to Jeanette's."

"I didn't mind any of those things," Rylan said sincerely, smiling at her a little.

"I find that hard to believe," Sabrina argued with him. "You have better things to do with your time than take care of me."

For the first time, Rylan dropped his guard completely. The smile he gave Sabrina was tender and loving, showing exactly what he felt inside.

He didn't know what he expected in return, but it wasn't the tormented expression that crossed Sabrina's face or the words that were spoken with utter conviction.

"Don't fall for me, Rylan Jarvik. It's the worst thing you could do."

For several long heartbeats the room was silent. Rylan was the one to break that silence, and when he did his voice was kind, his expression open. "Is there someone else, Sabrina, a husband or a fiancé who you haven't talked about?"

"No, it's nothing like that," Sabrina said, wishing she'd ignored his look and kept her mouth shut.

Rylan nodded before asking, "Is there something in my character you object to?"

"No," Sabrina said, looking surprised.

"Do you find me repulsive?"

"No!" Sabrina said, completely taken aback.

Rylan looked at her, praying they would not be interrupted because the next questions had to be asked.

"So you feel the problem is something with you?"

Sabrina looked away but still nodded in answer.

"Does it have something to do with the fact that you're comfortable talking to prostitutes?"

Sabrina's eyes closed in agony, but she still nodded her head yes. She realized that she would rather be beaten again than tell this man about her past, but he had guessed. Sabrina was afraid to look at him. She wanted to stay here—she was coming to love Token Creek—but not every person was Danny Barshaw. Not everyone would understand.

"I don't think a person's past has to define

her," Rylan began. "Especially a past that's been repented of."

Sabrina glanced at him but then couldn't look away.

"Did you think I would condemn you?" Rylan asked.

Sabrina nodded, still wishing that none of it was true . . . still wishing this was a man she could have for her very own. In all of her realization of his rescuing her, she had not admitted the most wondrous part of all: It had made her feel cherished and special.

"Sorry to bother you," Heather broke in from the door, Theta in hand. "Theta is ready for a little sit-down time in her chair."

"Thank you for letting us use your room, Theta," Rylan said, coming to his feet. Sabrina moved to sit a little closer and spoke as soon as the older woman was settled.

"You look nice in that gray dress, Theta. The color suits you."

"How are you feeling, Bri?" Heather asked.

"Still sore."

"As sore as you look?"

Sabrina smiled at her a little. "I'm afraid so. The skin around my right eye and cheek is very tender."

"I guess that would make sense since it's the blackest area."

"I wonder how long it will take before I'm presentable again."

"Try some cool compresses, Sabrina," Heather suggested. "I just remembered hearing something about cold helping with bruising."

"I'll do that," Sabrina said, thanking her.

"All right, Theta." Heather turned to that woman. "I'll check on you shortly." Heather made her way from the room, and Sabrina looked after her before glancing at Rylan. That man was smiling.

"Stuck with me again," he said.

"I don't feel stuck," Sabrina said, laughing a little.

"But you're afraid I'll want to talk about it?"

Sabrina sighed. "In some ways it's a relief to have someone know, and in other ways, I wish I had no past at all."

"Well, I hope we can talk about it some more, but rest easy that it won't be right now." Rylan made ready to leave, and Sabrina stared up at him. "I have a sermon to keep working on, and some folks to check on."

"Thank you for coming."

"I didn't really have time, but I forced myself."

Sabrina told herself not to smile, but it didn't work. Rylan smiled in return and exited the room. Sabrina asked herself if she'd just dreamed the whole conversation. Rylan Jarvik knew she had been a prostitute, and he hadn't acted as if he could catch something just by standing next to her.

Sabrina looked over at Theta, the older woman's stare not having altered in the least. *Is her mind working in there, Lord? Does she even know I'm here?*

Those questions went unanswered, and so did the one Sabrina asked of herself: Would it be easier to have no memory, trapped as Theta was, or to live with the ones she had?

* * *

"How is that?" Becky asked, standing close to where Sabrina lay on the sofa.

"I can't feel my face. Did you soak these cloths in ice water?"

"Yes."

Sabrina's shoulders shook with silent laughter. She had been sarcastic, but Becky had been her usual honest self.

"Well, what was I supposed to do?"

"I don't know." Sabrina's voice was muffled under the cloths, but she was still laughing.

"Well just lie there a bit longer. I'll come back to check on you."

Sabrina waved a hand and did as she was told. She had never been forced to lie still like this and realized it was good for thinking. There was nothing to look at and no one to talk to. Unbidden her thoughts went to Rylan.

Her mind concentrated on the way his face had looked and how he'd sat while they talked. It didn't take long for Sabrina to realize that Rylan was not surprised to learn of her past. His question had been quiet and thoughtful, and that shouldn't have surprised her either. She had lived in the world of this church family for long enough to know they didn't socialize with prostitutes or folks who lived in that area of town. Rylan had been the witness of many of her interactions with such folk. It shouldn't have been any great mystery that he would understand why.

Crystal's face suddenly swam into view. Sabrina wondered if there was a way to see her. With her face so bruised, the only time that would work would be at night, and Sabrina knew that the women of this household would not accompany her, nor would they allow her to go alone. It crossed her mind to ask Rylan, but she dismissed the thought almost immediately. He had already done enough.

Before Sabrina could work out a plan, Becky was there to check on her. For the moment, Crystal and her past went to the back of her mind.

* * *

"Just as you suspected," Chas said, getting a brief rundown from Rylan. "But you didn't talk about it much?"

"No. I think that might take some time."

"Does she know how you feel?"

"I doubt she's let herself think about that. She's too mortified that I know."

"Will you tell her you've told me?"

"Only if she accepts my love or is at least willing to talk about a relationship."

"And how will you handle the truth of this, Ry? It's no small thing."

"No, it's not, but her sins are not about me. I didn't even know her then. Her sins were against God, and she's been forgiven of those. I'm more concerned with how she'll view me with the way men have treated her.

I'm not going crazy with the idea that other men have touched her, but I want to know how her heart is doing when it comes to that same topic. If we can talk about that, I think we have a chance."

"You know I'll be praying," Chas said as they parted, and as usual Rylan took his words to heart.

* * *

Sabrina had been excited to have the handwork that Jeanette had brought her the afternoon before, but she had been worn out and left it until morning. It was strange not to be with the church family. She looked forward to Jeanette and Heather coming and telling her all about the sermon. In the meantime, she planned to sew. What she hadn't planned on was how much her face ached when she bent her head over the cloth.

She didn't last 30 minutes before she sat back a little discouraged. She had planned to be such a help. She had not wanted to be a burden. She was going to pull her own weight, but it wasn't looking like that at all, and her pride was taking a beating too.

"And what business do you have entertaining your pride?" Sabrina asked herself in the quiet of the small parlor. She realized she would have to tell Jeanette that she couldn't do the work. Sabrina leaned her head back, reminding herself to be patient and thankful that Jeanette had let her try.

* * *

"Well, I finished," Meg said to Brad as their wagon made its way home.

"Finished what?"

"Studying the qualities of an elder. And do you know what?"

"What?"

"You qualify."

Brad turned his head to look at her, and Meg looked right back.

"I didn't know you were studying them on your own."

"I didn't tell you. I just listened to all the things you talked about and then kept thinking about what each one meant. I can't find a qualification that you don't meet."

Brad smiled at her but then looked thoughtful. He said after a few moments, "It's a serious undertaking, but one I want to aim for."

"Does Rylan ever say how you're doing?"

"Yes, he's very encouraging and wants me to keep up the good work."

Meg tucked her arm in his and got a little

closer. Savanna, who tended to be quiet when they rode in the wagon, pointed at something and tried a few words that turned out to be gibberish.

"It's for her, Meg," Brad suddenly confessed. "It's not that you're not important, but not until Savanna was born did I realize how much I need to get this right."

"It sounds to me as though your heart is in the right place. I don't know how you could improve on that."

Brad moved his head enough to kiss her temple, his eyes going to the way Meg's waist was starting to expand. The next one was due in February. A wife and two babies. He still felt amazed when he thought about it. Amazed, thankful, awed by God's love for him, and a whole lot more.

* * *

"Can you join us for dinner?" had been Jeanette's invitation, and Rylan now found himself seated with that lady, Heather, and Sabrina. Sabrina had not been uncomfortable when he came in, but he thought she might be a little quiet.

He noticed that almost all the swelling was down around her eyes but then wondered when he would again see her face without the bruises.

"How did the sewing go?" Heather asked.

"Not very well," Sabrina answered. "I'm sorry, Jeanette. I thought I could help out, but my face aches when I bend over the cloth."

"Don't worry about it," Jeanette told her, and meant it. She could see that Sabrina was bothered by this and wondered if that's why she was rather quiet. Jeanette had romantic notions going in her mind and hoped that Rylan's presence was the reason for Sabrina's quiet, but she did her best not to think about it.

"This beef is good, Becky," Rylan said when she came in to check on them.

"Well, there's plenty, so you eat up. Bri, are you eating?"

Sabrina picked up her fork and started, not sure why she was suddenly thrown off with Rylan in the house. He was acting as if their conversation from Friday had never happened.

"Shall we tell you about the sermon, Bri?" Jeanette offered.

"Please," Sabrina said, sincerely wanting

to know about the morning and feeling something akin to relief at having the focus off of herself.

"We were in Colossians 3," Rylan began. "I was sharing today about the importance of making up our minds to live for Christ. We have to daily commit to thinking thoughts of eternity. Sinful habits come so easily, but that can't be who we are."

"What verses were you in?"

"The start of chapter three, the first five verses, where it says, 'If ye then be risen with Christ, seek those things which are above, where Christ sitteth on the right hand of God. Set your affection on things above, not on things on the earth. For ye are dead, and your life is hid with Christ in God. When Christ, who is our life, shall appear, then shall ye also appear with him in glory.' And then down in verse ten, which says, 'And have put on the new man, which is renewed in knowledge after the image of him that created him.'

"We have to remember who we are," Rylan continued. "We are in Christ, which means that we can't love this earth very much. We should love the people Christ died for, but not the things of this earth. The draw is very strong. We love our life here, but we have to remember how temporary this all is and what our purpose in Christ is."

"How do you memorize all those verses?" Sabrina asked, still thinking about the way he'd simply recited them.

"I study the text for many months before I bring it to the pulpit. It would be more surprising if I wasn't able to memorize it."

"I have a question for you about verse one," Heather said, but Sabrina was still thinking about what Rylan had said. She wasn't sure if she loved the things of the world, and yet the verses were there for a reason. She had never thought about if she loved her life here more than she loved Christ. It was something she would have to work on understanding.

"How about some dessert?" Becky asked as she came in with a pie and a handful of small plates.

Dessert was enjoyed with more conversation before Jeanette invited everyone into the parlor. Sabrina stood and began to remove dishes from the table. Becky objected, saying she was not up to it, but Sabrina ignored her. Heather pitched in as well, and in little time at all, everything was back in the kitchen. Becky had a swift word with Rylan, and the next thing Sabrina knew, he was standing at her shoulder.

"Why don't we head to the parlor before Becky's heart fails."

"Good!" Becky exclaimed. "She's supposed to be resting. Take her away."

Sabrina followed Rylan from the room, trying to be patient. She didn't think she needed to be babied, and she didn't know why Rylan had to be the one to look after her.

"You must have better things to do than keep me from working," Sabrina said, still following the big man to the parlor and trying not to look as agitated as she felt.

"Was that your way of trying to get rid of me?"

Sabrina's eyes narrowed when he looked at her. She might have made some remark, but they were at the parlor now, and Jeanette was waiting.

* * *

"I was going to ask you if you might be ready to get out of the house?" Rylan had waited until he was ready to leave and had gone so far as to ask Sabrina to walk him to the door.

"What did you have in mind?" Sabrina

wanted to jump at the idea of getting out but made herself ask.

"I thought I'd give you a tour of the livery. We could go when it's almost dark. There would still be enough light to see but probably not too many folks around."

"And the livery is closed today?"

"Yes, ma'am."

"I'd like that."

"I'll come back about seven-thirty. Does that work?"

"Yes. I'll be ready."

"Don't dress up. It's pretty dusty inside."

Sabrina nodded and then remembered the way Rylan had dumped her into the water. Her eyes flew to his, and she would have been willing to bet money he'd remembered the same event.

"I'll see you tonight," Rylan said, not willing to talk about the water incident that had indeed come to mind.

Sabrina agreed and watched Rylan head out the door, telling herself that the excitement she felt was simply over getting out of the house.

* * *

Cassidy settled into the Vicks' living room, Nellie, the youngest Vick, on her lap.

"She won't last long," Miranda said, taking in her daughter's sleepy gaze. Heidi came along next, her mouth moving before she got into the room.

"Heidi." Her mother stopped her. "Please go back out and try again."

Heidi turned, went out the door, and came back in again, only this time she was quiet. Cassidy looked to Miranda for an explanation.

"It's too easy to expect to be the center of attention or to interrupt someone when you enter the room talking." This said, Miranda looked down at Heidi, who had sat next to her. "That was much better. Thank you."

"I have a lot to learn," Cassidy said. "And I only have until January to learn it."

"Well," Miranda said with compassion, "you don't give birth to six-year-olds. You do have a little time before they start talking."

"That's true."

"I'm six," Heidi said, having now come close to Cassidy's lap.

"Yes, you are. I think that's very big."

"Nellie is just little. She's a baby."

"Did you want to hold her, Heidi?" Cassidy offered.

The little girl loved this idea, and climbed

onto the sofa to get in position. Cassidy handed the one-year-old to her sister, thinking she would wake up during the transfer, but it didn't happen.

Chas and Trace, accompanied by Franklin and Parker, joined them a short time later, and Chas invited everyone to play a word game that even the children could enjoy. The afternoon passed quickly, and as she always did, Cassidy shared her thoughts on the drive home.

"Whenever we go to the Vicks'," Cassidy said, "I'm more confused than ever about which I want. Nellie and Heidi are adorable, but the boys are so cute and just as much fun. I can't believe how big Parker's eyes are, and he worships Chas. I picture our little boy doing the same with you."

"Like Franklin does?" Trace asked with a smile.

"He can't stop staring at you. You'll have to bring Quincy in again and give him another ride."

"I think the next time he rides it should be at the ranch."

"Oh, that's a good idea. You would have a slave for life if you did that."

"I thought I had a slave for . . ." Trace tried

to say, but he had to stop because someone was poking him in the side.

* * *

"So did you learn most of your skills on the farm or after you came here?" Sabrina asked as the tour of the livery ended.

"I learned them mostly on the farm, but I honed them here. Pete was very patient and kept me on even when things didn't go well."

"Like what?"

Rylan stepped back from the back door that led to the alley and reached up to find a hook. He brought down a rather mangled-looking piece of iron and handed it to Sabrina.

"One of my first attempts at a hook."

Sabrina put her free hand over her mouth.

"You can laugh," he said dryly, and Sabrina did as she handed it back to him. Rylan replaced the hook, pulled the door shut, and would have started toward Jeanette's, taking the back way, just as they'd come.

"Rylan." Sabrina stopped him, looking up in the closing darkness. "Would you please take me to see Crystal? I want to talk to her, and I know no one at Jeanette's would understand."

Rylan looked down at her. He had not

expected this, but it made perfect sense. This was who she was.

"I don't mind walking with you, Sabrina, but have you considered that it's getting a little late?"

Sabrina did not need an explanation, but neither was she put off.

"I think I'll be able to tell if she has company."

Rylan did not need to know how she would know this, but he agreed without hesitation to walk her to Willow Street.

* * *

"How are you?" Sabrina asked. Both she and Rylan had been invited into Crystal's apartment.

"How am I? You can ask me that when I'm looking at those bruises!"

"Yes, I can ask. I haven't seen you in days."

"The question is whether you've seen that snake Zeke?" Crystal said, still not answering the question.

"No, I keep hoping he'll be picked up."

"He's probably on the run, thinking he killed you."

"I hope he's long gone," Sabrina said, and then got to the reason why she'd come. "I'm going to look for a new place. I won't be back here to live."

Crystal nodded, having known all along it was just a matter of time.

"Well, it's been nice knowing you."

"I'm not leaving town, just the neighborhood."

Crystal nodded, but her eyes told of her disbelief.

"Don't give me that look," Sabrina said, standing up to her. "I've never lied to you, and I'm not going to start now."

Her tone made Crystal smile and say, "You talk awfully feisty for someone who's a bruised mess."

Sabrina chuckled and stood. "I hope I'll be out and around in a week. Don't forget that I'm praying for you."

"Go on, now," Crystal said. "And take this walking mountain with you."

Rylan had to laugh, but he followed Sabrina to the door, waiting while she hugged Crystal. He had so much in his heart as they walked away from the apartment that he didn't know where to start. He wanted to tell Sabrina how special she was and how much he appreciated her, but not now, not in the dark when he couldn't see her face.

“I need to find an apartment,” Sabrina said when they were partway back.

“Why the hurry?” Rylan asked.

Sabrina was quiet and Rylan waited.

16

"JEANETTE IS WONDERFUL," SABRINA began. "So are Becky and Heather, but the house is hard for me."

"The house itself—the building?"

"Yes. It looks like a home my sister lives in, and the memories are painful."

"I'm sorry, Sabrina. I wish we had all known."

"It's not exactly something I can explain. 'Oh, by the way, every time I see your house I'm reminded of my sister—the one who got me involved in prostitution and then deserted me to marry a wealthy man.' "

"Tell me something, Sabrina," Rylan said,

her words cutting like a knife. "When was the last time you felt cared about?"

"I'm sorry I said that," Sabrina said, her voice contrite.

"I wasn't rebuking you. I really want to know."

"Well, I feel cared for here," she said, her voice now a little confused. "And Danny and Callie care for me."

"Before that," Rylan pressed.

"Oh," Sabrina said and then didn't speak for a long time. Jeanette's house was in sight before she said, "I can't really remember. I was probably 12 or 13—sometime when my father was still alive."

They were back at the house before Rylan could frame a reply, and there was no chance to speak of it further, but the entire evening stayed on his mind until he fell asleep that night.

* * *

"Well now," Rylan said to Jessie when he was in the store that week. "This looks fun."

"Oh, it is," Jessie spoke sarcastically. "I love it when the shelf breaks."

Rylan went down on his knees to have a look, having to shift canned goods and boxes out of the way.

"What happened?"

"It must have given way in the night. It was like this when I came down this morning."

Rylan saw that the board was beyond repair, but he also knew that Chas could cut one for her in little time at all. So could Jeb, but he and Patience were still on their trip, something Jessie must have been very aware of.

"Do you miss Sabrina?" Rylan asked.

"Well, she doesn't work for me on Thursdays, but if she were here, I'd have had her down the street looking for Chas right now."

"Tell me something, Jessie. How do you keep up with it all?"

"I don't know. I guess I've just been doing it for so long. I never remember a day in my life without this store."

Jessie was smiling at him, clearly not bitter about the thought, when Clancy came up.

"Did you break it, Pastor Rylan?"

"I didn't break it, but I'm going to talk to Mr. Vick and see if he can fix it."

Jessie began to protest, but Rylan waved a hand at her and kept talking with the little girl. "Do you think a bear came in and sat on this shelf?"

"I don't know," Clancy said, her eyes growing with the idea.

"Or maybe it was an elephant," Rylan suggested next. "How do you suppose he got in here?"

"He wouldn't fit," she said so seriously that Rylan had to laugh.

"Can I get a little help up here, please?" an irrate voice called from the front counter, and Jessie went that way.

"Well," Rylan said when they were alone. "What are you going to do today?"

"We might go to the creek," Clancy told him. "We can get wet."

"That sounds fun."

"Do you like to get wet?"

"I do, yes. Especially when the weather is this hot."

"Is it hot?" Clancy asked, and Rylan had to smile. Leave it to a child not to notice temperatures as warm as they were having.

Rylan had actually come in for some soap but noticed that Jessie was still busy. He gathered the fallen items and stacked them as neatly as he could on the floor. When he finally went on his way, the broken board was in hand. He would stop by and see Chas or leave it with Miranda if Chas was somewhere at a building site. Once he was free to look at it, that man would probably have the board cut and sanded in under ten minutes.

* * *

"Just a bit more," Heather said as she leaned close to Sabrina's face, using powder to cover the last of her bruises. At last she stood back and smiled at the younger woman. "Well, now, that's the face we all know and love."

"Do I look all right? I can go out?"

"I think so. Jeanette will be surprised to see you, and Jessie and the girls will go wild."

"Oh, Heather," Sabrina said, gratitude filling her eyes.

"Now my powder is a little bit pale for your skin, so let's try it out on Becky first."

The women went to the kitchen and stood, waiting for Becky to notice. She was bustling around as usual and did not immediately look up. Not that she hadn't started talking as soon as they walked in, but it took some moments before she actually saw them.

"Well, now!" Becky suddenly exclaimed, coming close to stare at Sabrina.

"Is it better?" the youngest woman asked.

"If I hadn't seen you the other way, I would have never known. What did you do, Heather, use some of your powder?"

"Yes, ma'am. Doesn't she look great?"

"I'm going to work," Sabrina said, only to have Becky come to full attention.

"At the shop?"

"Yes, and then to Jessie's."

"And then where?"

"After that I'll head to the worst part of town, and since it's Saturday I'll pick a fight with the first drunken man I find."

Heather didn't even try to hold her laughter, but Becky drew herself up like a small hen and got ready to give Sabrina what for.

"No," Sabrina cut her off. "I'm leaving now. I don't have time to be scolded. I'll see you both tonight."

The women stood still as she slipped out the kitchen door and went on her way, but they were not done talking.

"If only she would marry Rylan," Becky said wistfully.

"That would be perfect," Heather agreed. "He would take such good care of her."

Becky nodded before both women went back to work.

* * *

"Excuse me," Jessie said to the woman who could not make up her mind about a pair of shoes. "I'll check back with you," she added before heading to the door. Sabrina had just arrived, and Jessie got there as fast as she could, giving the other woman a hug.

"How are you?" Jessie asked.

"Better. Can you tell Heather used some powder?"

Jessie studied her and said, "The color is a little light for you, but you look good."

"Can you use me?" Sabrina asked.

The desperate look on Jessie's face made Sabrina laugh. Jessie would have enjoyed the moment with her, but she suddenly remembered the woman with the shoes.

* * *

"Well, now, I didn't think you were still in town." Bret Toben had come to Jessie's and found Sabrina behind the counter.

"Hello, Mr. Toben. What can I get you?"

"My mail, please. Where have you been?"

"At Jeanette's, taking it slowly. I ran into a man with a vendetta and found myself on the wrong end of his fists."

Bret's eyes narrowed, and as with the last

time, that surprised him. He didn't expect to feel angry, but he thought if the man were on the spot, he'd be tempted to shoot him.

"Any broken bones?" Bret asked, keeping his voice light.

"No, just some bruises."

Bret's eyes narrowed as he studied her, and Sabrina made a point of pushing his letter toward him, not sure he'd seen it.

"Are you still living at Sandgren's?"

"No. I haven't collected my things, but I will."

"My offer still stands," Bret said quietly and found himself alone. Sabrina had glared at him, turned, and walked away.

Bret made his way from the store, not sorry that she'd walked away in anger. He thought any emotion was a sign that he might be getting through. As long as she wasn't indifferent to him, he believed he might have a chance.

* * *

"How was your week?" Rylan asked of Sabrina on Saturday evening. He'd had a very busy week and had seen her only briefly. He had not been there for supper but came by afterward and asked Sabrina to go for a walk.

"A little bit long," Sabrina admitted, "but I

was finally able to sew again, and that was nice."

"No more pain when you bend over the work?"

"No. It's almost all gone unless I touch my face."

"And you worked today?"

"Yes, in both places." Sabrina smiled. "That was nice."

They were walking beyond Jeanette's house. The sun was dropping slowly in the sky, but there was still plenty of light, and because Jeanette's house was away from the businesses of downtown, it was quiet.

"Is it going to bother you if I ask you questions about your past?"

"No," Sabrina answered. It made sense to her that it might be a curiosity. "It's not a fun story."

"No, I imagine it's not. I assume your sister is older?"

"Yes, three years."

"Is she your only sibling?"

"She is. I think we were a pretty normal family for a long time. I mean, Sybil was always willful, but Mother was sure she would grow out of it." Sabrina suddenly shook her head in wonder. "I never saw what a selfish person my mother was until I came to Christ."

"What did that reveal?"

"I was able to see clearly for the first time that she never wanted bad news. She would say to all of us when we came home, 'Tell me the good news.' If my father tried to tell her something serious or sad, she would leave the room."

"Who died first?"

"My father. At that point Sybil went from willful to promiscuous. I couldn't tell my mother because that wouldn't have been good news, but Sybil was beautiful, and she loved the attention men paid her. She would hide the jewelry and gifts they would give her from our mother."

"Was she a prostitute?"

"Not right away. But when she realized the money she could make, she was out every night that last year my mother was alive, not walking the streets, but seeing men she knew and were willing to pay. My mother died without knowing what my sister had become."

"But she got you involved."

Sabrina sighed. "Yes, once my mother died we had even less money. My sister didn't like sharing her money, and she didn't like the house we had grown up in—it wasn't fancy enough. When our mother died, she gave me a little bit of time but then said it was time for me to make it on my own."

"How old were you?"

"Sixteen."

Rylan didn't know the last time he thought he could sob his eyes out. At 16 a young woman is supposed to be dad's girl, special in his eyes and treated like the treasure she is until that special someone comes along.

"What are you thinking?" Sabrina asked. Rylan had not realized she'd been watching him so closely.

"That it must have been awful, and that's not the way it's supposed to be when you're 16."

"I've asked myself how it is supposed to be, but I don't really want to know. In some ways it's easier not to know what you've missed." Sabrina shook her head again. "There I go, sounding like my mother, who wanted only good news."

"I think there's a difference between living in unreality and not torturing yourself with things you can't change."

Sabrina stared at him.

"What did I say?"

"I just appreciate your understanding."

"I'm glad, and speaking of appreciating, I wanted to tell you how much I appreciated your taking the time to see Crystal last weekend."

"She doesn't think I'll be back to see her, but I will."

"Of course you will," Rylan said dryly. "There's no chance you'll stay away from the roughest neighborhood in town."

Sabrina had to smile. "It's not my fault she lives there."

"Do me a favor. Just take me along."

Sabrina only smiled at him, and it was Rylan's turn to shake his head. This one needed watching, he was completely convinced of that.

"It's getting dark," Rylan said next. "I'll walk you back."

"It was nice to be out."

"We'll do it again," Rylan suggested as they turned toward Jeanette's.

"The walk or the talk about my past?"

"Both if you're amenable."

"Why is that?" Sabrina asked.

"Because I can't know who you are if I don't know what your life has been like."

"And you want to know who I am?"

"Yes, I do," Rylan said quietly.

Sabrina looked at him and he looked back, but they didn't speak on it again. He walked her inside, took a little time with Jeanette, and then left for home, wondering all the while what future walks and talks would look like.

* * *

"It's even hot in the shade," Jessie complained on Sunday evening. She was having a picnic with the girls, and they had invited Sabrina along.

"Enjoy it," Sabrina said. "Before you know it we'll be freezing and wishing for a little of this heat."

"Must you remind me?" Jessie said just before Clancy called to them.

"Come over. You can't get wet there."

"And of course that's our goal in life," Jessie murmured, keeping her voice low, "to get wet."

Both women stood and went to the bank of the creek. They did get wet, something that thrilled the little girls, but eventually they went back to the blanket to eat. Jessie had fixed a great supper of chicken, fluffy biscuits, two salads, and cookies. A jug of water helped to wash it all down.

Sabrina eventually lay back, saying she was going to pop. "I think if I'm not careful, I could fall asleep right here," she added.

"Wouldn't you be surprised come Monday morning?"

"Speaking of Monday," Sabrina remembered, "will it put you in a bind if I'm a little late? I want to ask around for an apartment or a room to rent."

"No, that's fine. Take the whole morning," Jessie added, wanting her to live in a safer part of town.

"Thank you."

"Where will you start?"

"Where should I start?"

Jessie had a few suggestions, with absolutely no idea if anyone wanted to rent a room, but that's what filled the conversation for the next hour. By the time Sabrina took herself back to Jeanette's, she knew almost every house in town.

* * *

"I thought Sabrina would be here," Rylan said to Jessie on Monday morning.

"She'll be here at noon," that lady had

answered. "She's looking for an apartment."

That conversation had taken place some 15 minutes past, but Rylan had yet to spot the woman in question. He walked the streets he thought she might try and tried to remember who rented rooms in their homes. He was about to give up when he spotted her. She had just come from a two-story house, walking slowly. Rylan's long legs covered the distance swiftly, but he was still just ten feet from her when she spotted him.

"Hello," Sabrina said.

"How's the search coming?"

"Not great," Sabrina said, not mentioning that the man in the house she had just left was willing to rent to her, but he had no wife.

"Have you tried Alder Street?"

"I don't think so."

"Here, come this way," Rylan directed, but Sabrina came slowly.

"You're rescuing me again, aren't you?"

Rylan stopped and looked at her before asking, "Would that be so bad?"

"I can't get used to it."

"Why not?"

"I'm all wrong for you," she made herself say, truly believing it.

"It's too soon to know that."

Sabrina didn't know what to say. He was not being cagey or obtuse, and Sabrina didn't know what to do with such a forthright attitude. She was on the verge of asking why he hadn't rejected her when he spoke again.

"I think we need a third party," Rylan said. "Someone to ask us questions about what we're thinking."

Sabrina looked thoughtful but didn't speak.

"I am mainly accountable to Chas. Would you object to our meeting with him?"

"I don't think so. Does he know about me?"

"Yes."

"Does Miranda?"

"He hasn't asked me if he can share with her, so I'm sure not."

Sabrina was silent so long that Rylan had a chance to figure it out.

"Would it be very hard if Miranda knew?"

"Women react differently, Rylan. They can't always cope."

"I'm sure you've experienced some awful rejections, but I can tell you that if Miranda Vick ever learns of your plight, all she'll do is cry with compassion."

Sabrina's eyes got a little big. Never had anyone called it a plight.

"You can think about it and let me know," Rylan said.

Sabrina could only nod. Every conversation she had with this man seemed to amaze her. At some point she was going to have to keep her head long enough to remember and have her questions answered.

* * *

Sabrina walked slowly away from Jessie's on Monday evening, trying not to be discouraged. She had not found a place to live, and for the rest of the day she'd been confused about her conversation with Rylan. She wondered if it would do any good to talk to Jeanette about it. But even as the thought formed, she wondered what she would ask the woman.

Sabrina was still working it out, many questions running through her mind, when she spotted a man who looked like Zeke. She stopped and watched him until he disappeared into the Boar's Head Saloon. Not rushing, and working to think clearly about what she was doing, she went to the saloon. The door was open, and she stepped inside, her eyes taking a moment to adjust to the darkness.

"Hello, Bri," Bret was next to her before she could find her bearings. "Come on in."

"Did Zeke Masters just come in?"

"I don't think so," Bret said, his voice growing cool. "Don't tell me you prefer Zeke's company to my own."

Sabrina's eyes, which had been scanning the room, swung to the saloon owner.

"You can't be serious," she said, her eyes going back to the room. She frowned when she spotted Deputy Varner in one corner and asked about him.

"Sure." Bret was offhanded about it. "He's in all the time."

Sabrina stared at him until he looked up and saw her.

"Have a drink," Bret tried next, but Sabrina shook her head.

"Thanks, but I'll be going."

"Bri," Bret called, having just caught on. "Did Zeke hit you?"

The nod Sabrina gave him was brief, and without further word she slipped back out the door. Bret went to the walk to watch her walk away, but she never turned back or noticed.

* * *

"I've been meaning to ask you a question," Sabrina said after she and Jeanette got to work on Wednesday. "Did you grow up here?"

"No. Theta and I are from Allentown, Pennsylvania."

"How did you come to Token Creek?"

"I met Owen Fulbright. He already lived here, owned the bank, and was building our home. It was hard to leave my family, but I was in love. I still am."

Sabrina smiled at her and then said the next thing that was on her mind. "I can't find a place to live. I've checked all over, but the safe places are all taken right now."

"Well," Jeanette said, still bent over the machine, "I think you should stay with me until something safe opens up. We like having you, and I think it might be sooner than you think. Who knows, maybe even the apartment upstairs will open. When I rented it to the man who's up there, he wasn't sure how long he would be in town. I took him because I thought even a few months' rent was better than letting it sit empty."

"Why doesn't it bother you that I stay at your house and eat your food?"

"Oh mercy, Bri," Jeanette said with quiet conviction. "All that God has given me, and I can't share with others? That would be sad indeed."

Sabrina hadn't looked at it that way. It was a hard house to see, but maybe she needed to move past Sybil's memory and see it as the home of a generous, godly woman.

"What does that thoughtful face mean?" Jeanette asked.

"I'm just thinking about how much growing up I have to do."

"Don't we all."

"Not you, Jeanette," Sabrina protested.

"Even me, dear. I've been wanting my own way lately, and God has had to remind me I'm not in charge."

Sabrina smiled at her. Jeanette smiled back. Sabrina decided to see the house differently from that moment on.

17

"What are you doing here?"

"That's what I came to ask you, Sybil. This house? Is it his?"

"Yes, and you have to leave."

"Why? You didn't tell him you have family? You didn't tell him you have a sister?"

"He knows about you, but he also knows what you do."

"What I do? What about you?"

"Keep your voice down, Bri!"

Sybil grabbed Sabrina by the arm and took her back toward the front door. They passed a woman in a maid's uniform, but Sybil ignored her.

"You can't stay."

"You're sending me back?"

"Yes."

Sabrina's eyes narrowed in anger. "How long do you have, Sybil? How long before he finds out what you really are and kicks you out?"

"We're married, Bri," Sybil said triumphantly. "He's in love with me and would never kick me out."

"If you're married, you can help me."

"It doesn't work like that. He's not going to want your kind around."

"My kind?" Sabrina gawked at her. "You act as if getting married changed who you are. We both know who—"

"You have to leave," Sybil cut her off.

Sabrina stared at her older sister, seeing that she meant every word. For a moment her eyes swept over the beautiful dress she was wearing and the perfectly coifed hair.

"I hope he lets you buy plenty of clothes, Sybil. You've got to look beautiful if you're going to distract him from your heart."

"Get out!" Sybil said, all triumph gone.

"Get out and don't come back. I never want to see you again."

Sabrina struggled out of sleep, wanting the images to go away and trying to come fully awake. She pushed to the side of the bed and sat up. It was not the first time she had dreamed about her sister, but this one had been very close to reality. She had gone to Sybil, who had disappeared without warning, and asked for her help, only to be told she had a new life and Sabrina was not going to be a part of it.

Sabrina went to the window and opened it wide. The night air was cool, and she stood for a long time letting it pour in on her.

Please forgive Sybil, Lord, wherever she is. Please save her and her husband. Help them to find You, Lord. Stir their hearts to yearn after You.

Sabrina prayed until her heart felt broken. She ached to see her sister and tell her about the changes in her own life and that Christ died for all. She wasn't sure Sybil would want anything to do with someone telling her that she sinned and needed to repent, but Sabrina wanted to try.

Eventually she went back to bed, crawling

beneath the covers and lying very still. She didn't sleep for a long time, but that was all right. She continued to pray for her sister, knowing God knew all about her and her needs. When she did drift back to sleep, Sybil was still on her mind.

* * *

"Tell us everything," Meg said when she saw Jeb and Patience on Saturday afternoon. The three Holdens had gone into town after hearing the Dorns had arrived home the day before. But this request took some doing. They hadn't seen Savanna in almost three weeks and couldn't get over how much she had changed.

"Your parents look wonderful," Patience began, Savanna still cuddled close. "They miss you but hope to come this fall."

"Oh, that would be wonderful."

"We told them all about Savanna," Jeb said, still wishing the three of them could have gone along. "They couldn't hear enough stories about her."

"You should see the box where your mother saves all your letters," Patience said. "Your father bought it for her. It's ornately carved, and she keeps it by her chair in the parlor. In the evenings when they're on their own, they get out the old letters and read about Savanna."

Meg closed her eyes against a sudden rush of tears. Brad put a hand on her back, asking God to bring his in-laws to visit this fall. It would be great if they could come when the baby was born in February, but winter travel was always a risk, and his heart told him Meg needed to see them sooner.

Jeb went back to talking about the visit, and Meg stifled the tears. Brad was pretty sure that would not be the end of it, but for now they concentrated on the Dorns and enjoyed the visit.

* * *

"Know who you are in Christ," Rylan preached on Sunday morning. "Live who you are in Christ, and be done with who you used to be. That's what's being said here in Colossians 3. We have been crucified and raised with Christ, so we must put aside the practices of the past. Let me read this list to you: fornication, uncleanness, inordinate affection, evil concupiscence, and covetousness, which is idolatry: anger, wrath, malice, blasphemy, filthy communication out of your mouth, and lying to one another.

"Not very pretty, is it? But that's who we were. Outside of Christ we are capable of any and all sins. Did you catch what I said? Outside of Christ, which is not who we are anymore. Know who you are, live who you are, and be done with who you used to be. Listen to this next list, starting in verse 12: the elect of God, holy and beloved, bowels of mercies, kindness, humbleness of mind, meekness, longsuffering, forbearing one another, forgiving one another as Christ forgave us, charity, the peace of God ruling in your hearts, called in one body, and thankful. Wow. That's a tall order, but that's the goal.

"I want to make sure you're aware of the verses that command all of this," Rylan said in closing. "Start in verse one where it says we have been raised with Christ. That's how we know who we are—we've been raised with Him. Then in that same verse we're told to 'seek those things which are above'—live out who we are. Now look at verse five where we are commanded to mortify the members which are upon the earth. In other words, be done with who we used to be.

"Take some time this week and study these over—know them, remember them. And let's not forget to pray for each other all week and check with each other as we live this out and put aside who we used to be."

* * *

"What are you doing?" Chas asked Miranda as she bent over a piece of paper after the service, shifting a sleeping Nellie to his other shoulder.

"I'm writing that down. I needed to hear it."

"About knowing, living, and forsaking?"

"Is that how you're going to remember it?"

"I think so. Be sure and check with me tomorrow about how I'm doing."

Miranda smiled at him, and Chas bent and kissed her cheek. They looked up to find the Rathman family headed their way. Daryl asked them to join them for dinner, and the afternoon began.

* * *

"I'll be fine," Sabrina said to Becky and Heather as the afternoon wore on. The women were both looking at her in horror, but for the moment were quiet. "I'll be more aware than last time, but I have to gather my things or Butch Sandgren is going to confiscate them. My rent is not paid past Tuesday."

"I'll go with you," Becky stated, wishing Jeanette had not gone to dinner at the Dorns'.

"That's fine," Sabrina said, "but not necessary."

"Well, now, that's a matter of opinion!" Becky mumbled and said she was going to change.

Sabrina looked at Heather, but that lady was biting her lip in anxiety, and suddenly Sabrina had had enough. She wasn't angry, but she was going to say what was on her mind.

"I can't live like you do, Heather, in fear."

"Is that what you think?"

"Isn't it true? I can't stay indoors for the rest of my life as you all want me to."

Heather looked amazed. That was what they wanted, to protect and shelter her from this man, but what kind of life was that?

"I'm sorry, Bri. I didn't really see it for what it is."

"Thank you."

"Are you really all right with Becky going with you?" Heather asked, knowing it would take some work not to fear for her anymore.

"It's fine," Sabrina said, "but as I said, not necessary."

Heather nodded and Becky came back with an old dress on and a hat on her head.

"Becky," Heather said a little sternly,

"when you come back I have to talk to you, but while you're gone, you let Sabrina do as she needs. Do you hear me?"

"I hear. Is she going to be safe?"

"That's not the point," Sabrina cut in with conviction. "I need my things; I'm going to get them; and that's the end of it."

"It's too bad Timothy has the day off," Heather said. "It would be nice to have the wagon."

"Can we hitch the horse ourselves?" Sabrina asked, thinking it would be nice to get it all in one trip.

"We could try," Becky said, suddenly all for it.

Heather had to laugh. Sabrina laughed with her, but Becky was already headed for the door, Sabrina in her wake.

* * *

"Easy there, big fella," Sabrina crooned to the huge animal that was nearly asleep on his feet. "Just be calm."

Becky grunted and pulled on the tongue of the wagon. "How does Timothy move this?"

"Here, let me help you," Sabrina said, her eyes popping a bit when she pulled.

"See?" Becky said. "It's heavy!"

The women stood across the tongue from each other and thought about the man who worked for Jeanette. He was well past his first flush of youth, but he had been hitching the buggy and wagon for years.

"Let's try again," Becky said, and this is what the women were doing when Rylan walked in.

"What does it weigh?" Sabrina asked in exasperation.

"This is an interesting sight," Rylan commented, startling both women, who jerked upright and looked at him.

"We need to get this wagon hitched!" Becky took no time in saying. "How does Timothy do it?"

Rylan smiled at Jeanette's cook, went to the wagon, and moved the block that Timothy had put in front of the back wheel.

"Well, I never!" Becky said as she watched him. Sabrina put a hand over her mouth to hide her laughter as Becky gave Rylan an earful. The big man took it in stride, calmly bringing the horse out and hitching the wagon in a ridiculously short period of time.

"May I drive you ladies somewhere?" Rylan offered, working not to stare at

Sabrina—she looked beautiful in the dark blue dress she was wearing. It had been trimmed in a lighter shade of blue that matched the color of her eyes.

"We're moving Bri from her apartment," Becky said, biting her tongue when she wanted to say more.

"Well, I hope you'll let me help."

Sabrina stood back while he helped Becky into the wagon and then turned to her.

"Did Heather send for you?"

"No, was she supposed to?"

Sabrina shook her head and didn't try to explain, quietly allowing Rylan to help her into the wagon.

* * *

"Moving out?" Crystal asked, standing at the edge of the building, a woman beside her that Sabrina thought might be Paula.

"Yes, it's time. Are you Paula?"

"Yes."

"I'm Bri."

"That your boyfriend?" she asked, her eyes following Rylan as he came down the stairs with the headboard in his hands.

"My pastor," Sabrina said shortly, turning back to Crystal. She sensed no need in

Paula, only interest in the nearest man. "Why don't we meet for dinner or supper sometime at the hotel."

"All right," Crystal agreed slowly, still very curious about this woman. "I could come Tuesday."

"Dinner or supper?"

"Supper," Crystal said, telling herself she deserved a night off.

"I'll meet you there a little after five."

"You'd better show up," Crystal said.

Sabrina only smiled at her and turned to go up the stairs. She heard Crystal question Paula about wanting to talk to her in the past but kept moving up the stairs, not working to hear the answer.

* * *

"Thank you for all your help, Becky," Sabrina said when the wagon was unloaded.

"It's no trouble," Becky said in her brusque manner, turning for the house. Sabrina looked for Rylan, who was taking care of the wagon and horse, going so far as to walk inside the barn.

"Thanks for your help," Sabrina said, wondering why he was so easy to be around.

"You're welcome. Was it hard to lose your place?"

"A little," Sabrina said, realizing how true it was. "Crystal and I made plans, and that helps."

Sabrina hadn't been looking at him, but when he didn't reply, she looked up. Rylan was staring at her.

"You're special. Do you know that?"

"What made you say that?"

"I'm not sure you hear it enough, and it's the complete truth."

"Because Crystal and I have plans?"

"Exactly. Not every woman can reach out to a woman in Crystal's situation, and even if she could, she might not want to ever have a part of that life again."

"I guess I have Callie Barshaw to thank for that."

Rylan frowned, wondering what he'd missed.

"Did you not know that she used to work in Denver's night district?"

"No. I mean, if I did know, I'd completely forgotten."

"We went back to the bordello to get my things," Sabrina told Rylan as the memory came to mind, "and she came in with me. Lil, the woman who owns the building, invited Callie to take a room with her. Callie was in complete control. She didn't let her say a word out of line.

"This week Bret Toben was in to get his mail and said something inappropriate to me. I just walked away. Callie told me I have to draw a hard line and know how I want people to treat me."

"Why did you leave Denver, if Callie was such a help?"

Sabrina sighed. "I lived with Danny and Callie in a nice neighborhood, but it wasn't that many blocks from the night district. I worked at the laundry, and there was one man who knew me. He wasn't a problem, but then I started seeing others, and some wouldn't go away. Some even came to the Barshaws' door. I wanted nothing to do with that life, but the men finding me wouldn't let me forget it. Danny said the move was for the best, and they put me on the train."

"Token Creek's gain."

Sabrina opened her mouth, not able to believe he was real. "Where did you come from?"

"The same place as Danny Barshaw."

Sabrina looked at him for a long time and then remembered Chas.

"Did you talk to Chas about our meeting with him?"

"This morning. He's expecting us tomorrow night."

"When were you going to tell me about this?"

"This is the first I've seen you alone, and he knew I hadn't had a chance to check with you and might need to reschedule."

Sabrina looked at him.

"Do I need to reschedule?"

"I guess not."

"Do try to calm all that enthusiasm."

Sabrina laughed a little and said, "Becky said something about pie. Are you coming in?"

"Yes, ma'am."

Rylan watched her smile, trying not to see it as a good sign but admitting to himself that it was just what his heart wanted to believe.

* * *

"We can't be in a panic every time she leaves the house," Heather said to Becky, having found her in the kitchen. Jeanette was there as well, quietly listening. "She charged me with being afraid, and she's right—I have been. I can't push my fears onto her." Heather turned and looked at Jeanette. "We've all done it."

Jeanette nodded. Heather was right.

"I just have one last thing to mention," Heather continued, knowing she was free to have her say. "If we can't live with the way Sabrina lives her life, then she needs to move out. Maybe another church family could make room for her."

"No," Jeanette said. "She needs to stay. She didn't ask to be attacked. That was not her fault. She does go to the rough part of town—not foolhardily, but to reach out to others. I just have to do what you said, Heather, and not push my concerns on her."

"She needs to marry Rylan," Becky put in, as if this would just take care of the whole issue.

The two other women were ready to laugh at her face and tone, but they heard steps on the kitchen porch. Sabrina and Rylan were coming their way.

* * *

"Chas still hasn't shared with Miranda. If you're comfortable with it, he'll do that before we get there, and then she can join us when we meet."

Rylan had come to Jessie's on Monday and tracked Sabrina down. They now stood in one of the back corners of the storeroom to talk.

"What if she doesn't respond the way you figured? What if she needs more time?"

"Time for what?"

"To get used to the idea. She might not want me around for a while."

Rylan looked down into her face, his heart squeezing so painfully in his chest that he could hardly breath. Sabrina misunderstood his hesitation and spoke again.

"I understand, Rylan. We can meet another time."

Rylan's hand came up and gently touched her cheek. He couldn't help but touch her.

"I'm sorry for all the rejection you've known, Sabrina—so sorry."

Sabrina looked into his eyes, not sure what to do. She wasn't prepared for his hurt. She realized in the space of several heartbeats that she could take the hurt on herself but not see it on him.

Sabrina said the first thing that came to mind. "What am I going to do with you?"

"Chas will help us figure that out."

Sabrina stared at him, not sure if that was possible.

"So wait on Miranda?"

"Not at all. Just know that I'll understand when you need to cancel."

Rylan ignored her doubts and said, "I'll come to Jeanette's and get you at seven o'clock."

"I'll be ready."

Rylan let her get back to work. Sabrina's mind didn't linger on the evening. She figured Rylan would be back at some point to tell her she was right and knew there was no sense worrying about it in the meantime.

* * *

"Do you know where Lewis was this morning? He came in late," Nate questioned Thom Koeller as Monday wore on.

"No, I didn't see him. Why?"

"Never mind, and don't mention that I asked."

Thom nodded. He was the newest man to join the ranks of deputy and wanted to keep this job. If that meant keeping his mouth quiet, he would do it.

* * *

"Are you going to be all right?" Chas asked Miranda, her eyes still red.

"I think so. I just don't want her to mistake my tears."

Chas nodded. He had told Miranda as soon as Rylan had given him permission, and as he knew she would, she sobbed with hurt for the other woman.

Do you know, Chas? Do you have any idea how awful that would be? she had asked him over and over, her heart torn with the grief of it all. Now Rylan and Sabrina would be there within the hour, and Miranda was still teary over the news.

They worked on the dishes, put the kids to bed, and waited in the living room. Miranda had made a cobbler with berries, and even had fresh cream. She was desperate to see the other woman, and it was almost seven o'clock before it occurred to her that Sabrina might be dreading this night. She spent the rest of the time praying for Sabrina, that she would know how much she was loved.

* * *

"Are you all right?"

"I am. I just didn't expect us to actually go."

"I think you'll enjoy Miranda when you get to know her."

"I like the way she is with her children. You can tell they love her, but they still obey."

"When have you noticed this?"

"On Sundays. They all want to sit in Chas and Miranda's laps, but they always obey."

"You'll have to tell them that. It will encourage them."

"What exactly are we doing tonight?" Sabrina suddenly asked.

"Just starting to get to know each other."

"You and I, or all of us?"

"I think it will be all of us, but it's to help you and me talk about our pasts and who we are."

"You don't have a past."

"Or so you think."

Sabrina came to a dead halt, her mouth open. Rylan stopped with her.

"I can't believe how selfish I've been. I've been so worried about your falling for me and wanting to protect you from that, I haven't even asked you about yourself."

"You haven't been selfish. And when you think of questions, I'll answer them."

He had made it sound so simple. Sabrina began to wonder what his past was like and if it could really be that easy.

18

"HOW ARE YOU?" MIRANDA asked Sabrina as soon as she saw her.

"I think I'm all right."

Miranda looked up at her and couldn't stop the tears that flooded her eyes. "I told myself I wouldn't cry. Please forgive me."

"There's nothing to forgive, Miranda," Sabrina said, putting a hand on the other woman's arm. "You're so kind to care."

"Listen to me, Bri. If ever you want to talk about anything, I'll listen. I might not be much help, but I'm a good listener."

"Thank you," Sabrina said, and the two women hugged. They had stayed right by the front door to talk but now turned to join the men in the living room.

"Take the sofa," Chas invited. "You too, Ry. Get comfortable."

Sabrina relaxed when Rylan sank down next to her, and relaxed further with Chas' first questions.

"How was your day? Were you at Jessie's?"

"Yes. It wasn't too busy. I spent the morning in the storeroom."

"Do the little girls talk to you?" Miranda asked.

Sabrina had to smile. "They're so funny. At times they quarrel, and at other times they're the best of friends."

The four continued to talk about the day, and then Chas asked a different question.

"Why do you think you're here tonight, Bri?"

"Rylan has said things that make it seem he's interested in me. At the risk of sounding insulting, I'm not sure he really understands." Sabrina said this and then glanced at Rylan before looking back at Chas and Miranda.

"What is it you don't think he understands?" Chas asked.

"What that time of my life was like. He's not sheltered; I don't mean that, but he doesn't really know."

"I think you're the only one who knows exactly what you went through, Bri, but Rylan doesn't have any false images about that life. He knows it was awful for you."

Sabrina nodded, wanting to believe that he could really love her and overlook that time but finding it almost impossible.

"I think I said that wrong," Sabrina spoke up again. "He seems willing to put all that aside, but I feel that just can't last. At some point, he's going to see the full import and change his mind."

Chas nodded and turned to his pastor. "Ry, what did you hope we would accomplish during these meetings?"

"As you can tell, Sabrina believes she's all wrong for me. She doesn't seem to take my word for the fact that I don't believe I'm all wrong for her. I was hoping a third party would help us sort through the words."

"What's your biggest fear?" Chas asked next.

"That Sabrina will never accept my love."

"And you, Bri?"

It took a moment for Sabrina to admit this,

but she said very slowly and quietly, "I fear that we'll be married, maybe for a few years, and some man will come to Token Creek who knew the old Bri, and it will become known that Pastor Rylan Jarvik married a prostitute. I fear that such information will destroy the wonderful testimony he's built in this town."

Rylan's eyes closed in grief. Miranda's eyes were huge as she tried to hold back the tears, but it didn't work.

"If you were sure that would never happen," Chas pressed her, "would you accept Rylan's love?"

"I want to, but I still fear for him. I fear for me too. What if on our wedding night he remembers that he's not the first? I fear that if we go ahead and marry, and things suddenly become clear to him, he'll no longer want me.

"I wouldn't blame him," Sabrina went on. "But I want to spare myself the heartache, selfish as that seems."

"Why would Rylan hold something against you that God has forgiven?"

Sabrina did not have an answer for that. She knew Rylan wouldn't do that, but wasn't that just what she was saying?

"Had you not thought of that?" Miranda asked when she stayed quiet.

"I guess I had, but then I forgot. I don't think he would, but I still worry about it. Maybe I just need more time."

"Well, we have plenty of that," Chas said, and then noticing Sabrina's pale face, he suggested they pray together. They talked about a few more things before they spent some time in prayer. When they finished, Chas accompanied his wife to the kitchen to get the coffee and dessert.

"Are you all right?" Rylan asked.

"Who takes care of you?" Sabrina asked. "I feel as though the whole evening has been about me. Who takes care of Rylan Jarvik?"

"It's sweet of you to ask, but I haven't been hurt the way you have."

"I did choose, Rylan. You understand that, don't you? Sybil did not hold a gun to my head. I chose that life."

"Yes, I do understand, but tell me what you did as soon as the Barshaws gave you a different choice."

Sabrina didn't answer. She didn't need to.

"And then," Rylan went on, "tell me what you did when you understood that Christ died for you?"

"I believed," Sabrina said.

"Why?" Rylan whispered, leaning a little closer to her. "Why, my sweet Sabrina, would I ever hold your past over you and use it like a whip?"

"You wouldn't," Sabrina whispered back.

They're eyes held for a long time. In fact they were still looking at each other when the Vicks returned with dessert.

* * *

"If someone asks me about us, are you comfortable with my telling them that we're working on a relationship?" Rylan asked Sabrina as he walked her home.

"I am comfortable with that," Sabrina was able to say for the first time. The evening had been wonderful. Hard at times but still wonderful.

"I'm glad to hear it."

"Rylan," Sabrina suddenly asked, "what would you do if word got out about my past?"

"That's not who you are in town, and that life is past. I guess I would tell folks the truth—that it was in the past, has nothing to do with today, and doesn't need to be discussed."

"But would you be embarrassed?"

"Of you?" Rylan sounded as astounded as he felt.

Sabrina would have looked at him, but it was dark.

"Sabrina," Rylan said, "I would be concerned only for your being hurt. Nothing you could do would embarrass me."

"You're too good to be true, Rylan."

"Is that the way Callie feels about Danny?"

"I don't know," Sabrina said, not having thought of it before but glad Rylan mentioned it. "I just figured out that I need to write Callie. I think she could be a help to me right now."

"That sounds like a good idea. I'll pray she'll have answers for you."

"Goodnight, Rylan," Sabrina said at Jeanette's front door.

"Goodnight, Sabrina."

"Are you ever going to tell me why you call me Sabrina?"

"I plan on it, yes," Rylan said, a smile in his voice as he wished her goodnight one more time and turned and walked away.

* * *

Dear Callie, Sabrina started her letter when she got to her room on Monday night.

I need your help. I think I'm in love with Rylan Jarvik, and he says he

loves me, but I fear for him. I feel I can't give myself to him completely because of all I've lost. He's so special that I don't feel worthy of his love.

Did you ever feel that way about Danny? What did you do to get past the feeling of being damaged or used goods that no one would ever want? Is it too soon? Am I asking too much of myself, since last year at this time I was still living in the night district?

Sabrina stopped. The words had taken a lot out of her, and now her mind was swept back. She pictured each woman that she had lived with in the small apartments. Had any of them found a way out? Right across the hall had been Zoe. She was older, nearly 40 but trying to look 20. Wilma had been young—not as young as Sabrina but less educated and very trapped.

Tears poured down Sabrina's face as she remembered them and she cried out to God on their behalf. "I couldn't stay, Lord," she whispered, "but I love those women. Please save them. Give them a hunger for You that will send them searching and not just accepting that dark life forever."

Sabrina could not articulate another word. She sobbed at the small writing desk, her tears so harsh that Jeanette heard her. She stood in the hallway outside her bedroom, not sure what to do. Heather heard as well and came with a lantern, but neither woman disturbed her. They both returned to their bedrooms, hearts heavy but unsure they would ever know why.

* * *

"Well, now," Sabrina said when she saw Crystal the next night. "Taking the night off?"

"Yeah," Crystal said, but she was pleased. It was the only dress she owned that was not meant to attract male attention. She didn't even remember having it until late in the day and almost on a whim put on the brown high-necked dress. She was aware that Sabrina always looked nice and hadn't wanted to be shown up.

The women took a table in the corner. It was a bit dark, but neither one seemed to mind.

"How are you liking it at the mansion?" Crystal asked right away.

"The mansion," Sabrina said on a laugh. "It's nice. They're all very sweet and treat me well."

"They seem like your type."

"How did you get started?" Sabrina asked, tired of wondering.

"Does it matter?"

"No, I was just curious."

"I'll make a deal with you," Crystal suggested. "I'll answer questions if you answer questions."

"I think I can live with that," Sabrina said, not as relaxed as she appeared.

"Why are you willing to talk to me?"

"My sister was a prostitute. You're not all that scary."

"Was?" Crystal asked, but Sabrina shook her head.

"My turn. How did you get started?"

Crystal laughed but still said, "I grew up in this town, on the wrong side. My father taught me how to steal, but I didn't like spending time in jail. This turned out to be easier."

So many questions sprang to mind, but Sabrina only nodded.

"How did your sister get out?"

"She was shrewd and beautiful. When a rich man came along who fell for her, she used every trick she knew to entice him, and it worked. They're married."

"There was someone who wanted to marry me once," Crystal volunteered, "but he certainly wasn't rich. He was a bigger thief than my father, and I said no."

"What happened to your father?"

"He tried a big job—robbing the train before it could get into town—and got shot."

"I'm sorry, Crystal."

Crystal looked away. She hated it when people said that, but it wasn't so bad coming from Sabrina.

"You gonna marry Rylan Jarvik?" Crystal suddenly asked.

"I don't know."

"You should. He's a good man."

"Why do you say that?"

"He doesn't think he's better than the rest of us."

"That's true," Sabrina agreed. "He understands who he is and how much he needs God."

"He doesn't look like a preacher."

Sabrina laughed but didn't comment because their food was arriving.

"Do you mind if I pray?" Sabrina asked when the waiter left them.

"I guess not," Crystal said, but she didn't bow her head. She watched Sabrina, not able to help herself.

"Thank You, Father, for this food and this time Crystal and I can have together. In the name of Your Son, I pray. Amen."

"Why do you say it like that?" Crystal asked the moment Sabrina's head came up. "In the name of the Son?"

"Oh," Sabrina said, a little stumped but still honest. "I can't remember why. I'll have to get back to you on that."

"It's doesn't matter."

"It's a good question," Sabrina said. "I wish I could remember where that comes from."

"You mean it comes from somewhere in the Bible?"

"Right," Sabrina answered, picking up her fork as though she were asked these types of questions all the time. She was new at all of this and suddenly wished she was Rylan with all the answers.

"Why did you come to Token Creek?"

"I was ready for a change of scenery. Denver holds a lot of bad memories."

"Is your family gone?"

"All but my sister, and we haven't been close for a long time."

It never occurred to Crystal that this woman was alone too. Sabrina seemed so confident and clearheaded.

"Excuse me," the waiter interrupted, his voice sounding tired. "The men at the table by the door are wondering if you ladies would like company."

"No, thank you," Sabrina said, not even looking across the room but going right back to her dinner.

For a moment Crystal was so filled with envy that she could hardly think. Sabrina hadn't even glanced at the other table! Crystal thought she would give up everything to be that sure of herself.

"What's the matter?" Sabrina asked, catching the odd look on the other woman's face.

"You didn't even look," Crystal said before she could stop herself.

"Unless Rylan is sitting over there, I'm not interested," Sabrina stated simply. "And he wouldn't do that. If he came in, he'd come right to the table and say hello. No games. And you said you were taking the night off."

Crystal had to smile at her. She had never met anyone like her, who wasn't a prostitute but who talked about it without stumbling over each word.

"Am I being laughed at?"

"No," Crystal said, but did not go back to her meal.

"You need to eat," Sabrina said. "No wonder you're skinny."

"I'm padded where I need to be," Crystal said, her voice a bit smug.

"You still need to eat," Sabrina said, well aware of the other woman's full chest and sorry she felt it was all she needed.

Crystal didn't argue, but she did pick up her fork. She kept waiting for it, waiting for Sabrina to try and talk to her about God, but it didn't happen. They visited about everything under the sun, learning that their tastes in colors and interests were similar. The evening ended, and with talk of doing it again, they went their separate ways. Crystal walked home in a state of wonder, having expected Sabrina to talk to her about God and not sure how she felt about the fact that she didn't.

* * *

"Why do we pray in Jesus' name?" Sabrina asked Jeanette at the breakfast table.

"We need the reminder that everything we have is because of Christ," Jeanette said, reaching for her Bible. "Let me read a verse to you, Bri."

"We might have covered this in church before you moved to town, but Colossians 1:17 says, 'He is before all things, and by him all things consist.' We want to remember when we pray that we need to do it in Christ. His name is everything. He came to us from the Father, and when we pray to the Father, we ask in His Son's name. If we can't ask in His Son's name, then something is wrong with what we're praying."

Sabrina nodded, thinking about it because Rylan had also said that verse spoke of creation.

"Did that help?" Jeanette asked.

"I think so. I just need to figure out how I would describe it to someone who doesn't believe like we do."

"Your friend with whom you had dinner?"

"Yes. I prayed before we ate and said 'in the name of Your Son.' She wanted to know why. I was embarrassed to tell her I couldn't remember."

Jeanette smiled at her. "I think your honesty is refreshing. You just told her the truth."

"I also told her I would get back to her on it."

"Then the door is still open. That's wonderful."

"I guess it is," Sabrina said, not having thought of it.

"Why don't you ask her here for dinner next time? You can join us or cook something yourself."

Sabrina stared at her, seeing no choice but to lay it on the line.

"Jeanette, Crystal is a prostitute."

"How sad for her," Jeanette said quietly. "But what's even sadder is your thinking that I wouldn't allow such a woman in my house. I've been a hypocrite, Bri."

Sabrina didn't know what to say. That wasn't the way she saw Jeanette at all, and she was completely without words.

"Do you remember that day in the shop, Bri, when I told you I had more growing to do. I'd wanted to be in charge, and God was showing me otherwise?"

Sabrina nodded.

"That was about you. I was so angry with your moving to Willow Street that I refused to visit you. It took me a long time to get over your moving there. Not until you were able to reach out to others did I come out of my selfish little world."

Sabrina still could not speak.

"You reach out to others in the most amazing way I've ever seen."

"But you reach out, Jeanette, all the time."

Jeanette's smile was sad. "I reach out in my own safe world to the women of the church family. I sew for the community, but I can't remember the last time I had a chance to share Christ with someone."

"Jeanette, I don't—" Sabrina began, but stopped.

"Know what to say?" she asked. "It's all right. I just wanted you to know that I'm sorry for the way I acted about the apartment, even though you weren't aware of it, and that you may certainly invite your friends here."

Sabrina was still nodding when Jeanette went on.

"And while I'm being honest, I really want you to marry Rylan."

Sabrina started to smile.

"Don't you laugh, Bri Matthews," Jeanette said, trying not to smile as well. "I mean it."

There were many things Sabrina could have said to this, but she kept them to herself. She did realize one thing, however. If Jeanette could see what was going on, there were probably others in the church family who could too. She couldn't help but wonder if they would be as enthusiastic as Jeanette.

* * *

"Hey, Nate," Rylan said when that man came by the livery.

"I was hoping you'd be working," the sheriff said. "I keep seeing Miss Matthews, but not to talk to. How is she doing?"

"She's fine. Back to normal life."

"She's got guts, Rylan. I still see her on Willow Street and even out with Crystal."

Rylan had to smile when he agreed, thinking about how plucky she was.

"Well, I wish I could tell you to pass on to her that we've picked up Zeke, but it hasn't happened. I think he left town. With how many times he hit her, he might have even managed to scare himself."

"You think he's afraid he killed her?"

"I wouldn't be surprised," Nate said, shaking his head a little. "I'm glad she looks like herself again. The first time I saw those bruises, I wasn't sure."

"It was bad," Rylan agreed, remembering as well.

Lewis Varner chose that moment to come from the bank. Both men watched him head the other direction before Rylan spoke.

"Did he remember Sabrina's and my coming that night?"

"Yes," Nate said, his voice growing tight, "but insisted he wrote a report that Thom must have lost."

"How did he explain the fact that we didn't see him write anything?"

"He said he did it after you left."

The men exchanged looks before Nate went on. "I'm keeping my eye on him. And whether he knows it or not, Thom is too."

"I hope it works out for you, Nate."

"Yeah" was all Nate said, the word filled with doubt.

The sheriff didn't linger but went on his way. Rylan went back to work, remembering to pray for the sheriff and his deputies as well.

* * *

"I have a little surprise for you," Jeanette said to Sabrina on Friday before they could even leave for the shop.

"What's that?"

"You're taking the day off."

"Today? I thought there was lots of work to be done."

"No, we're in good shape, and we've got half the day tomorrow."

"All right," Sabrina agreed, thinking about what she might do.

"Now Trace will be here soon," Jeanette continued. "He'll want to visit with his mother, but then he'll take you back to the ranch."

"I see," Sabrina said, a teasing glint entering her eyes. "You not only have given me the day off but planned how I'm to spend it."

Jeanette smiled at her own high-handedness but could see that Sabrina was not offended.

"Doesn't it sound fun?" Jeanette checked with her.

"Very. What does Cassidy think?"

"It was her idea. We've been plotting against you since Sunday."

Sabrina had to smile. It was such a nice plan, and if the truth be told, she loved surprises. Changing out of her white blouse and navy skirt, Sabrina got ready for a day at the ranch.

19

"WELL, RYLAN," JEANETTE SAID on Friday morning when he came into the shop. "You look like a man looking for something."

"I need a dress shirt, Mrs. Fulbright," Rylan said. "The collar on mine is wearing."

"Let's see," Jeanette said, taking the shirt he'd brought with him. "I think I might be able to replace this collar and match the fabric, but I'll also make you another one so you can use your old one as a backup."

"Thank you very much. Where is your assistant today?"

"I sent her to the ranch."

"Well, now," Rylan said, his smile coming

into full bloom. “Does she need a ride home?”

Jeanette, who had hoped Rylan would ask that very thing, was happy to tell him what Sabrina’s plans had been.

* * *

“Where is Bri?” Trace asked his wife after dinner. He’d slipped upstairs to change the shirt he’d gotten soup on and come back to find her gone.

“At the stream. I told her I was going to take a nap, and off she went.”

“If I recall she liked it out there last time too.”

“I don’t know if she’s ever alone,” Cassidy said. “I think she likes how calm and quiet it is.”

Had Cassidy but known it, she had guessed the very reason Sabrina liked the stream. She was already under the branches of a tree, a quilt beneath her, her stockings off, and her feet in the water. The weather had cooled with August speeding by, but it was still warm enough to soak her feet. Sabrina sighed unconsciously as she wiggled her toes in the water. Looking down at her feet, her mind went immediately to Rylan.

I didn't see this coming, Lord. It's all a little strange. I feel like I'm living someone else's life, but it's mine. I never asked You for a husband, Lord. It was not something I thought I would have or even want.

Sabrina's head went back as emotions filled her. *All I wanted was Your forgiveness. That was enough—more than enough. I just wanted to know I was saved from my sin. And now You've sent this wonderful man, this man I don't deserve.*

Sabrina worked at not feeling that way, but those thoughts still plagued her. She laid back, the air warm around her, as she studied the sky through the leaves above. In places it looked like lace. Sabrina was picking out her favorite pattern when she heard footsteps. Rylan was headed her way. Taken by surprise, she came awkwardly to her feet and waited for him to approach.

"Hi," Rylan said quietly, not sure what her look meant. "Did I disturb you?"

"No, my mind was just miles away. Did you not have work today?"

"I got everything on my schedule done, and I must admit that when I heard you were here, I put a few things onto next week."

Sabrina smiled, but Rylan didn't smile in

return. She found herself wondering what his look meant.

“I think you have something on your mind,” she said at last.

“I do, but I don’t want to say anything that will sound like some man from the past.”

“But you want to say something.”

“Yes. I want to tell you how beautiful you look, but I don’t want you to hear anyone else’s voice, the voice of someone who’s looking for something.”

Sabrina nodded with understanding and said, “I don’t think of anyone else when you talk to me, but thank you for being careful.” This said, she turned back toward the pond. “I wish there hadn’t been anyone else. I wish it was only you.”

“It can be, from this moment forward if that’s what you want.”

“I do want that, but there’s still some fear.”

“Of the physical?”

Sabrina nodded, realizing it was true.

Rylan’s arm came out. He turned Sabrina to him and drew her into his embrace. He pulled her close, his mouth so near hers that if either of them moved, they would be kissing. Sabrina looked up at him with huge eyes as he began to talk.

"I need you to understand," Rylan began quietly. "I'm not any of those other men. I am not a man controlled by my urges, who sees you as a thing to be used. You say the word, and I'll stop. Even holding you this close, you shake your head no or say stop and that's what I'll do. I'll never use you and throw you away. I'll cherish you at all times, especially when we touch, and you can always, *always,* tell me no."

Sabrina looked into his wonderful face and relaxed. She moved her arms enough to hug him back, laying her cheek against his chest. She could hear the thunder of his heart and simply hugged him tighter.

"I love you," Rylan whispered, bending close to her ear.

"I love you too, but I still want better for you than me."

"That's why we're going to keep meeting with Chas and Miranda." Rylan spoke practically, knowing that once she was sure, he could woo and romance her to his heart's content.

"Rylan," Sabrina said, suddenly stepping back. "I have something to show you."

Rylan watched as Sabrina turned a little and showed him her bare foot. There, on the outside of her ankle, was a small tattoo, a flower. Rylan looked at it and then into her eyes.

"Was that normal among women in the night district?" Rylan asked, as calm as if they'd been discussing the weather.

"Somewhat," Sabrina answered, not having thought about it.

"How did you decide to get one?"

"A customer wanted me to. He didn't want anything else, just to pay me to let him put on tattoos."

"How many do you have?"

"Two."

Rylan nodded, knowing he had to be careful of his thoughts at this point.

"Is the other one in a private place?"

Sabrina nodded, and Rylan did as well, still looking utterly calm. Suddenly Sabrina was back next to him, gripping his arm.

"Why, Rylan?" Sabrina begged. "Why are you able to overlook this? Why are you not angered and repulsed by it?"

Rylan put his hands on her shoulders, his touch light and undemanding.

"Hear me, Sabrina. I'm not dismissing the severity of your sin, but I understand the greatness of the cross. Your sin has been covered. It's gone. You're not that person anymore."

Sabrina looked up at him, realizing how true it was. She could not have been more different than the woman Danny Barshaw dragged away from that crowd. And it was all about the greatness of the cross.

"Oh, Rylan," Sabrina suddenly said. "I think I'm starting to see. The cross is huge. It's why we're who we are."

"Exactly. It's why I don't tell Nate Kaderly no when he wants me to talk to a hurting soul across town. It's why you head back to Willow Street and talk to Crystal, and why I found you out on that Saturday night. It's why I stand in the pulpit each week and call my congregation to greater holiness. The cross is just that big."

Sabrina sighed, her heart full, so full she wasn't able to talk about it. She couldn't form the words in her head. She just knew that she never wanted to be separated from this man.

Rylan was in the same place. He had known this woman was out there for him somewhere, a woman who would love people as he did, not afraid of getting her hands dirty and doing the hard work that it took to be a pastor's wife.

At the same time they heard someone approaching. It was Cassidy, a smile on her face at the sight of Rylan.

"I was thinking Bri might be needing company, but I can see you beat me to it, Ry."

"Hello, Cass," he greeted. "I'm inviting myself to supper again."

"You let me join you in the shade, and you can stay all weekend."

The couple, newly aware of each other and their love, welcomed Cassidy to the quilt. The three talked for more than an hour before Brad and Trace came by. Before the evening was over, both households joined together for a meal. Six adults and one entertaining toddler spent the evening together, conversation roaming far and wide. And although Rylan and Sabrina said nothing about the change in their relationship, it was obvious to everyone but Savanna that Rylan Jarvik had found someone who fit perfectly into his heart.

* * *

Nate Kaderly watched Lewis come from Crystal's apartment, asking himself why he kept the man on. He had enough to keep order in Token Creek without having to watch his own men. He followed at a discreet distance, long enough to see that the deputy was headed home.

Token Creek's sheriff opted to go back and question Crystal herself about why Lewis was there, fairly certain his own man would not give him an honest answer. Her place was dark when he got back, however, and he realized that for now he would have to let it drop.

* * *

"I've been curious about your parents," Chas said to Sabrina on Monday night. "How old were you when they died?"

"My father died when I was 12, almost 13; my mother when I was 15."

"How did you live after your father died?"

"My mother kept selling things, and my sister brought money home and told her it was from her job at the cannery."

"And your mother believed her?"

"Yes. Sybil never showed Mama how much she had, or Mama might have been suspicious. If she noticed that Sybil had a new dress every week, she never said anything."

"That might have led to bad news," Rylan said, remembering what she'd told him.

Sabrina agreed, and Rylan explained to

the Vicks what Mrs. Matthews had been like. They talked about Sabrina's life at the Barshaws' and her work at the laundry. They eventually got to Sabrina coming to Token Creek and what that had been like.

"I never even considered trying to get hired as a seamstress, but when I saw that sign in Jeanette's window, I felt I'd been set free." Sabrina shook her head. "When I think of how much I hated my sewing lessons, I could kick myself. I wouldn't have made it without Mama's teaching.

"And then," Sabrina went on, warming to her subject, "I was reminded of it all over again when I had dinner with a friend last week. She has no skills to fall back on. Her father taught her to steal, but she didn't like going to jail, so she turned to prostitution. I thought about teaching her to sew, but unless she's ready to leave town I don't think it would help her get out of her present life."

"Could she leave town like you did? Or maybe head back to where she belongs, like Eliza?" Rylan asked.

"She's from Token Creek," Sabrina said. "But I'm still thinking on it. I still want to help her. I just haven't found a way yet."

"We'll think on it too," Chas said.

"You seem different this week," Miranda said when there was a lull. "More at peace, Bri. Did something happen?"

"I think it did. Rylan and I talked on Friday about the cross, and I realized some things. The cross is huge, and I had completely forgotten about grace. God's grace toward us, certainly, but also grace in Rylan's heart that he isn't offended or angry with me about my past."

"Are you offended about your past?" Chas asked. "How are you doing on forgiving yourself?"

Sabrina had to think about this. After a time she admitted, "I'm still working on that. I have so many regrets. I don't know if that's not forgiving myself or not."

"We do have to be careful with regrets," Rylan took this, having continued to think on their conversation from the ranch. "We're forgiven, for one thing, but beyond that, God is sovereign."

"Which means what?"

"God is absolutely in control of all things at all times," Rylan said, and then watched Sabrina nod rather slowly.

"I'm thinking of Paul right now," Rylan continued. "In Philippians he lists all the things he had, all the position and religious training, but then he says it counts for nothing. He saw it all as worthless after the cross. I don't sense any regret in him. I don't think that's the point. But he knew that his old life, even things that might have been considered fine, were all worthless. So we don't have to have regrets about sins we have repented of. We can be as logical as Paul was and see them for what they are: worthless outside of Christ. In the same way, we have to see how worthless life was before Christ, but without regrets."

Sabrina took some moments to let this soak in. She realized she wasn't forgiving herself when she spoke of regrets. And it was worse than that. She was actually saying that God hadn't been watching, that He should have been more aware and had her in a different place.

"Did that make sense?" Chas asked her.

"Yes, and I have some changing to do. I've been viewing God on my level, as though He's a little bit helpless."

Both Chas and Miranda shared about the times they had seen this in their own lives before the evening continued. As before, Sabrina left with a great sense of hope and knowing Rylan Jarvik just a little bit more.

* * *

"What happened to you?" Sabrina asked the moment Crystal opened her door and she saw the mark on her face.

That woman didn't answer but turned away. Sabrina walked in and shut the door behind her. She watched Crystal fill a glass with amber liquid and went to the kitchen to start coffee, grabbing the bottle as she went. She worked swiftly, but it took some time for the coffeepot to boil. Thankfully Crystal had not finished the glass when she came with a steaming cup.

"Here," Sabrina said quietly, "trade me."

Crystal gave up the glass after taking one more swallow, and Sabrina set it out of reach. The other woman was steady with the coffee cup, but the slight glaze in her eyes and the bruise that sat high on one cheek gave her a drunken look.

"Tell me who hit you."

"The same one who always does. He uses his badge to get in, and then he never pays."

Sabrina's heart sank, but she didn't comment.

"Most times I can cover it, but this one got purple right away."

"What's his name?"

"Varner!" she spat. "He makes me sick. Can't stand the sight of anyone from Willow Street but certainly wants our favors!"

"Drink your coffee," Sabrina said, getting the pot to give her more.

Coffee or not, it didn't take long for Crystal to look sleepy. Sabrina made her comfortable where she was on the sofa and checked to make sure the stove was closed up. Crystal was dozing when she let herself out, telling herself she would be back. She hadn't been able to tell Crystal about praying in Jesus' name, but she was determined to do that.

* * *

Rylan was finished with supper and working on the dishes when he heard the knock at the door. He'd been praying for Brad and another man, Daryl Rathman, because they were serious about becoming elders.

"Sabrina!" Rylan said, glad to see her and immediately going onto the porch. "How are you?"

"I'm all right, but I have something to tell you."

Rylan didn't interrupt while she explained Crystal's story, but he had an immediate answer for what she should do with the information.

"Leave it to me. I'll see Nate myself."

"Will he believe you?"

"Yes."

"What if Deputy Varner is there?"

"I'll decide what to do about that when I get there."

Sabrina nodded, but she had a new look on her face, one that Rylan hadn't seen before. He naturally asked her what she was thinking.

"I just realized what you go through when I go to Willow Street and you worry about me."

Rylan's head went back with his laughter. Sabrina smiled at his obvious enjoyment before saying, "Will you walk me home?"

"On one condition."

"What's that?"

"I get to hold your hand."

Sabrina could not define the feeling of pleasure that spiraled through her. Feeling shy for the first time in years, she nodded, feeling utterly breathless when Rylan took her hand.

"No one's ever held my hand before," she admitted as they walked.

"Mine either," Rylan said, still getting used to the pain that no one had ever cherished her.

"There's something else I want to tell you too. I don't know much about kissing."

Rylan turned to look at her but could only see her black hair because she didn't look up.

"How does that work?" he asked gently.

"I wouldn't let men kiss me. I didn't like it." Sabrina shook her head. "It sounds ridiculous when something far worse was going on, but I still wouldn't let them."

The admission made Rylan want to hold her on the spot. Her voice was so vulnerable, her heart so bare. Instead he only tightened his grip on her hand.

"I'm glad you told me."

"Me too," Sabrina agreed, glad to hear him sounding so normal. For some reason it had been important for him to know. She'd almost dreaded telling him. It seemed silly now but the relief she felt was amazing.

Rylan could feel it in her. One more thing disclosed. One more step closer. Sabrina's steps had changed, and she even squeezed his hand back. As he left her at Jeanette's front door, he knew with confidence that they were going to get through this. Of this he was certain.

* * *

"She told Sabrina this?"

"Yes. She saw the bruise on Crystal's cheek."

Nate sat down at his desk, looking well past his 46 years.

"I saw him coming from Crystal's on Sunday night. It never occurred to me that he hit her."

"Crystal said he gets in with his badge and never pays."

"I have to be done with him. I wanted to give him every opportunity, but I can't have him acting like that."

Rylan didn't speak, but he was reminded once again of how much he appreciated this man. He could so easily feel as Varner did, that the folks on Willow Street were lower-class people, but he wasn't like that. He came as swiftly to a call down there as he did uptown.

"Thanks, Rylan," the sheriff said, coming to his feet.

"Sure, Nate. I'll see you later," Rylan said briefly and went on his way, sensing that the other man did not need or want his company any longer.

* * *

"How did it go?" Meg asked, meeting Brad at the door. Both he and Daryl had met with the elders this night, and Meg had prayed for them all the while.

"It went well. They are a great group of men. They asked us lots of questions and gave us some things to think about and discuss with our wives. We ended with prayer," Brad said, not able to fully explain what he'd seen and heard. To hear the elders pray for the church family was a very special thing. It made him want the office even more and excited him to keep on in the good work.

"I prayed for you," Meg said, and Brad put his arms around her. He was too emotional to speak, so he just thanked her and held her close. In time he hoped he would be able to explain what it had been like, the humility and joy, the serious moments and the moments when they laughed and teased one another.

And he had not felt like an outsider. The elders were excited to have him and Daryl with them. In truth, he couldn't remember the last time he was so encouraged.

Brad suddenly told Meg his thoughts, and that sweet woman, asking all the right questions, learned about the whole evening. They didn't get to bed for almost two hours.

* * *

"Stay close to the bank, Franklin," Sabrina cautioned on Thursday night. Chas and Miranda had gone out to supper, and Sabrina was on a walk with the children. Naturally they had ended up at the creek.

Parker, who was coming down with a cold, had not left Sabrina's side, and Nellie was happy on the quilt, stuffing a toy block into her mouth and drooling all over it.

"Bri!" Heidi had run up, panting with excitement. "I saw a fish."

"Did you? Let's go and look, Parker. Come on. I'll hold your hand."

"Where's Papa?" the little boy asked.

"He and Mama are still out to supper. They'll be back very soon."

"It's Pastor Rylan," Franklin suddenly shouted. "Are you coming to get wet, Pastor Rylan?"

"I think I just might," he said, having come right up to the little boy, his eyes taking in the group and not missing a thing about Sabrina. She was in a pale blue skirt and a pink blouse, that gorgeous mass of black hair hanging down her back and shoulders. She had pulled it off her face, and the effect was more than a little eye-catching. Rylan knew better than to stare, but it was tempting.

"Pastor Rylan." Heidi was there, tugging on his pant leg. "Come down."

Rylan hunkered down to her level, his eyes on her adorable little face.

"Mama is eating with Papa, and we're with Bri."

"I see that. Are you having fun?"

Heidi nodded, her blue eyes big.

"I wish I had my fishing pole," Franklin said next.

"That would be fun. Although, if my memory serves, Sabrina doesn't know how to fish."

"That's true," Sabrina admitted, smiling at Franklin's surprised face.

Rylan took Parker in his arms at that point, and Sabrina smiled at the sight. The six of them sat on the bank, Franklin and Heidi brave enough to get wet and everyone laughing at Rylan's gentle teasing of the youngest boy.

"Can you breathe like a fish?" Rylan asked, doing things with his face that made Parker giggle and forget about his cold. "You try it."

They laughed uproariously at Parker's attempts, and that little guy relaxed enough to join his siblings by the water. With only Nellie beside them, Sabrina asked Rylan how he was.

"Missing you for some reason," Rylan answered honestly.

"I know why," Sabrina said, and Rylan waited. "We held hands. I think it makes for more awareness."

Rylan had not thought of this but knew she was right. That, along with the fact that he knew he loved her. It was interesting to see how his feelings for her were growing stronger, and as positive as that was, it was also going to bring about more challenges.

"What are you thinking?" Sabrina asked, not forgetting the children nearby.

Rylan smiled, "Just about you and me and how fun and challenging a relationship is."

Sabrina had to smile as well, not at all surprised to hear him view it this way. She was sure they would talk on it some more, but Franklin was looking for Rylan's attention.

That man went to the creek bank, but not before he reached out and cupped Sabrina's cheek, his eyes telling her how much she was loved.

20

"WHERE ARE WE GOING?" Sabrina asked, Rylan leading the way but not saying much.

"You'll see."

It was a gorgeous Sunday afternoon, warm but not hot, and Rylan had shown up at Jeanette's looking for Sabrina. He'd been cryptic about the fact that he was glad to see she'd changed her dress, and then asked her to come along. Too curious not to, Sabrina trailed him, laughing at his pleased smile and trying to get information from the first step.

"Your legs are too long," Sabrina complained at one point, causing Rylan to slow a bit, but Sabrina wasn't done. "Honestly, you're as excited as Franklin when he thinks he's going to fish."

The words were no more out of Sabrina's mouth than she came to dead halt. Rylan stopped with her.

"Come along, Sabrina," Rylan coaxed.

"That's it, isn't it?"

"What?" Rylan asked, working not to smile.

"You're going to teach me to fish."

"Maybe."

Sabrina laughed at the wide eyes he gave her and wasn't fooled at all.

"Do I have to touch worms, Rylan Jarvik? Because if that's the case, this little outing is going to be off to a bad start."

"No worms," he said.

Sabrina studied him to see if he was teasing and then slowly followed. He took her to a tree-lined section of creek, and she saw that he'd already been there. Fishing equipment was set up, as was a quilt to sit on. Sabrina saw a small basket and a jug of tea. She looked at Rylan, who was watching her, and smiled.

"This is very nice."

"What exactly?"

"Well, it looks as though you made a little picnic."

"Just the tea," he said. "The basket is full of worms."

Sabrina laughed as he hoped she would, and the next thing she knew he was showing her how to fish. He took care of the worms, and Sabrina looked the part in fairly short order, but Rylan was the only one to catch anything. An hour passed, and she still had no fish. Eventually they washed their hands in the creek and sat and ate the food Rylan had brought, Sabrina peppering him with questions all the while.

"When did you learn to fish?"

"I can't remember exactly, maybe when I was five or six."

"Who taught you?"

"My father and oldest brother."

"I thought you only had one brother."

"No I have two older brothers and an older sister."

"You're the baby? I thought your sister was younger."

"No, I'm the baby."

"When was the last time you saw them?"

"Two years ago."

"But you all write to each other."

"I hear from my father or mother every week, and from my sister at least once a month."

"Your brothers?"

"Usually their wives."

Sabrina nodded, trying to picture them all and wondering what kind of people they were to produce a son like Rylan. She stared at the water rippling along the creek for a while, watching the way it skipped along the rocks, and then looked back at Rylan.

"Does Sybil look like you?" Rylan asked.

"You can tell we're sisters, but her skin is very fair and her eyes are a darker blue."

"Who's taller?"

"She is. She's almost six feet. I think I heard you say you're the tallest?"

"Yes," Rylan smiled. "They still call me their big little brother."

Sabrina smiled, wishing she could meet his family, especially his mother and father.

"I never knew you would be beautiful," Rylan suddenly said.

"What do you mean?"

"I was fairly certain God would bring you along, but I didn't know what you would look like. Your looks weren't important. But here you are, with just the right heart, and beautiful too."

"Just the right heart?"

Rylan nodded but didn't try to explain. He didn't know if he could, and Sabrina didn't seem to need it. He put out his hand, and Sabrina reached as well. They sat in silence for a while, giving Sabrina room for her thoughts.

If she'd been asked to describe Rylan before today, she would have said he was a big man with a handsome face and square jaw, dark brown hair and eyes, and a wonderful smile and heart. But now she would have to amend that. He didn't have just any heart, it was the right heart. She thought such a statement would be far truer of him than herself.

Sabrina looked down, realizing that he was not just holding her hand but touching her fingers. She watched him finger each one, brushing his fingers along her smooth nails.

"I didn't know anyone could have such perfect hands," Rylan said almost to himself.

"They're a little smaller than yours," Sabrina teased gently.

"Overall, but your fingers are long!" he said, pressing their palms together with studied concentration. With the bottoms of their hands lined up, Rylan could still curl his fingers over the tops of Sabrina's by almost an inch.

While Sabrina was still watching, he pressed a kiss into her palm and folded her fingers over it. He then looked into her eyes.

"I think you're going to have to kiss me, my sweet Sabrina. When the time is right."

"Why is that?"

"I'm not trying to force you into leading, and we have to be careful with our thoughts and actions before we're married, but I want our kissing to be something you're comfortable with."

"What about you? What will make you comfortable?"

"Knowing you're comfortable," he said, and saw that the answer frustrated her.

"Rylan, stop taking care of me."

"But that's my job, to take care of you, and because we're not starting in the same place, both knowing nothing, I have to tread a little carefully here."

Sabrina was quiet, and Rylan took her hand again.

"This is not going to be easy. We're going to be finding our way for a long time. Even after we're married, things will come up that neither of us thought of. And that's all right. We'll handle it as it comes."

"I understand that, but why must I kiss you?" Sabrina asked, finding the idea rather daunting.

"So I know you're ready for that. From that point forward, I'll take the lead."

Sabrina frowned, not sure how to say what she was thinking.

"What did I say wrong?"

"Well, it's just that you make it sound like a future thing, as though I don't want to kiss you now."

"You wish we had already kissed?"

Sabrina nodded, and Rylan looked surprised but also pleased.

"So you won't be afraid if I kiss you at some point?" he double-checked.

"I don't think so."

"But you're not sure?"

Sabrina wrestled the words in her mind for a moment, and then did her best to explain.

"Most of us avoided big men. Naturally they could do the most damage if they grew angry. Or if you wanted them to leave, you were helpless to do anything about it. Sometimes your size can be scary, even though I know you're not any of those men."

"That makes sense," Rylan said, his face thoughtful. "Why would the men get angry?"

"'Self hate' was what Zoe, one of my neighbors, called it. Men, usually those who were married and hated themselves for what they'd just done, would grow abusive. They had to take it out on someone. Sometimes they used words, and sometimes they used fists. A big man could put you off the streets for weeks, and few of us could afford that."

"That's why you were so calm when Zeke hit you. You'd been hit before."

"More times than I can remember," Sabrina admitted, glad that most of it was a blur. "I was usually pretty fast if I saw it coming, and since I'm not little, I could defend myself against a man who wasn't that big. Occasionally I was taken by surprise."

"How often did you think about getting away from it?"

"I had no skills, no money saved, and no place to turn, so I tried not to think at all. I tried not to concentrate on what I was doing, or I would never have survived."

"And during this time you had no thoughts of God?"

"I didn't think He could look on sin, and I knew I was sinning. Danny was the first one to show me I'd been kidding myself. When I realized God had known all along, I was pretty shook up, but at the same time I was trying to figure out who Danny and Callie were. I'd never met anyone like them, people who were willing to take me in and give me a chance."

"And this is why you reach out. This is why you don't give up on Crystal and you stayed with Eliza until the end."

Sabrina nodded, knowing that what he said was true.

"I don't wish your past on anyone, Sabrina, but God can certainly use you now because of it."

"Isn't that true of all of us?"

"I think it is. I remember what you said about hating your sewing lessons. For me it was work on the farm. I would finish as fast as I could so I could find friends to play with, and if my father was looking for a volunteer, my hand would never go up.

"My father finally got through to me concerning the value of what I was learning, and

I will always thank him. When I came to Token Creek, one of the first people I met was Pete Stillwell. He offered me work, and I've been there ever since. It's given me a path into the community that's been invaluable. I don't know if there's a soul in town who doesn't know that I'm a pastor. I've had questions come while I was shoeing horses and while I was dripping with sweat in the forge."

"That wouldn't be the case if you were a hypocrite, Rylan," Sabrina said. "You're real with people, and they can trust you."

"I care for people. It's hard at times. Not everyone wants my friendship, but I still care and pray for them."

Silence fell between them for a little while, and then Sabrina asked, "Can we start back before it gets dark? I want to check on Crystal."

"Have you talked to her since you saw the bruise?"

"No, and she's been on my mind."

"Let's head that way. Why don't you carry the tea, the basket, the fishing pole, and the quilt?"

Sabrina was reaching to do just that when she caught herself. Rylan laughed when she looked at him. Sabrina picked up the basket and the pole and then waited, her look saying much. Rylan folded the quilt and grabbed the jug, still looking very pleased with himself as they started toward Willow Street.

* * *

"Nate and Thom are in the neighborhood," Rylan said when they were almost at Crystal's. "I think I'll say hello."

"All right."

"Stay here. I'll walk you back."

"Why, Rylan," Sabrina worked to sound hurt. "You know my safety is always on my mind."

Rylan dramatically rolled his eyes before saying, "You and I are going to work on defining 'safe,' Miss Matthews. We need some increased unity on that topic."

The smile Sabrina gave him was nothing short of cheeky as he went on his way and she knocked on Crystal's door. Crystal invited her inside, and Sabrina wasted no time.

"How is your eye?"

"It's fine. I've got a little powder on tonight. You can't even see it."

"We can go to supper Tuesday if you want."

Crystal almost mentioned that she couldn't take the night off but changed her mind. Yes, she'd been forced to take nights off with the bruise on her face, but she didn't want Sabrina to stop asking.

"I've got the answer to the question you asked me," Sabrina said.

"What question?" Crystal frowned

"About why I prayed in Jesus' name. It's a way to remember when we pray, we need to do it in the name of Christ. Jesus Christ, God's Son, came to us from the Father, and when we pray to the Father, we ask in His Son's name."

"Who told you this?"

"Jeanette Fulbright. She's been a believer in Jesus Christ for a long time."

"Is that what you call it, believing in Jesus?"

"Yes. Specifically, I believe that His death, burial, and resurrection are real, that He died for my sins, and that I need a Savior or I'm lost."

"Did Mrs. Fulbright tell you that too?"

"No, it was a man and a woman who live in Denver."

"Did they know your sister?"

"No. I was pretty much alone, and they took me in."

Crystal looked at her, not sure what to say. She wasn't sure what questions to ask, but she was curious. It was a relief when one came to mind.

"Did you feel like you had to believe to be their friend?"

"No, I wanted it. I wanted to know I was forgiven."

"But how can you know?" Crystal asked next, but Sabrina didn't get to answer. Someone was knocking on the door, and Crystal rose to answer it.

"We have to talk," Lewis was there saying, pushing his way inside and locking the door behind him.

"Get out of here," Crystal started to say.

"Not until we talk," he said, and then spotted Sabrina. "You have to leave."

Sabrina wasted no time turning to Crystal.

"Do you want me to leave?"

"No, you can stay. The deputy is leaving," Crystal stated flatly, and Sabrina felt proud of her.

"I lost my job," the man gritted out. "We have to talk."

"It had nothing to do with me!"

The ex-deputy glared at her, and then his

eyes swung to Sabrina. He looked at her and realized that Crystal was telling the truth.

"You talked to the sheriff."

"As a matter of fact, I didn't," Sabrina spoke honestly. "But if you're going to hit women and do nothing when someone gives you a report about being hit, you don't deserve to be the law in this town."

The words that came out of the deputy's mouth were nothing new to these women, but his angry actions put them on guard. Lewis didn't come near them or pick up anything to threaten them, but his agitated actions kept the women away, their eyes watching his every move. Sabrina had just spotted the iron skillet that she thought she might be able to reach if he came toward her. She was weighing her options when someone else knocked on the door.

* * *

Rylan waited patiently for someone to answer the door of Crystal's apartment, and when that didn't happen, he knocked a little louder and called Crystal's name.

"We're busy!" a man's voice shouted, and Rylan tried the handle to find it locked. Not giving his next action a moment's thought,

Rylan put one hard shoulder into the side of the door. One swift hit and it flew back on its hinges. He stepped inside, his eyes locking with Lewis' after that man had spun around in anger.

"What are you doing here?" Lewis growled.

"I could ask you the same question," Rylan said, remaining calm. "Did you want him here, Crystal?"

"Not likely. My bruises haven't faded from his last visit."

Rylan stepped aside, giving clear passage to the door, his meaning clear. Lewis' mouth went off again, but no one else spoke. He was almost out the door when Nate and Thom appeared.

"Is there a problem?" Nate asked, and Crystal wasted no time. She complained to the sheriff about Lewis' entrance and attitude, and without a word to anyone in the apartment, the other lawmen walked Lewis away.

"Are you all right?" Rylan asked the women when they were on their own. They both said they were, but Crystal was a little pale. "Let me check this door for you," Rylan offered next. Finding nothing was broken, he adjusted the lock. Sabrina didn't comment, her mind still on Lewis' visit, but she did remind Crystal about supper on Tuesday night.

"I'll meet you at the hotel just like before."

"I'll be there," Crystal said, and even hugged Sabrina back when that woman went to her. Rylan said goodnight, telling Crystal to be careful, and he and Sabrina left.

Rylan waited only until they were a block away from Willow Street, in the lee of a building, to pull Sabrina into his arms. His heart had almost stopped in his chest when he'd heard Lewis' voice coming from Crystal's apartment.

"Having you visit Crystal is going to be the end of me," Rylan admitted.

"It's always interesting, isn't it? And do you know what?" Sabrina said, pulling back a little, even though the dusk was making it hard to see. "We were talking about how you can know you're forgiven."

"Which means you'll be going back," Rylan said, his voice dry. He could feel Sabrina shaking with laughter. Rylan's tone turned sarcastic. "Oh, yes, go ahead and laugh at my pain. Every time you're on Willow Street, someone tries to hurt you."

"Not every time," Sabrina said. "Just nearly."

Rylan had to laugh. He took her hand and finished the walk home, honestly wondering how his heart was going to survive.

* * *

Sabrina got a letter from Callie when the mail came on Monday. She didn't allow herself to look at it until the end of the day. She walked back to Jeanette's and went to the garden, sitting on the stone bench there.

My dearest Sabrina,

There is no way to tell you how much I long to hold you and tell you in person how much you are loved. Your question brought back many memories. Both Danny and I have laughed and cried over our remembrances of that time.

To answer your question: It took a while. I saw Danny probably much the way you do Rylan. Perfect. No real shame in his past. None of his sins of unthankfulness, an occasional bad attitude, or a struggle

with lust ever seemed to compare with my past. I shouldn't have been keeping score, but that's what my mind did.

So what did I do? The turning point might surprise you. I didn't keep weighing the two of us, or try to find some sin in his life that made me feel better. I simply recognized that I was not that person any longer. I was saved from all of that, and was being saved every day. It was one of the most freeing things that ever happened to me. It wasn't about me but about what Christ had done with my sin.

By the time Danny told me how he felt, I was not surprised. I realize that not every man could handle having a former prostitute for a wife, but I knew that the man who let me get away was a fool. I was growing in my faith and I was working hard to be holy. I was kind, caring, wanted a home of my own to keep, and deeply wanted a godly husband and children.

Sabrina stopped reading, her mouth open a little in surprise. Having confidence that she had something to bring to a relationship had never occurred to her. She felt almost grateful that Rylan cared for her, too grateful in fact—as though she should forever be in his debt that he would overlook her past and love her. But that was all wrong, and she knew that Rylan didn't feel that way either.

"Well, now," Becky said as she came upon her. "I didn't know you were out here."

"Hi, Becky. I'm just reading a letter."

Becky sat beside her, a basket in her lap.

"From Denver?"

"Yes."

"You're not leaving us, are you?"

"No," Sabrina said, and knew how true it was. It also caused her to remember something.

"Are you going to put something in that basket?" Sabrina asked, slipping the letter into her pocket. "Would you like some help?"

The women worked side by side in the garden, talking about the day and what Becky had planned for supper. Sabrina didn't miss a single berry or squash, but her mind was hatching a plan the whole time.

* * *

Not until Thursday did Sabrina get a chance to see Rylan and give him the gift she'd bought. She went there directly from the shop, telling Jeanette she might be a little late to supper. Rylan answered the door right away, surprised and pleased to see her. They faced each other on the porch, and Sabrina took something from the fold of her skirt.

"What's this?"

"A ticket to Denver so you can see your family. I know it's only one way, but I thought if you had it, you could save for the return ticket."

Rylan looked at it and back up at her.

"What about you?"

"That's just it. If you don't go now, then we might become married, and it will be even more expensive to go. It's been two years. I want you to see your family."

Her sweet face, watching him intently, caused Rylan's heart to clench with love. He could have crushed her in his arms but made himself stand still and gather his emotions.

"I have something I need to show you."

Rylan was in the house for only a minute before returning, two letters in hand. The couple sat side by side on the bench before Rylan began.

"I wrote to both my father and Danny Barshaw. I don't think I need to tell you what I wrote. You'll be able to tell by their letters.

"'Dear Ry,' my father writes, 'I don't know that I've ever known a man who wrote to ask his own father if he could marry. I've certainly known men who checked with the bride's father, but never the groom with his own. To say you make me proud is so inadequate it's not worth the ink.'

"'Your Sabrina sounds as precious as a woman can be. To have found someone who will partner with you in your love for Token Creek and the church family is a gift from God. I am not concerned about you marrying someone we have not met. I know Chas keeps in close touch with you, and you have never shirked a single question we have sent your way. My only regret is not being able to see you married or at some point on your honeymoon, but you know that we understand.'"

Rylan looked at Sabrina, whose mouth had fallen open a bit, smiled, and started on Danny's letter.

"'Dear Rylan, do you want to know something special? I saw your father for the first time in years the day after your letter arrived! He told me of your letter, asking if you could marry Bri, and my heart was blessed.'

"'I do not hesitate to give you my blessing to marry our Bri. She is precious, and I know that you will treasure her always. Our only regret is not being there with you or having you visit us here. Keep us informed of your plans and know our prayers are with you.'"

Rylan stopped long enough to look Sabrina in the eyes before speaking again.

"So you see, we need to set this ticket aside until there is enough money to make the trip together. That's what everyone wants, including me. Don't ask me, my sweet Sabrina, to go to Denver without you. It wouldn't be any fun at all."

"I thought I was giving you such a lovely gift, but you're right," she answered with utter practicality. "We'll have to go together sometime."

Rylan had to smile at her matter-of-fact tone, and Sabrina smiled in return. And it was at that moment the most natural thing in the world to lean toward each other and kiss for the first time. It was brief, and for a few seconds they moved back and looked at each other.

"Are you all right?" Rylan asked, his voice soft and deep.

"I am. Are you?"

Rylan nodded before they leaned one more time. The second kiss was sweeter than the first, and Sabrina sighed when Rylan put an arm around her and she was able to put her head on his shoulder. She was planning only to drop off the ticket and get home to Jeanette's, but they started to talk about their families, and she was a good deal later than she planned.

21

CASSIDY, NOW FIVE AND a half months pregnant, walked the short distance back to her house to get the loaf of bread she had forgotten the night before. Trace and Brad were on their annual cattle drive, and the women were staying together. It had been decided early on that Cassidy would stay at Brad and Meg's, so as not to uproot Savanna. And truth be told, they were having an amazing time.

It felt like the days before Cassidy and Trace were married, when Cassidy would come to Meg's on Wednesday afternoons and the two women would sew and visit. The first two days the men were gone, they worked on their own laundry and some special jobs that had been waiting, but now they were doing things together, including meals and long conversations in the evening.

Meg well remembered the cattle drives when she went to stay in town with Jeb and Patience—and they had come for supper one night—but this time together with her sister-in-law was causing the men's absence to be less painful and to pass swiftly.

Cassidy was nearly to her porch when she heard a wagon coming up the drive. She looked over to find Jeanette and Rylan in the wagon. She stood still and watched as her pastor brought the wagon between the two houses. Meg had heard as well and had come out her back door as they pulled up, Savanna in her arms. The tears in Jeanette's eyes told the women the news was not good. They both knew before being told that Theta Holden was gone.

* * *

Brad and Trace had gone to see their mother before they left, but that did not make her funeral any easier. The Holdens had lived in the area for many years, and many folks were at the graveside for Rylan's words.

"I have two very good friends in Token Creek, and they happen to be brothers," Rylan said, looking at the Holden men, their faces sober as they stood across from Rylan, Theta's coffin between them. "Brad and Trace befriended me when I first arrived here, and I count myself blessed to know them.

"I knew their mother in a different way. Theta and I never had a normal conversation, but I knew much about what Theta believed because of her sons. Theta Holden understood that this life is temporary. She taught her sons from an early age that they must not settle here too permanently. She told them about her own faith in Christ, and that heaven awaited her. Her sons could see the genuine belief in her life and wanted it for themselves.

"I have no doubt that if Theta could have spoken, she would have told her sons how pleased she was that their faith was real. She would have been blessed beyond words that they both found believing wives and were having children who would know exactly where their salvation lies."

Rylan's eyes swung to Jeanette before he continued. "I'm sure there were moments when time seemed to crawl, but in truth the time that Theta lived at Jeanette's passed swiftly. Jeanette and I were talking last night, and she vividly remembers the day her sister was born, even though she was only three years old. 'A live doll to play with' was how Jeanette saw it."

More than one person smiled at the image before Rylan went on. "But the relationship progressed far beyond that. They were not just sisters but friends. Theta moved here with her husband and two sons many years ago, and the relationship she shared with Jeanette only became stronger. Theta's sons were Jeanette's sons. They shared joys and sorrows as one. When Jeanette's husband died, Theta was there with love and support. There was nothing they wouldn't do for each other, so when Theta's needs became special, it never occurred to Jeanette to do anything else but bring her into her home to live.

"And I'm sure you can guess who gained the greater blessing. Theta was not able to tell us how she felt, but I know that God used

Theta Holden to strengthen Jeanette Fulbright. She has shared with me many times how Theta's silence caused her own heart to quiet. And when those times came, God always used His Word to remind Jeanette of something she'd forgotten. Something she needed to have fresh on her heart again.

"Heather, Becky, and Timothy will all miss Theta. They have selflessly given to her for years and also have known God's blessing because of it. Theta has touched many of us repeatedly, and I know her memory will continue to do so."

Rylan closed in prayer then. He had not asked anyone else to share—the family had not wanted that—but few hurried from the graveside. Indeed it was more than an hour before the friends and family broke up and took Jeanette up on her invitation to come to the house.

* * *

"I'm not sure what I'm going to do with myself," Heather said to Sabrina after the service. A large group had gathered at Jeanette's, and those two women were in the kitchen helping Becky. "I already miss her."

"Give yourself time," Sabrina said. "Don't rush your heart."

Timothy sat at the table and pretended to read the newspaper. They all heard Becky sniff but knew she would not want to talk. They worked along, making food for the ones gathered and talking to those who wandered through.

Sabrina thought about the way death affected a family and then realized that was what they were. With Theta gone, not a person who lived in the house was related to another, but that didn't change what they had become.

As if she had suddenly had the same feelings, Jeanette was there. She didn't question how anyone was doing but finished loading a tray with fresh fruit, her hand touching each one of them as she passed by. She slipped back out, Heather behind her with another tray. Sabrina made no move to leave. Even when the next tray was ready, she waited for Timothy to notice and continued to work in silence alongside Becky. She was strangely comforted by this small act and a feeling that for the moment this was where she belonged.

* * *

Cassidy found Trace on the porch, sitting across from his mother's empty chair as he had done so numerous times in the past. Cassidy came close, sat on the arm of his chair, and slipped an arm around him.

"How are you?" she asked.

"I don't know," he admitted. "I'm glad she's not going to stare blankly from that chair anymore, but at least when she was there, I could be with her."

Cassidy laid her cheek on the top of Trace's head, and he reached for her hand.

"The truth is, Cass, I haven't had her for a long time. None of us have. I'm sad for me," Trace spoke as he realized, "but more than that, I'm happy for her."

Cassidy felt tears coming and didn't try to speak. Trace had not cried, and the reason was just as he'd stated: Theta Holden had been gone for years.

"We can still tell the baby all about her, Trace," Cassidy whispered. "You have so many memories to share. These last years will fade, and our baby will know all about the mother you remember."

Trace choked up at that point but didn't try to speak. He held his wife's hand a little tighter, wondering when it was really going to hit him that his mother was gone for good.

* * *

It took Rylan a while to find Sabrina. She had slipped outside to sit in the garden. It seemed as though every corner of the house was filled with people, and she had wanted some time alone. Rylan was certainly welcome, but she was thankful when he only sat beside her, his arm going around her shoulders, and left her to her thoughts. Some time passed before she was ready to talk.

"I kept seeing Mirabel's tiny casket today. I couldn't believe how strong the memory was."

"I thought of her too."

"I prayed for Eliza even while you were sharing. She just kept coming to mind."

Rylan nodded and said, "I hope she kept reading that Bible I gave her. I don't want her all cleaned up and going to hell."

Sabrina turned her head to look at him. "I don't think I've heard that phrase. What did you mean?"

"Just that she walked away from prostitution, and that's great, but unless she repents before God and believes in His Son, she's a former prostitute who will spend eternity separated from God."

Sabrina suddenly reached for his hand. "I'm so glad you said that, Rylan. Something's not right between Crystal and me. Since that night with the deputy, she's been avoiding me. I don't know what it means, but I have to remember what you said. It's about eternity, or it's not worth a thing."

"It's what makes reaching folks like Jessie Wheeler and Nate Kaderly very hard," Rylan said. "They're moral, kind, and hardworking. It isn't immediately obvious how lost they are."

Sabrina laid her head on his shoulder and sighed. "Are you ever overwhelmed by all the sin and lostness?"

"I'm tempted to be, yes. But then I work not to lose sight of the cross and my fear of God, and I believe again that He is able. You're not giving up on Crystal, are you?" he suddenly thought to ask, hoping she was not.

"No, but I've got to figure out what went wrong and find our friendship again."

"I'll pray you can do just that."

Sabrina angled her head so she could look up at him.

"I love you, Rylan Jarvik."

"I'm certainly glad to hear that," Rylan said before using his arm to draw her in close. Her hugged her for a long time, both of them quiet again. Not until Becky came looking for them did either one feel a need to speak.

* * *

"I can't remember the last time I was so tired," Meg said, sitting on the side of their bed, thankful that Savanna had gone right to sleep.

"Here, let me get your buttons," Brad offered, but Meg didn't move. She was looking at his face, studying the weary lines and sad eyes.

"Are you all right?"

Brad looked down at her. "It's not real yet. I don't mean her death but the chance that she might return to normal. That's what really died for me today."

"Oh, Brad, it's so true, isn't it? It's almost like hope died."

"Yeah. If you had asked me a week ago if I still had hope, I would have said not much, but I realize now that's not true. I'm grieving that loss more than anything else."

Meg put her arms around him and told

him to come to bed. Brad helped her with her dress, and with as little ceremony as they could manage, they slipped under the covers. Sleep did not come as fast as they expected. Their minds didn't relax as fast as their weary bodies, each one thinking about how swiftly their world could change and how precious life was.

Brad ended up reaching for Meg's hand and then started to pray. He thanked God for all the time they'd had with his mother, both before and after her husband's violence had put her in such a state. He asked God to forgive and save his father if he was still alive. And then he asked God to forgive and save himself and Meg, so that none of this time would be wasted. He finished by asking that they would use what they'd learned to grow more and to pass God's Word on to Savanna and the baby, as Theta had for him.

* * *

Jessie had asked Sabrina to sweep the boardwalk in front of the store on Monday morning. She had been working on it for a while and was almost done when she spotted Crystal. She had been coming up the street but stopped short when she saw

Sabrina. Sabrina could see that Crystal was going to turn and walk away, but she had questions and wanted answers.

"So tell me," Sabrina began when the women were still 15 feet apart, "what happened?" Sabrina finished when Crystal was directly in front of her.

"I don't know what you mean," Crystal said, and Sabrina decided to speak plainly.

"Listen, Crystal, I'm not going to force myself into your life. You didn't meet me at the hotel, and you haven't answered your door since. That's fine. I just wondered what I did. I thought you'd have guts enough to tell me."

They were just the right words. The shorter woman's eyes narrowed and her chin came up.

"I don't need your type of friendship. All you want to do is tell me I can have a better life. You haven't said it, but I know it's coming."

"I do believe you can have a better life, but my friendship isn't contingent on that."

"Sure."

"Tell me something," Sabrina forced herself to stay calm when she was confused and getting frustrated. “What happened to make you suddenly feel this way?”

Crystal’s defiant stance melted a little, and she said quietly, “I can’t have what you have, Bri. I just can’t.”

“Why not?”

“I don’t know how to read, and I can barely write my own name. What kind of job can I get in this town except the one I have?”

“Crystal,” Sabrina said just as quietly, glad she had not become angry. “You need a friend like me. I can teach you those things.”

Crystal stared at her.

“And I’ll always believe you can have a better life, but if you don’t want to hear it, I won’t talk about it,” Sabrina said, not forgetting what Rylan had shared in the garden but praying that Crystal would change her mind about what she was willing to hear.

Crystal wanted what Sabrina was offering, but she was afraid too. She happened to look over just then and spotted Paula coming from the Boar’s Head. She looked awful, as if she’d been up all night. A cold feeling swept up Crystal’s spine, and she turned back to Sabrina.

“I’ll meet you for supper tomorrow night.”

"I'll tell you what, come to Jeanette's and I'll cook something." Sabrina's voice dropped at this point. "Then we can start working on reading."

"I can't come to Jeanette's," Crystal started to say, but Sabrina cut her off.

"Yes, you can. I'll expect you at five-thirty. If you don't show up, I'll come looking for you."

Sabrina didn't wait for an answer. She turned to get back to work, her heart pounding with emotion and questions. She didn't know if Crystal would make an appearance, but Jeanette and the others would be warned, and she would try to be ready for anything.

* * *

Sabrina wasted no time on Monday night. As soon as supper was served, she explained to Jeanette, Heather, and Becky who would be coming the next night.

"I'll make something for us, and we won't be any trouble."

"You can eat with us, Bri," Jeanette said, but Sabrina had to shake her head.

"I'm not sure Crystal would be comfortable with that. I just hope she shows up so I can prove to her she's welcome. We'll eat in the kitchen or on the porch. I'm going to be helping her with something, and we'll need a little privacy anyway."

"I hope we'll get to meet her," Jeanette said, meaning it with all her heart.

"I'm sure you will. She won't be comfortable until she can see for herself that you don't hate her."

"Is that what she thinks?" Heather asked in her sweet, compassionate way. "That we all hate her?"

"Well, I don't know if hate is the right word, but she would have a hard time believing that she was welcome. And I don't know," Sabrina had to add, "she might not even show up. But thank you for letting me invite her."

"Thank you, Bri," Jeanette said, and Heather nodded. Becky was quiet during all of this, staring at Sabrina as if she'd never seen her before. Sabrina didn't have time to find out what she was thinking. Tonight was her meeting with Chas and Miranda. Rylan would be arriving for her in less than an hour.

* * *

"I can't believe how changed she is in the last month alone," Chas said to Rylan when the men were alone in the living room. Miranda and Sabrina had gone to the kitchen to get dessert. "You've heard from both your father and Danny Barshaw. When are you going to ask her to marry you?"

"I have a plan for that, but I need the church family's help."

Chas' smile threatened to stretch off his face, his romantic heart giving him away. By the time Rylan was done whispering what he had in mind, Chas had all he could do not to rub his hands together and start to work on the spot.

* * *

"What did I do wrong?" Sabrina asked Becky, who was once again working not to laugh, this time at the thinnest gravy she'd ever seen.

"I don't know, but you can't give the girl this stuff! What am I going to do with you?"

"I was trying not to be any trouble."

"And when have you ever been trouble?" Becky asked next. Sabrina gave up.

"Did you make enough for Crystal and me?"

"Of course I did. Enough here for an army! Go on to the front door so you can catch her before she runs off."

Sabrina did as she was told, and not a moment too soon. She went so far as to walk down the front walk and see that Crystal had come partway up the street and stopped.

"Come on," Sabrina called to her.

That woman finished the rest of the walk, her modest brown dress in place, and stood staring up at Jeanette's imposing home.

"I've never even been close to this house."

"You'll like it. It's beautiful but also homey."

Crystal stared at her.

"Come on in."

"Is anyone else inside?"

"Sure. Everyone. They'd like to meet you."

Crystal followed Sabrina up the walk, a feeling of unreality coming over her. But she was in for the surprise of her life. She met the women inside, as though nothing was out of the ordinary. They ate supper in a beautiful garden room, and then she started learning the alphabet with Sabrina, who was the same today as she had been every other time they talked. Crystal walked away three hours later, her heart stirring with hope that she would have said was long dead.

* * *

"And then we worked on the alphabet—she already knows some of it," Sabrina told

Rylan when he came to the shop on Wednesday, "and I could tell she was so pleased with her progress. We worked for two hours!"

Rylan watched Sabrina's animated face and could tell that she was losing her heart to this woman. He knew that feeling well. There were many in town that he ached for, Nate Kaderly among them.

"I prayed for you," Rylan said when she took a breath, and she smiled when she caught herself.

"Am I driving you mad?"

"No, it sounds great. Does she want another lesson?"

"Yes." Sabrina's eyes shone up at him when she answered. "Next week."

Jeanette had sat quietly for all of this, not even suspecting that Sabrina was teaching the other woman to read. She could see why she would want that kept quiet.

"What did you think of Crystal, Jeanette?" Rylan asked.

"She broke my heart," that woman admitted. "Her eyes were guarded when we met, but she looked so vulnerable when she followed Sabrina into the conservatory that I almost wept."

"She's not had an easy time of it," Rylan said.

"But she might have a chance now," Jeanette added.

Neither Rylan or Jeanette could have missed the way Sabrina sighed.

* * *

Sunday morning the three women met as usual at the front door for the walk to church. This was not a new routine because Becky had always stayed with Theta. Theta's absence was still being felt keenly, but each woman was dealing with it in her own way.

"All set?" Jeanette asked when Heather joined them at the door.

Before she could answer, however, Becky joined the group. She was obviously dressed to go out, and evidently going to church with them for the first time. Jeanette had all she could do not to comment. She, Heather, and Sabrina said not a word, or dared to even look at each other, but went out the door and down the street.

* * *

"In two weeks' time," Chas announced at the end of the service. "We're going to have a church picnic. Our hosts will be the Holden families. If the weather cools on us by then, we'll bundle up and build a big fire. Bring plates and such, and two dishes to pass. We'll head out directly after the service and eat around one o'clock. If you have any questions, see Miranda, me, or anyone from the Holden family. Even Savanna."

Everyone laughed at Chas' zany brand of humor. He grinned with pleasure, and the congregation was dismissed. Rylan, who had stood quietly at the front, wasted no time getting to the women from the Fulbright house.

"Welcome, Becky," the big man greeted.

"Thank you, Pastor Rylan," she said, nearly all of her bluster subdued.

"How are you?" Rylan asked the rest of the women, his eyes lingering a moment longer on the youngest woman.

"We're doing well. Can you join us for dinner?" Jeanette asked. "We have plenty, and there's something I need to tell you and Sabrina."

"That sounds fine," Rylan agreed, telling the women he would see them shortly.

They all started for home, and Sabrina could not keep her curiosity to herself.

"What did you think, Becky?"

"I like it," she said, her voice clipped, but not unfriendly.

"I do too," Sabrina said, her voice soft, causing all the other women to smile with her.

22

"THE APARTMENT ABOVE THE shop will be open by the end of the month," Jeanette told just Rylan and Sabrina when the meal was over. "Mr. Aspenson caught me as I was leaving yesterday. He's found a house to live in. I could have told just you, Bri, but I thought I'd save the news in case you wanted to discuss it with Rylan. You're welcome to it if you want it, Bri, but I hope you know by now that we don't want you going anywhere." This said, Jeanette stood up. "I assume you might want to talk about it, so I'm going to leave you alone."

Rylan and Sabrina thanked her, watched

her walk from the room, and then looked at each other.

"What do you think?" Rylan asked.

"I don't know. It wasn't so long ago that I would have jumped at it, but now I'm not certain."

"What changed?"

"My attitude and Jeanette's."

Rylan looked confused, so she went on.

"I decided not to see this as my sister's house, but as the house of my friend Jeanette Fulbright, a warm and generous person who cares for me."

"And Jeanette?"

Sabrina thought a moment. This one was harder to explain.

"I don't know exactly how to say it, but Jeanette wasn't very open when I first moved here. She was easily shocked and put off by things. No, that's not true. She was put off by people, and I didn't know what to do about that. It's only been recently that I felt I could have Crystal come here. And now that I do, I don't know if there's a reason to move."

"I can see the softening in her," Rylan agreed. "Have you told her you've noticed changes?"

"No, but I think I should."

"So you really are all right with being here?"

"Very much so."

"Good, because I want you here until we marry. The shop is closer to my house, but I just like having you here. I like knowing you're a part of this put-together family."

Sabrina nodded, very content, but her heart was also doing funny things in her chest. Rylan had mentioned marriage. Sabrina didn't want to say anything, but her mind was going to that topic more and more. It was simply lovely to know that Rylan's mind was on the same thing. Not that she doubted. It was just very nice to hear.

* * *

Heather sat in the conservatory and wrote in the journal she'd started not many days after Theta's funeral. She could not believe how much she missed Theta Holden, and something inside of her needed to remember the little things she had learned over the years. She needed to remember the big things God had taught her along the way as well. She wrote furiously at some times, and slowly at others. It helped to be in the room she was sure Theta called her own.

It was fruitless to speculate about what Theta might have been thinking, but Heather was not the same person for having known her. If it took her years, she was determined to write Theta's story, at least as seen through her own eyes.

* * *

"We have to talk," Jeanette said, having tracked Becky down on the second Sunday she'd joined them at church. She was in the kitchen as usual.

Becky looked at her but didn't speak.

"Why, Becky? Why after all these years?" she asked, not needing to be more specific.

Becky looked out the window for a long moment, her eyes on the garden. When she began to speak, she kept her gaze there.

"I'm not a young woman anymore, Jeanette. I always thought I would make time for God later, but suddenly time moved away. Theta's gone, and to me it feels like she just got here. And Bri," Becky started but took some time to find the words. "She's not selfish, and I am. She shames me."

"I don't think of you as selfish. You do for others all the time."

"But that's to please myself, Jeanette." Becky finally looked at her. "I have to get to church before I grow any more selfish. I have to hear what God might want to say to me."

Jeanette could have wept on the spot. She had never pressed Becky to come to church, but had always made her welcome clear. And then Theta had come to them, and Heather as well. Heather was vocal about her beliefs, and Becky had wasted no time volunteering for Sunday morning duty. It had seemed to make her content, and Jeanette had let time take over.

"I love you, Becky," Jeanette took a risk in saying, knowing the other woman did not like to hear such sentiments.

Becky swallowed several times. Jeanette wanted to give her privacy if she needed to cry, so she turned away.

"I love you, Jeanette." The words were whispered so softly that she barely heard them, but hear them she did. Jeanette stopped just long enough so that Becky knew the message got through and then continued on her way.

* * *

"How does it look?" Sabrina asked Jeanette on Thursday, holding up a very large shirt in blue chambray.

"Very nice," Jeanette praised her, standing

next to her as she sat at the machine. Sabrina had used her own money to buy the fabric, and Jeanette had taught her how to use the sewing machine. She had just finished the shirt for Rylan, hoping it would fit and that he would be pleased.

"I think you need to deliver this," Jeanette suggested.

Sabrina smiled before asking, "Can you spare me?"

"Go on," Jeanette ordered. "I'm quite certain you'll find him at the livery."

"I'll try to be right back."

"Sure you will," Jeanette said, and Sabrina had to laugh. Just remembering to have her wrap it in paper, Jeanette sent her on her way.

* * *

"Well, hello," Rylan said when Sabrina reached the wide doorway, having spotted her coming up the street. "Making a delivery?"

"I am." Sabrina held the wrapped garment out. "Here you go, Pastor Jarvik."

"Jeanette finished my shirt," he said, even as he reached for the parcel.

"Are you sure?"

"Yes," he smiled. "I wore it on Sunday."

"I think you're mistaken," Sabrina argued, trying to look convincing. "You'd best open it."

Rylan was thankful that his hands were not covered in grease, or worse. He tore the paper back and saw the blue shirt.

"Did you make this?" he asked, holding it out for inspection and liking it very much.

Sabrina nodded.

"With the machine?"

Again the nod, her smile a little shy.

Rylan bent toward her but didn't kiss her. "This was a terrible place to open a gift. Half the town is probably watching."

Sabrina looked into his eyes and whispered, "Does that matter?"

Rylan didn't hesitate. He bent the rest of the way and kissed her on the mouth, both of them looking much too pleased.

"One of these day I'm going to have a question to ask you," Rylan said.

"I'll be sure and have an answer," Sabrina said in return, and then forced herself to say, "I have to get back."

"My loss," Rylan said, his eyes warm.

Sabrina gave him one more smile and went on her way. She got back to the little blue dress shop without mishap, but if she'd been pressed, she could not have said how.

* * *

Timothy had Sunday off, so Rylan put Jeanette's two-seat wagon together for their ride to the ranch. Sabrina had insisted that Jeanette take the front seat, so she was in the back with Heather and Becky. Becky had gone again to church but not spoken to anyone about what she'd heard.

"I love this drive," Heather said when they were partway there.

"Isn't it beautiful?" Jeanette agreed. "I remember when Theta and Wes bought the ranch. I hadn't been much out of town before then, and it was such a treat for Owen and me to come this way."

Jeanette spoke of Theta often. It seemed to be her way of honoring her sister's memory and easing the pain. It was also nice for the rest of them, who didn't always know the stories she told.

"Look at all the wagons!" Sabrina said, not realizing how many folks were ahead of them on the drive. Rylan pulled their wagon under the Holden Ranch archway, and the fun began.

* * *

"I've been looking for you," Rylan said to Sabrina when dinner was over. They had laughed, talked, and eaten for nearly two hours, and now the games were getting started. Rylan and Sabrina had planned to sit together but gotten into conversations and been drawn apart.

"What's up?" Sabrina asked.

"Let's go for a walk," Rylan invited, his hand coming out.

"Are we allowed to do that when the games are about to begin?" Sabrina asked, even as she took his hand and gladly went along.

They both had long legs, and in no time at all were a ways away from the group. The hills rose all around them, but there was a knoll that Rylan wanted to climb, and they talked as they started that way.

"Do you have a favorite verse in each chapter of Colossians?" Sabrina asked.

"Let me think," Rylan said as they climbed, still holding hands. "I don't know if I have one in each chapter, but I have several."

"Which ones?"

"Well, I can tell you one that I pray about a lot is Colossians 1:7, which says, 'As ye also learned of Epaphras, our dear fellow servant, who is for you a faithful minister of Christ.' I often pray that verse and ask God that I would be a faithful minister of Christ and a servant. I would love it if others could say that of me."

"I think they can," Sabrina said, and Rylan thanked her. "What's your favorite part of preaching?" she suddenly asked.

"Well, the study of the Word is beyond compare, but I also love the looks on folks' faces when a new truth hits home. It's wonderful to watch. In fact I had a hard time with you at the beginning."

"Why was that?"

"So many thoughts are wondrous to you, and your face shows it all."

"I didn't know that."

"It's true."

"But not so much now?"

"No," Rylan smiled, "your face still shows it all, but I'm not trying to keep from looking at you these days."

Sabrina laughed and continued to climb. She wasn't winded, but she was ready to turn and take a look when Rylan tugged on her hand.

"A little higher," he invited, having taken

his time and enjoyed every minute. "I think the view to the other side is pretty fun."

Sabrina learned he was right. They got to the top and a small valley fell away, with dips and hollows that made Sabrina want to run down the other side.

"It's magnificent."

"I thought you might like it," Rylan said, keeping his arm around her shoulders, and wanting to wait until the perfect moment. "Oh, and we have to look back down on the ranch. It's a great view from here too."

It took a moment for Sabrina to see it. Her eyes took in both houses and the barns, but then she saw it, or rather them. Seemingly every person in the congregation was lying in the field, their bodies spelling out four words: *Will you marry me?* The question mark was far from perfect, but Sabrina got the message.

"Oh, Rylan," Sabrina laughed, turning to look at him. "You planned this!"

"I certainly did. Have you got an answer?"

"Yes!" she shouted before throwing her arms around the man she loved.

* * *

On the ground, the man in charge of the words—Chas Vick—saw the hug and shouted for everyone to move. Rylan didn't know about this part, but with much laughter and a little too much dust, the congregation spelled out: *Congratulations.* They hadn't organized an exclamation point, but when they all came to their feet and cheered, it was just as good.

Rylan and Sabrina took the fastest route down and were instantly surrounded by folks they loved and who loved them in return. Congratulations were many and heartfelt, and the next hour sped past as the picnic wrapped up and folks headed back to town. Not until Rylan had dropped most of the women off at the front door and taken the wagon back to Jeanette's barn did the newly engaged couple have time to speak alone.

"Who will marry us?" was Sabrina's first question.

"I have a friend, Willis Ruggles, who lives in Evers. I think he'll be happy to come over."

"When?" was her next question, and Rylan had to smile. He'd been wondering the same thing.

"How about we put a few dates into a letter and let Willis let us know."

"I like that idea as long as I have time to make a new dress."

"How much time do you need?" Rylan asked.

Sabrina thought about that, knowing Jeanette would help, but also that she still had two jobs to keep track of.

"Does two months put us too close to Christmas?"

"I don't think so. I think having you for a Christmas present sounds perfect."

And that settled it. Rylan wrote his letter the next day and heard back within the week. Pastor Willis Ruggles would be happy to marry Rylan and Sabrina on December 24, 1881.

* * *

"It's mean out there today," Bret Toben said to Sabrina as November rushed to an end. He had come for tobacco but also took time to linger near the stove. The wind was howling down Main Street, and no one lingered out of doors.

"You need a warmer coat," Sabrina told him, still working to organize the mail that had been delivered.

"I understand congratulations are in order," Bret said next, his voice a little flat.

Sabrina glanced at him and kept her thanks brief.

"You don't look especially pleased," Bret said next, suddenly at the counter.

Sabrina turned then and faced him. "What can I get for you, Mr. Toben?" she asked, not willing to talk with him on a personal level.

"The usual," he said, and took pleasure in having her remember.

Sabrina got his tobacco, and even checked to see if he had mail. Once his coin was on the counter, she stood expectantly, assuming he would leave.

"Am I invited?" Bret asked next, keeping his voice light.

"No," Sabrina answered, no sting in her tone.

"Crystal tells me she's invited."

"That's true. She is," Sabrina answered, wishing she could hand him off to Jessie, but that lady had actually been talked into taking a few hours off.

Bret nodded, not upset and still impressed by this woman. He genuinely enjoyed talking to her.

"She also told me how you helped her," the saloon owner said.

Sabrina nodded, never having told anyone but Rylan and Jeanette.

"It's good of you, Bri," Bret said as he

finally picked up his tobacco. He was on his way before Sabrina could frame a reply, but she still appreciated his words. She was also encouraged that Crystal had told him. It meant they were making progress with her confidence. She still couldn't get the other woman to agree to come into the church and see her married, but they were making progress. There was no denying that.

* * *

"Are they the most adorable couple you've ever seen?" Heather asked of Jeanette and Becky, the women still wearing their wedding finery as they drooped in their chairs with fatigue.

"Perfect," Becky agreed. Even she felt too tired to do anything.

"When I think about Rylan's face when he looks at Bri, I could sob my eyes out," Jeanette admitted.

"I think you're tired," Becky said.

"I know I'm tired," Jeanette corrected her.

"They looked so happy," Heather said, her voice a bit dreamy.

"We need to find you a husband," Becky suddenly said.

"At my age?" Heather squeaked, causing the women to start to laugh. If there had been any doubt, it was gone. They were all too tired, and the only remedy was sleep.

* * *

Mr. and Mrs. Rylan Jarvik made their way through the cold darkness to the parsonage. They had been married for nearly five hours, laughing and visiting with the church family and friends from town. Jeanette had hosted their reception, and it had been enjoyed by all.

But now they were alone in their living room. Rylan lit a lamp so they could see, and for a moment they stood looking at each other. When Rylan put his arms out, Sabrina walked into them. They kissed for a while, not aware of the fire not being lit, how low the lantern's oil was, or their coats still being on.

"Can I tell you a secret?" Sabrina said between kisses, still standing in Rylan's arms.

"Please do," Rylan said, a smile in his voice.

"I'm a little scared and wish I could just sit on your lap."

"Now that's a wish I can grant," Rylan said gently as he began to work the buttons on his coat. Sabrina took hers off as well, and by the time she was done, Rylan had lit the fire and sat down on the sofa.

"Come here, my sweet Sabrina," he invited.

Sabrina's heart melted as she moved to sit on his lap, her arms going around his neck.

"Tell me where this came from," Rylan said, his arms keeping her close and thinking she had a very good idea.

"I just needed it, and I've dreamed about sitting on your lap but didn't want to tell you until we could."

Rylan looked into her eyes.

"Don't forget that we have no plans tonight. There is no rush. Things will happen when they happen."

"I remember."

Rylan told her how much she was loved before they sat for a while in silence.

"Shall I tell you a secret?" Rylan asked after a time, his eye having caught the white fabric that had been stitched into the bodice of her dress.

"Yes."

"I can now relax when you wear a white blouse."

"Why haven't you been able to before?"

"Because my sweet Sabrina, whenever you would wear a white blouse, I would remember your getting wet in the livery that day."

Sabrina's mouth opened before she said, "I'd forgotten all about that."

"I wish I could have," Rylan said dryly. "Now I won't have to think about other things every time you wear that dark skirt and white blouse. It's been a challenge at times."

"You're wonderful. Do you know that?"

"I'm glad you think so."

"I mean it, Rylan. You worked to keep your thoughts pure even when they were about me."

"Shall I tell you one more secret?"

Sabrina nodded.

"I have no regrets. My wife is worth every second of hard work."

At the moment Sabrina couldn't find the words to tell him just how much he meant, so she simply kissed him one more time.

Epilogue

May 1882

SABRINA FINISHED DUSTING THE living room, shifting pillows into greater neatness, and seeing that all was just right. She never knew when folks would stop in, and when they did, this was the room they were most likely to occupy.

She went to the kitchen next, having already cleaned there, and started on a loaf of bread. It had taken some doing, working alongside Becky, but her bread was turning out very nicely these days, and she had less mishaps in the kitchen all the time.

"Sabrina," Rylan said, coming down from upstairs to find her. "Have you seen the ledger?"

"I put it on your desk."

"Oh," Rylan said, thinking he'd looked.

"Not there?"

"I don't know." Rylan suddenly became vague, coming over to stand close, his eyes catching hers. "Why don't you come in and show me?"

Sabrina smiled, knowing exactly where his mind had gone. They had learned that his desk chair held both of them very nicely. Sabrina visited him in his office whenever she had the chance.

Rylan's voice and his hands on her waist had become coaxing. He had almost convinced her to finish her bread later when someone knocked on the front door. Telling her not to forget where they had left off, Rylan went to answer it. Sabrina could not help but hear the shouts of joy and laughter that were coming from the living room. She came from the kitchen to find Danny and Callie standing there.

"Callie!" Sabrina shouted, running to the other woman and wrapping her arms around her smaller frame. "I can't believe you're here!"

The reunion was a tearful one, Sabrina and Callie unable to stop crying, and Danny bringing numerous greetings from Rylan's family. Rylan and Sabrina had just invited them to sit down when Danny and Callie looked at each other.

"We have someone with us, Bri," Danny said, his voice as kind as ever. "But she was afraid you wouldn't want to see her."

Sabrina's hand came to her mouth.

"Is my sister here?" she asked, even as she moved to the door. "Where is she?"

No one had to answer. Sabrina had seen that Sybil was standing just off the front porch, her face guarded.

"I can't believe you're in Token Creek," Sabrina said, having stopped about eight feet in front of her.

"I'm glad to see you, Bri," Sybil said quietly. "I'm sorry about what I did and the things I said."

"Oh, Sybil," Sabrina said and felt free to hug her.

Sybil felt her sister's arms and broke down. She had not expected forgiveness, even though the Barshaws had assured her otherwise. They had told her all—that Sabrina was loved and cared for, had turned her life over to God, and was no longer selling herself. But none of it had been real until Sabrina's arms came around her.

"Come in," Sabrina invited. "Meet my husband. Did you bring your husband with you?"

"No," Sybil said, her voice sad as she tried to control herself. She hadn't cried like that in years.

"Are you still married?"

"Oh, yes," Sybil answered cheerfully enough, not willing to tell Sabrina that her husband had figured out who she was. He hadn't divorced her, but he had changed toward her and that was worse.

"Come inside," Sabrina invited again. "Come and meet Rylan."

Sybil followed slowly, her heart knowing some relief that her sister was all right but also somewhat deflated that she didn't appear to need her.

* * *

"Is she all right?" Sabrina asked the men when they returned after supper, seeing they were alone.

"Yes," Danny answered. "She took the nicest room the hotel offered and said she would see us in the morning."

"Do you think we will see her?" Callie asked.

"I honestly don't know."

The men had joined the women in the living room, Rylan sitting by Sabrina and taking her hand.

"I can't figure out why she came," Sabrina said, having thought about how little Sybil had said all day and how uncomfortable she'd been. She had wanted nothing to do with staying the night, even though they had plenty of room, and had touched almost none of the supper she and Callie had served. Sabrina had tried to ask questions as well as share her life, but Sybil had been almost completely unresponsive.

"I think she came out of guilt," Danny guessed. "She had to know how you fared."

"She's miserable," Callie said. "She might be out of prostitution, but she sold her soul to marry Evert Clebold and all his money."

"Did he ever learn who she was?" Sabrina asked.

"She didn't say as much, but we got the impression that that's exactly what happened."

Sabrina wanted all the details then. Danny and Callie explained the way Sybil had come to them two months ago—having tracked them down through Lil—and wanted to know about her sister. They had offered Sabrina's address so she could write, but Sybil never wanted that. Not until they told Sybil they were making a surprise trip to Token Creek did she let her guard down and say she wanted to come, as long as Sabrina had no idea.

"The stark envy in her face every time Rylan looks at or touches you," Callie said with a small shake of her head, "was almost more than my heart could take."

Sabrina nodded, things becoming clear. It had seemed to her that her sister was angry, but Callie was right. She had been seeing envy.

The four talked about the situation for a while but then switched to their own lives. It was wonderful for Sabrina to hear about the church family in Denver and even some of Danny's recent forays back to the night district.

The Barshaws wanted to know all about life in Token Creek and the church family. They were anxious for a tour the next day. They wanted to meet as many folks as possible, the ones Sabrina talked about repeatedly in her letters. They planned an early start but still talked until late. By the time Sabrina and Rylan went to bed, the Barshaws sleeping down the hall, they were both weary.

"Are you going to be able to sleep?" Rylan asked, not wanting her to think about Sybil all night.

"I think so. I'm tired, and to tell you the truth I'm not expecting Sybil to be here in the morning. She was never very honest, and I doubt that's changed. At some point in the evening, I accepted that I've had all the time I'm going to get."

Rylan nodded, thinking about Sybil's face when he and Danny had left her at the hotel. He was fairly certain his wife was right. Rylan was still thinking about it when Sabrina came close and laid her head on his chest. She had angled herself in such a way that they could look at each other, something she often did.

"I love you," she said, tears coming to her eyes.

"I love you," Rylan said, his hand stroking her cheek and hair. "Why the tears?"

"I don't know. Seeing Sybil just brings so much back."

"If she's here in the morning, will you tell her you think you're expecting?"

"It feels cruel, Rylan. She's so obviously not happy, and I've found you."

"Maybe she'll find Christ, and the despair will leave her face."

"I hope so, Rylan. I pray it with all my heart."

"And let's not forget the miracle that she came at all. Danny and Callie are a nice surprise but not all that shocking. Sybil's being here is amazing."

Sabrina smiled at him.

"What would I do without you?"

"I'm not planning on your finding out," he smiled in return, and started to pull her close.

"There's something else you're not planning on my finding out as well," Sabrina said, not willing to kiss him just yet.

Rylan began to smile.

"Tell me why you call me Sabrina."

"Someday," he said, still pulling her close.

Knowing from his voice that she would not find out tonight, she came without hesitation, her arms going tightly around him—her wonderful, amazing husband who had just the right heart.

About the Author

LORI WICK is a multifaceted author of Christian fiction. As comfortable writing period stories as she is penning contemporary works, Lori's books (6 million in print) vary widely in location and time period. Lori's faithful fans consistently put her series and stand-alone works on the bestseller lists. Lori and her husband, Bob, live with their swiftly growing family in the Midwest.

To read about other Lori Wick novels, visit **www.harvesthousepublishers.com**

Books by Lori Wick

A Place Called Home Series
A Place Called Home
A Song for Silas
The Long Road Home
A Gathering of Memories

The Californians
Whatever Tomorrow Brings
As Time Goes By
Sean Donovan
Donovan's Daughter

Kensington Chronicles
The Hawk and the Jewel
Wings of the Morning
Who Brings Forth the Wind
The Knight and the Dove

Rocky Mountain Memories
Where the Wild Rose Blooms
Whispers of Moonlight
To Know Her by Name
Promise Me Tomorrow

The Yellow Rose Trilogy
Every Little Thing About You
A Texas Sky
City Girl

English Garden Series
The Proposal
The Rescue
The Visitor
The Pursuit

The Tucker Mills Trilogy
Moonlight on the Millpond
Just Above a Whisper
Leave a Candle Burning

Big Sky Dreams
Cassidy
Sabrina

Contemporary Fiction
Sophie's Heart
Pretense
The Princess
Bamboo & Lace
Every Storm
White Chocolate Moments